The Secrets He Kept

The Secrets He Kept

Jackie Walsh

hera

First published in the United Kingdom in 2019 by Hera Books

This edition published in 2020 by

Hera Books
28b Cricketfield Road
London, E5 8NS
United Kingdom

A CIP catalogue record for this book is available from the British Library.

Print ISBN 978 1 80032 111 3
Ebook ISBN 978 1 912973 20 0

Printed and bound in Great Britain by Clays Ltd, Elcograf S.p.A.

Prologue

Smiles, tears, love, lies, deception. It all ends now. Blood flows from the wound, forming a warm blanket for me to lie in. The room blurs, my eyes flicker to a close.

I knew it would free itself someday. The truth, the one I had imprisoned. It would break loose, and reveal its story. My story… Her story… His story.

The room is soaked in anger. It's stuck to the walls, the floor, the ceiling, almost visible in its intensity. Thick, dark anger, brought on from years of lying, of playing along with her charade. I should have stopped it. I know that now. But it's too late. The truth is out there, stirring fear. Nurturing hate in its victims. All three of them.

It came to me, years of thinking the worst before finding out what had really happened. What we had done, how we had lied to her. The pain seeped from her every word. Determined to bring it all out into the open. To fix the unfixable.

Then he came, anger flying out of his mouth. Why had I told her? He didn't want her to know. I tried to explain it wasn't me but he wouldn't listen.

I thought it was all over, that they had left me to cry my tears. When the doorbell rang again.

Chapter One

'Aaron… Cian,' Tom calls out from the kitchen, alerting the boys that breakfast is ready. When I enter the room he hands me a cup of coffee, kissing me on the head, filling me with that sense of safety I get every time he's near.

'Morning, love, you look great.' His dark blue eyes stare into mine so I kiss his lips and linger a moment. 'Are we all set for tomorrow?' he says, when I pull away.

'Just about.'

Placing two bowls on the kitchen table, Tom goes to the fridge, takes out a carton of milk and a bottle of water for me.

'I'm sure it will be a great day tomorrow, Sal. I'm looking forward to it.'

I'm looking forward to it too, looking forward to it all being over. For the crowds to be gone and peace restored, but I don't want to say this and spoil Tom's excitement. He loves doing things for the boys, bringing them to swimming classes, taking them to their favourite ice-cream shop and lugging them to football matches in the club, where the boys are still too young to understand what's going on. But they love standing at the side of the pitch, laughing at their dad shouting at the referee.

Moving my gaze to the window, I watch the heavy rain splash the glass and wait for the boys to run in from the playroom. They're almost three. 'The big surprise' we called it the day we found out I was pregnant. 'The bigger surprise' when we found out it was twins. After years attempting to provide Amber with a sibling had failed, out of the blue, just like buses, two arrived together.

'Do you want me to drop you in?' Tom says, noticing the bad weather.

'No, I'll take my car, I've to pick up the cake on the way home.'

The boys come rushing into the room, hoofing themselves up onto a chair, pulling the breakfast bowls closer to them. Tom winks at me with that old reliable smile, letting me know he has everything under control. He will take care of them. I can relax.

As Aaron and Cian shovel Rice Krispies into their mouths like the winner is going to get a prize, I glance at the clock on the wall above the window.

'Look at the time, I better get going.' I kiss both boys, hugging them tightly before making my way upstairs to Amber's room.

Like most fifteen-year-olds on a Saturday morning, Amber is still asleep when I open the door. Her gentle breath warms my skin when I kneel over to kiss her. Amber stirs, eyes still closed as she mumbles, 'See you later, Mom.'

Before closing the door behind me, I take one last peek at her, then gently release the handle.

'You might need this,' Tom says handing me an umbrella when I get downstairs. 'And this.' He takes the bottle of water that he'd left on the table from behind his back and laughs. 'I don't know what you'd do without me.'

'Neither do I,' I say, hugging him briefly before taking the bottle and pushing it into my overloaded bag.

''Bye, Mom.' Cian and Aaron sit at the window repeatedly shouting goodbye to me. Their little hands waving, air kisses blowing guilt my way. It's like I'm leaving for a fortnight's holiday, every time I go to work. Tom is standing behind them also blowing me a kiss. I hate leaving them, leaving Tom. But I don't have a choice so I smile, wave and pull out of the driveway.

Now I'm Sally the hairdresser.

—

The city is slower to wake on a Saturday. Less traffic. I get to the car park in no time, pick a spot nearest the exit and grab my bag from the floor. The rain has eased to a damp haze. It feels good, waking my senses, preparing me for the day ahead. Quickening my step, I continue my short journey towards the hair salon.

Cake, sticky tape, paper cups. I close the list in my head and continue down the street. It's eight in the morning, the birds are done, their song replaced by the opening of shutters, footsteps, the odd greeting. 'Good morning.' 'Terrible day.'

Moore Street is not the prettiest street in Dublin but it has a comfortable feel at this early hour. Traders pulling their stalls into position. Same stalls. Same positions. Fruit and veg, flowers and fish. The pungent smell from the fish stall forces me to hold my breath. I hurry past but the stench still manages to creep into my nostrils.

At the top of the street, I cross the main thoroughfare and enter the coffee shop on the corner.

'The usual, Sal?' Graham, the coffee guy, already has his hand on the barista machine preparing my order when I step inside. There's no one else here but in an hour's time the queue will be out the door.

'Thanks, Graham.' I hand him the exact change which I always have ready in my pocket. Then take my order and leave.

When the boys were born, I cut my working hours to three days a week. Perfect, time for everyone, including myself. But circumstances beyond my control forced me back to work full time. And even though I'd prefer to be at home with Tom and the kids, it's not the worst thing. I get to put make-up on first thing in the morning. Scan my thinning closet for something fashionable to wear and put my feet in high-heeled shoes. My day is spent in the company of adults, though at thirty-seven years old, I'm regarded as one of the old folk now.

–

Elsie is sitting in the usual spot outside the shop front when I arrive. Everything she possesses packed into two bags tucked tightly on either side of her worn frame. For the last two years she has sat under the narrow shelter provided by a small awning jutting out from the salon. This is the spot where she opens her sleeping bag at night and dreams about having a roof over her head someday. Elsie never speaks about the circumstances that led her to being homeless. But everything about her suggests it was not always the case. Her clothes, her skin, her knowledge of which restaurants to visit and which to avoid. I've been tempted to ask her how she lost it all and to tell her I nearly did too. But something in her dignity stops me, tells me not to go there, just let it be.

'Thank you, Sally,' she smiles, her teeth still holding up under the strain. She takes the bag from my hand, immediately opening it to get at the coffee and croissant.

'Hold the door,' Amy shouts, rushing towards me while balancing four paper cups in a cardboard tray. Standing back, I watch her go through in front of me. Amy's hair is pink today. Last week it was orange. Hail the employee discounts.

'Morning, all,' I say, walking into the buzz. The shop doors aren't open to the public yet and already I feel more alive.

'Morning, Sal.' Megan's head appears up from behind the reception desk as she plonks a big book on the counter top. Her eyes don't waste time looking at me. As my boss, Megan is too busy locating all the bits and pieces she needs to efficiently navigate the day ahead.

'Hi, Meg.' I walk towards the staffroom to the sound of Jason Mraz. Which is another thing I like about this place, keeping up to date with what's going on in the world of music. Peppa Pig has no pull here.

The smell of Coco Chanel welcomes me when I push the staffroom door open. Which can mean only one thing, Marie is here.

Leaning forward, she shakes her head. Black glossy hair floats like great wings from side to side. A wild bird set free. But not for long. Marie captures the hair into her grip and wraps it tightly into a bun.

'Hi, Sally, love the highlights,' she mumbles, balancing a hair clip between her teeth. My fingers push at the fresh blonde streaks Sienna did for me yesterday, luminous above my flushing skin. Receiving a compliment from anyone other than Tom makes me blush. I always shy away from kind words. It took years before I said 'thank you' instead of coming up with some ridiculous explanation for having got something right.

'Thanks.'

'I guess you heard?'

'Heard what?' And here we go. The news. There's always some bit of news.

'About Sienna. She left Alan.'

'What? She did not.'

'She did.'

Sienna had been living with her partner for over ten years. She has two children and was, allegedly, for the past two years, enjoying a second relationship with Conor, a younger guy who supplies hair colour to the premises on a twice-weekly basis. It took a while for the rest of us to figure out hair colour was not the only thing he supplied on a twice-weekly basis.

'But...' I'm totally shocked hearing Marie relay the story... and yet a part of me is not. Sienna does what Sienna wants to do. Always has and I suppose always will.

My mind rambles to my default mode. The victims. The poor children and Alan her partner. I could never do anything to hurt Tom or my kids. I've seen first hand the devastation it can cause.

Anna is next to walk through the door, her face the colour of well-nourished grass, her eyes pickled. Anna currently holds the trophy for the most exciting social life. Out on the town almost every night. Drinking and dancing like there's no tomorrow.

'Hi, all, don't talk to me, my head is banging.'

Dropping her bag onto a chair she searches through the front pocket and pulls out a packet of paracetamol. Putting two pills into her mouth, she lifts a plastic bottle half full of water from a shelf, opens the bottle, smells inside then downs its contents.

'Morning, Anna,' Marie says, extra loudly, smiling at me in the process. 'Beautiful day, isn't it?'

'Fuck off,' Anna barks, before walking out of the room.

Ten more minutes pass before the first client arrives in through the door. The young girl has blonde shoulder-length hair. She's standing at the reception desk talking to Megan whose head is stuck in the computer. After a bit of toing and froing, Megan walks to where I'm standing.

'Can you take this one?' she says. 'It's just a blow-dry. Your first appointment is not due until half nine.'

'Sure,' I say, the interaction just a courteous exchange, it's not like I have a choice.

'Great.'

–

Megan directs the young woman to the wash basins where Louise, our new junior, waits with a head full of attitude and a towel in her hand. It will take a few minutes for Louise to finish, so I check my phone and see a text from Amber.

Shit, what does she want now? Most of my lunch hours are spent going from one shop to another picking up something that Amber just can't live without. I know I shouldn't spoil her. But since she inherited the role of chief babysitter, her requests are worded to persuade me she deserves it.

The young girl, Charlie, arrives back from the basin. Hair dripping, she sits on the seat in front of me. Beep, beep. Another text. I want to take the phone out to check the message but there are rules. No phones allowed while with a client.

I could conveniently move it out of my pocket and leave it face up on the counter so I can read the message. I want to make sure Amber is okay.

'You can get that if you want,' Charlie says.

'No phones allowed during work.' Smiling, I plug the hair dryer into the socket below the counter while glancing up at Megan. She would have no qualms about pulling me up if I did check my phone.

'Really?' she says, taking her own Samsung in her hand. 'I'd die without me phone.'

The noise from the dryer puts an end to the conversation and I wait, wondering what Amber's beep has in store for me? Will it be Penny's, H&M or Mac?

I switch off the dryer to brush through Charlie's hair. 'Are you going anywhere nice?'

'Yeah, I'm going to a party tonight… It's me boyfriend's party.'

'Well… we have to have you looking your best then, don't we?' Lifting her hair at both sides, I show her what it would look like if I clipped it into an upstyle.

'He's sixteen… Kenny's his name… d'ya wanna see him?' Charlie seems more interested in flicking through the photos on her phone than in her new hairstyle.

I'm becoming concerned, my phone has beeped three times since Charlie sat down. I need to finish this head quickly and find out why Amber is being so insistent. I've told her a hundred times that I'll answer her messages as soon as I get a chance.

'This is him,' Charlie says, lifting her phone into my view. I glance quickly.

'Handsome,' I say, barely noticing the picture.

'Here's another one of him.'

I look again. This time I don't glance. This time I stare. The photograph shows a man with his arm around Charlie's boyfriend's shoulder. The young boy is holding a trophy. The man by his side is wearing a pink shirt, blue jeans and a smile that I would recognize anywhere.

Without asking, I take Charlie's phone from her hand and hold it closer to my face.

'Who is that?' I ask, pointing to the man I know is my husband, his arm wrapped around Charlie's boyfriend.

'Oh, that's Kenny's dad.'

Chapter Two

That's Kenny's DAD.

That's KENNY'S Dad.

THAT'S Kenny's Dad.

No matter which way I hear it, the words slice like razorblades through my mind. How could this be? What is going on? Fear flushes through my body, blurring everything in sight. The phone drops. I hear a gentle bump as it lands on the tiled floor. Bouncing, bouncing, bouncing. Everything goes dark.

–

Now I'm staring at two pairs of shoes. My own silver block-heeled sandals from Penny's and black-wedged, runner-style Louis Vuittons. They can only belong to one person, Megan. Inhaling deep breaths as per the instructions being delivered to me, I lift my head slowly.

'Are you okay, Sal?' Megan hands me a glass of water which I accept with shaking hands. The icy cold fluid sends a jolt through my body forcing me to face the reason I became weak. The photo. The boy. The dad. What is going on? Why am I sitting on a chair in the staffroom with my colleague trying to bring me back from the dead? What the hell happened? Did I really see my husband in that photo?

'Is she okay?' Sienna opens the door and sticks her head round.

Megan answers, 'Yes, she's fine, she's fine, go back to work.'

Megan is sitting on the bench beside me. I know she's here, but all I can see is Tom, standing with his arm around a young boy. The pink shirt. The familiar smile.

Swallowing the remainder of the water, I stand up and tell Megan that I'll be fine. That the boys had a bug yesterday, maybe I caught it from them but I'm grand now. I sound stupid, no one gets a bug for ten minutes.

'Do you want me to ring Tom?'

'No! No, just give me a moment, I'll be fine, honest.' Tom is the last person I want to see. Even the mention of his name makes me want to check out again.

'You can't continue in work, not after getting weak, Sal.' My God the woman is persistent.

'I'll be fine, Meg, honest, just give me a minute.'

My heart is beating so hard, it's almost audible. This can't be true. It must be some kind of sick joke or maybe I just imagined Tom in the photo. I've been so tired lately, running and racing I can't trust my own eyesight.

Moving towards the door I realize I have to catch that young girl, Charlie, before she leaves. I need to see the photo again. I want to know the man with his arm around her boyfriend was not my husband.

'Is she still here?' I say.

'Who?'

'Charlie, the young girl whose hair I was blow-drying, I need to speak to her. Is she still here?' My palm is on the handle of the door when Megan comes alongside me and pushes it closed.

'No, she left.'

'But…' I'm not going to say anything about the photo she showed me. Not now and definitely not to Megan. Her concerned gaze is already bothering me. Anyway, she'll think I've gone mad if I tell her.

'Did that girl say something to upset you, Sally?'

'No… I was feeling unwell before I came in this morning, probably should have stayed at home.' I turn from Megan's stare, sipping the last drop of water from the glass that shakes in my hand.

'Why do you need to talk to her?'

Think, think. 'I just want to finish her hair… I didn't get to finish it.'

'Don't worry about that, Marie did it.'

Megan takes the empty glass from my hand telling me to sit back down, take a few more minutes. No doubt the shop is busy as hell but Megan is taking the time to stay with me, making sure I'm okay. It's an odd feeling, having someone take care of me. Usually it's the other way around. Sally Cooper, looking out for everyone who needs her help.

I allow myself to indulge in the moment, to savour the attention but soon the image in the photograph jumps to the front of my mind again – along with the possibility that maybe it *was* Tom. Maybe Tom has another son somewhere. No, even the idea sounds completely crazy. There is no way he could keep that a secret for… what did Charlie say? Sixteen years. That would make Kenny a year older than Amber on her next birthday. That would mean… no it's impossible. Don't go there, Sally. You know it has to be a mistake. Tom does not possess the ability to keep this hidden for all those years. He's never even been capable of keeping a secret for a day. When he decided to have a surprise party for my thirtieth, I was the first to know.

Megan is getting restless now, I can tell. She's rubbing her knees and glancing around the room waiting for me to suggest she goes back outside.

'I'm fine now, Megan, definitely feeling a lot better. You go back to work. I'll give Tom a call if I feel I need to go home.'

'Are you sure, Sally? You're still very pale.'

'I'll be fine, you go.'

With Megan safely out of the room, I kneel forward, take deep breath after deep breath and wonder what will I do?

Shaking my legs and arms, I try to get the blood in my veins flowing. I don't feel normal. Will I ever feel normal again? Leaning into the mirror, frightened eyes stare back. I pinch my cheeks. *Get it together, Sally Cooper.*

The texts, I remember the beeps on my phone. Whipping the phone out of my back pocket, I open a message. Amber, asking me if I could pick up a bottle of the new fake tan from Penny's that everyone is raving about. Wiggling my fingers, power slowly returns allowing me to text her back. *I will do my best.* But I add that I'm not sure if I'll get out of the salon today the shop is so busy.

With a fuzzy head, I check myself in the mirror before leaving the staffroom. The sound from the radio, the hairdryers, the chatter, all seems so noisy now, irritating me. The shock of what I thought I saw has me on edge. Was it Tom in that photo? The man I've slept beside for the last sixteen years. The man I've trusted, the father of my children. There's no way Tom could have a secret child. That young girl Charlie must have it wrong. She's mistaken, thinking the man with his arm around the boy is his father. Charlie may never even have met the boy's father. Tom was probably in that photo because the boy won some player of the year award or something like that. After all, Tom used to coach one of the teams in the club before life got too busy for us. That's what this is. Tom was just congratulating the boy when the photo was taken. That's if it even was Tom.

Taking a deep breath, I walk to where Megan is waiting for me at the reception desk.

Megan smiles at me. 'Okay now, Sal?'

I nod at her, turning the book on the counter and reading from my client list. I'm finding it hard to concentrate. The words blur but eventually come into focus.

I realize I can't just leave it at that, presume Charlie has it wrong. Why would she say the man in the picture was the boy's father if she didn't know? I need to see her again. I need to see that photo again.

Chapter Three

Strong coffee helps. It slows me down when I'm swallowing it and speeds me up when I'm finished. Megan didn't want me to stay at work. But I didn't want to go home, so I insisted I was fine and capable of doing my job. Going home without a plan of action would be a bad idea. I'd walk in the front door, attack Tom with all kinds of accusations handing over any advantage I have. Yes, I will have to confront him. I know that. But I want to gather as much information before I do. Surely if Tom has another child there must be some evidence lying around the house.

When Tom heads out for his usual Saturday evening match drinks with the lads – the ones he feels so entitled to after minding his own kids for the day – I'll search through his things.

With my head in a tizzy and my heart unfamiliar with the new beat, I welcome my next client and take her to the basins. Agnes is an older lady and unlikely to show me any photographs from a phone. She brags the traditional way, telling me how great the grandkids are. How fabulous her daughter's house is and how happy she is that her gay grandson has finally found a partner. My mind is doing its best to ignore the elephant in my brain. I pay as much attention as possible to Agnes.

Nodding, smiling, agreeing. Thanking God that hairdryers are noisy.

–

By lunchtime I'm feeling a bit stronger. There is no client booked in for my service for half an hour so I take the opportunity to approach Megan.

'Feeling okay?' she says, without looking up from the computer. How does she do that? It's like she has a secret pair of eyes hidden somewhere on her head.

'I'm fine, Megan, sorry about this morning, I don't know what came over me.'

Megan moves her attention to the big book at her side. 'No need to say sorry, Sal, as long as you're okay?'

'Yes, thanks.' I stall, wondering if I'm doing the right thing asking, I don't want to raise a flag. But then again it's the only way I'm going to find out.

'I was wondering if that young girl, Charlie, the girl whose hair I was doing this morning…'

'Yes?' Megan swirls around in her chair and looks at me. Suddenly I have her attention.

'Did she leave a number when she was making the booking?'

'She didn't make a booking, Sal, she just walked in off the street.'

'Oh.' My face obviously can't hide the disappointment. Megan has shuffled her chair closer to me.

'Sal, do you want to tell me what's going on?'

I do, I really do, but it's crazy so I can't. Shaking my head while moving away, Megan grabs my hand.

'You know I'm here, Sal, if you need me.'

Don't cry, Sally, for Christ's sake, don't cry in the middle of the shop. Trying my best to hold it together I head for the staffroom. Megan is so kind and caring with everyone, not just me. She's like a mother to us all, even though she's about ten years younger than me. I know I could trust Megan but I'm just not ready yet. Not ready to let anyone else know what I thought I saw, especially when I probably just imagined it.

–

The clock eventually reaches six. My feet are sore, my body tired and I can't wait to go home. I need to see Tom to hear his voice and feel his touch. I'm sorry now that I even considered what Charlie said to be true. Tom and I have an honest relationship. We share everything, even the bad stuff. I know the man inside out. If I couldn't trust him I wouldn't be with him and Tom knows that. He knows why too.

Tears, fights, my mother standing at the window (sometimes all night long), waiting for my father to decide whether to come home or not. The night I heard her pleading with him, begging him not to leave even though he had just verbally abused her, threatening that he would not come back if she didn't cop on. I knew then, that was not the life for me.

Chapter Four

Tom is standing in the kitchen wearing that ridiculous apron with the ballet dress printed on the front. The smell of garlic soaks the air. Waving the spatula in his hand he pays a compliment to the dinner he's making and walks over to me.

'Hi, love, how did your day go?' I want to tell him what happened but I decide now is not the time. I'll sit and eat with my family first.

'Fine, but my feet are killing me.'

He leans in and kisses me before I pull my shoes off.

'Make yourself comfortable, Sal, you're in for a treat.' Tom returns to the pot boiling on the stove.

'Mommy, Mommy.' Cian runs in from the kitchen with a parcel in his hand.

'I got a present already.'

His eyes are wide with excitement. I kneel down and kiss him on the cheek.

'That's great. Who gave it to you?'

'Rena.'

'Rena?'

Amber enters the room, her eyes glued to her phone. 'Yeah, she dropped them in earlier, said she can't come tomorrow – something, something, I can't remember.'

'Oh.'

This doesn't surprise me. Ever since Rena witnessed Cian and Aaron fighting with each other, using language that surprised even me, she hasn't been too keen to bring her one-year-old son into their company. I've asked her into the house once or twice for a coffee. She's a nice woman, helpful, and she gives Amber the odd babysitting job but I guess she wants to protect her only child from the unruly influence of the Cooper twins. She's new to all this, she'll cop on.

'Can we open it?' Cian says.

'Sure.'

'Daddy says we have to wait until tomorrow,' Aaron says, walking in holding his present.

'Well, Daddy's not the boss anymore. Mammy is home now. You can open it.'

-

With Amber out of the house and the twins finally asleep I pour myself a glass of wine to settle into the sofa when the photo jumps into my head. I've tried to block it out, forget about it but it just keeps rearing its threatening image. Maybe I should have a look around the house, check through Tom's things while he's not here, see if there's any sign of another life.

Investigating my husband feels weird. He's the man I've loved and cherished since the day we met seventeen years ago. The man I spent five euros — or was it pounds? — to dance with at a charity fundraising night. We still joke about it, how I got a bargain, how I was robbed. Could this man have kept this secret from me? My heart weighs heavy so I take a sip of wine.

I've never spied on him before. I don't agree with it but some people do it all the time. Check their husband's phone, computer, receipts from his pockets after a night out. Sienna is a wagon for it, maintaining you can't trust any man. But I've never felt the need to spy on him. Tom has always been up front with me and I with him. Except of course for that one time when it took him forever to admit the mess he had landed us in. But searching through his things, that's just silly, Tom couldn't have a secret life. Could he?

If I did have a look it would put my mind at rest, help me forget about the photo. Deciding it wouldn't do any harm I leave my glass down on the table and reluctantly go upstairs to the bedroom. First stop, his bedside locker. The house is silent when I open the top drawer, the sound of my rummaging breaking the peace. An old driver's licence, money, business cards. Then the second drawer. Books, books, books. The third drawer. An old instant camera that was never opened. Batteries. Photos. PHOTOS.

Lifting a pile of photos from the drawer I place them on top of the bed and spread them out. The first photo to grab my attention is one of Amber. She's about three years old, sitting on Tom's knee, licking an ice cream that's almost as big as her little face. Tom looks carefree and happy. No secret behind those eyes.

The next photo I see is of our wedding day. Jesus, we look so young. Tom looks like he's at a debs' not a wedding and I'm not much better with my homespun make-up and borrowed veil. No indication that Amber was already with us below the ruffle of my dress. Which reminds me: eight thirty, still half an hour before Amber returns home. I better get a move on.

There's no sign of any boy or anyone else I don't recognize, so I place the pile of photos back in the drawer and think. Where else could he be hiding something? Tom doesn't have an office or a man cave like some of the husbands we know. He relinquished any dreams of peace and quiet when Cian and Aaron arrived. But he does have stuff in the shed at the end of the garden, which I can't go to now because it has no electricity so it will be pitch black. If I take a torch, I'm not guaranteed I wouldn't injure myself in the chaos out there. That will have to wait until daylight.

I'm about to leave the room when I remember the old suitcase Tom has stored under the bed. It's where he keeps important documents: insurance policies, house deeds, birth certs, passports, how to succeed in business manuals, all that stuff. Gripping the handle, I yank the heavy case out and again feel a twinge of guilt shoot across my chest.

The case is ancient; two leather straps hold it secure so I pull them open and lift the lid. Why am I doing this? This is just wrong. *You're doing it because of what you thought you saw in the photo, Sally.*

But it's not just that. For the past few months Tom has seemed distracted, worried about something. Just like the last time he was holding onto something he couldn't tell me. Eventually he did, had to, but he was able to keep it to himself, able to carry on like he hadn't almost ruined our lives, before eventually plucking up the courage to tell me. Is he doing the same thing now?

There are no obvious surprises in the case, no strangers' birth certs, no pictures of extra kids.

'Where are you, Mom?' Amber yells, wondering why I'm not on the sofa in front of the TV.

'Sshh.' She's going to wake the boys. I better shove this back under.

'Mom, Mom.'

Now she's at the top of the stairs. I'm about to close the case when I see a white envelope sticking out from under a pile of brown ones. I glance at the address, *Tom Cooper c/o 12 Sycamore Gardens*, then quickly fasten the lid. Probably something to do with one of his clients in work.

Amber walks into the room? 'What are you doing?'

'I'm… I'm looking for something.'

'What?'

Think quick, Sally! 'Oh… just one of my earrings, you know the ones with the little gold trinket dangling from the green stone.'

Amber looks down at the dressing table at her side and lifts the earrings in her hand.

'These?'

'Gosh, I must be going blind.' Pulling myself upright, I walk over and take the earrings from her hand.

'Did you get the tan?'

'What tan?' Shit, I forgot the tan.

'I sent you a message, Mom. You replied, said you'd get it.'

'I think I said I'd try to get it Amber, if I got a lunch break.'

I'm not going to tell her I did get a lunch break. But instead of rushing from one shop to another fulfilling Amber's empty dreams I sat with Marie and Sienna in Arthur's pub next door to the salon and actually had lunch.

Amber frowns as she walks away. It seems to me I see a lot more frowns than smiles on that beautiful face lately.

'If you're going to continue frowning, Amber, you really should use cheaper make-up.'

'I don't know why you put up with not getting a lunch break, Mom. You should join the union, they shouldn't get away with that.'

Amber's at an age where she thinks she knows exactly how the world should be run and she's not afraid to share her opinion. Maybe the kid is right. The simplicity of it all. What's obvious in the daylight of youth becomes blinded by the shadows of adulthood.

'I got my highlights done when the shop was quiet on Wednesday, Amber – cost me nothing. Quid pro quo.'

A grunt of disdain, before she moves her attention back to her mobile phone and walks into her bedroom, closing the door behind her.

Chapter Five

I'm sitting with my feet up on the sofa, sipping wine, when I hear the key turn in the door. I wasn't expecting Tom for at least another hour, if not more. My heart jumps. What am I going to say? I've spent hours going round and round in my head, rehearsing the words 'Do you have another child, Tom?' 'Is there something you would like to share with me, Tom?' But the words have suddenly disappeared, the sound of Tom's footsteps scaring them away.

He enters the room. 'You still up?'

I'm usually already asleep in bed at this time on a Saturday night. A full day of bleaching and braiding sends me into a coma once Amber is safely in her bed. But tonight my mind is restless.

Tom is hanging his coat over the back of a dining-room chair when it strikes me. This man – standing looking at the TV, stretching his back while scratching his neck – there is no way he could be hiding such a big secret from me. Tom loves me, I know that. Even if he had got someone pregnant before he met me, he would have told me. Wouldn't he?

I was twenty-one when I first saw Tom's smile. Myself and my friend Emer were walking down Jones Road in the shadow of Croke Park when a gang of lads approached us. Tom was one of them, holding a flag on his way to the match, his tall fit body hidden beneath a Dublin jersey. Emer had made me go to the match, said the craic would be brilliant. She had got the coveted tickets from her boyfriend. Tom was one of his mates. The long-awaited win had injected everyone with the energy to celebrate until four in the morning and that's when he kissed me. When our destiny was sealed. After a few months dating, Amber's conception accelerated our plans. I never doubted that I wanted to marry Tom. I loved him from the start, his gentleness, his kindness, his way of making me feel like I was the only girl in the world. The idea of spending my life with him was a dream come true. So getting married earlier than we planned didn't matter to me, or to him. We were both happy about it. My father wasn't so thrilled but he put his hand in his wallet, which unlike his heart was always full, and made the day happen.

Tom's phone beeps. He takes it from the pocket in his jeans and glances at the screen before putting it down on the table. If he leaves the room now, I could have a quick look in the contacts, see if there's a Kenny.

'I think I heard one of the boys stirring, Tom, will you check?'

'I didn't hear anything.'

'All right,' I sigh, lifting my feet to the floor. 'I'll go.'

'No, I'll do it.'

With Tom out of the room, I jump up from the sofa and grab his phone. The screen lights up the moment I swipe it. No lock. He's certainly not trying to hide anything here, which is good. Still, my eyes troll through the contacts list while my ears listen out carefully for his familiar thud on the stairs.

Amber, Alan, Brian, Colm… on and on until I reach K.

Kilkenny Golf Club, Karina Ryan, Kohl Tyres. Kenny's… My stomach rises, retreating when I see the name beside it. Golf Shop. Kenny's Golf Shop, where Tom gets all the tools he blames when he's had a bad day on the course.

A door above my head closes. Tom's footsteps on the stairs. I place the phone on the table and move back to the sofa.

Go out, light, please go out.

The screen is still lit up, taking forever to go dark. But it does. Just as Tom walks in through the door.

'They're both out cold up there,' he says, opening the drinks cabinet and taking out a bottle of Baileys.

'Do you want one?' He holds the bottle up in the air to tempt me.

'No, thanks.'

'The lads had to head off early so I only had the three pints.' He says this like there's a quota he's supposed to hit. 'They're all up at the crack of dawn for the captain's day tomorrow.'

Oh, here we go. Tom was raging when I arranged the twins' birthday party on the same day as some big golf tournament he wanted to play in. I explained to him there was nothing I could do about that. The twins' birthday is the same day every year. It always will be and this was the closest Sunday to the day. He suggested that I could have had it on the Saturday but I reminded him that I have to work on Saturdays, and that we both knew whose fault that is. That shut him up.

With his Baileys in hand he moves to the far end of the sofa. Usually I stretch my feet over his legs but this time

I pull them away from his touch. I don't know why but the picture jumps to the front of my head. The pink shirt. The day we bought it sticks in my head because Aaron got sick on the floor of the shop after eating a whole packet of jellies, while Tom was at the till. I was in a panic trying to clean it up with a crumbling tissue I found in my pocket, when the woman came out from behind the counter in a panic waving her hands for everyone to step away. Tom looked at me, both of us trying not to laugh at the woman's reaction to a bit of baby puke.

The wine in my blood stream is making me braver and weaker at the same time. Will I say something? Or should I wait and look for some real evidence. Something to suggest that it was Tom in that photo before I go jumping down his neck.

'Do you have another child, Tom?' The words slip out of my mouth before I have time to stop them. The wine must be conducting my brain. Tom is in the middle of laughing at something Graham Norton is proclaiming when he turns to look at me.

'What?'

'I'm asking you if you have another child, Tom?' My heart thumps like a bass drum threatening to drown out his answer. He laughs. Just a short chuckle before turning his attention back to the TV. What do I do now? He thinks I'm joking.

'I'm not joking, Tom, do you have another child? A teenage boy.' Taking the remote in his hand he lowers the volume on the TV and twists around in the sofa to face me.

'You're for real, are you? You're actually asking me if I have another child?'

'Ehh… yes?'

The look on his face describes exactly what he's thinking. That I'm crazy. 'What makes you ask that, Sally?'

'I saw a photo today of a teenage boy and I thought I saw you in the picture with him. The girl with the photo said the man was the boy's father.'

'What?' He moves forward to the edge of the seat and places the hand that isn't holding the Baileys on my foot. I pull my foot away. 'What are you talking about, Sally?'

'Today in the hairdresser's, a young girl showed me a photo of her boyfriend with his father. It looked like you in the picture.'

'Why are you saying this? That's not possible.'

'I'm telling you what I saw.'

'It must be some guy who looks like me, Sally. It certainly isn't me.'

'So you're telling me you don't have another child.'

'For fuck's sake, Sally, how much of that wine did you drink? This is crazy talk.'

He heads back to the drinks cabinet to fill up his glass. And for some reason, I feel like he's an intruder in the room. Someone who doesn't belong here.

'You really need to stop drinking so much wine, Sal. It's beginning to play games with your mind.'

He returns to the sofa, raises the volume on the TV and tunes back in to the entertainment. I'm sitting here feeling like a fool. It has to have been someone else in the photo. Someone who looked like Tom. Someone with the same expression, the same pink shirt. I've been so tired lately. Working full time, caring for the twins and worrying about Amber and how distant she seems. Maybe my imagination is playing tricks with me. And with the party tomorrow...

Oh no… Shit. I forgot to pick up the birthday cake on the way home from work. I don't fucking believe it.

Grabbing my cell, I quickly Google Thunder's Bakery.

The boys are expecting Thomas the Tank Engine to be stationed in the middle of their party table tomorrow. They've been talking about it all week. Well, actually I have, trying to rouse them, get them all excited.

I flick through the screen. *Please be open Sunday… pleeeease.*

> Opening hours. Mon – Sat 9 a.m. to 6 p.m.
> Closed Sunday.

Fuck. I can't believe it. The cake. What will I do? The most important day for Cian and Aaron and I'm off somewhere in my head playing the victim. Worried about a stupid photograph that some stranger shows me of what might or might not have happened in the past and all the time neglecting the present. The boys, the party, the family I love.

Chapter Six

'How did you forget to pick up the cake?' Amber is pumping air into balloons and judging me at the same time.

'I was run off my feet yesterday, Amber. It slipped my mind.' I hear myself explaining my actions, or lack of them, to my fifteen-year-old daughter who is shaking her head in despair. That's not right.

Washing crayon marks off the Thomas the Tank Engine that I intend sticking on the top of a Tesco birthday cake, I turn around to face her.

'Amber, when you're a full-time working mother, looking after a house and raising three children, maybe then you can qualify to question me.'

'Don't worry, that won't happen.'

'Why not?'

Amber holds three balloons in both hands and walks towards the playroom.

'I intend marrying someone with lots of money.'

'Well, that's disappointing to hear,' I shout after her. 'I would have thought if you wanted loads of money you'd be able to earn it for yourself. Not wait for some man to give it to you.'

'Why do you presume I'm talking about a man,' she says, raising her foot to close the door between us. She couldn't let me win even that one.

Lifting the tea towel, I dry off the train engine and consider how disappointing it is to hear my daughter say she does not want to end up like me. What's wrong with me? I thought I was a great role model, earning my own living while keeping the ship afloat. But what does Amber see?

Someone whose dreams of opening their own salon never came through. Someone rushing and racing, tired every night, unable to keep their eyes open to the end of a movie. Someone who spends less and less time with their friends. Gradually skipping going out on Thursday night with the girls, until eventually stopping altogether.

Is that what Amber sees? A tired old woman, not yet forty, whose life has become so busy she does nothing except fulfil the basic needs for her family's survival.

Of course she doesn't see that when she looks at Daddy. Tom. The calm one. The one who never loses his head. He gets to play golf, enjoy a few pints with his buddies. With 'yes' being the most common word Amber hears coming out of his mouth, I'm not surprised it's always Tom she goes to when she wants permission to do something.

Like the first time she wanted to go to Wrights Disco. They both confronted me in the kitchen to raise the subject after I had been adamant she wasn't allowed go until she was fifteen. Shoulder to shoulder they stood in front of me. 'Sure, she'll be fifteen in a couple of months,' Tom said while Amber listed all the girls in her class that were allowed to go. With no energy left to fight them, I eventually gave in.

It wasn't Tom the bouncers rang when Amber was found puking at the back of one of the sound speakers, barely conscious, having downed half a naggin of vodka.

It wasn't Tom who had to drive out and lift his little baby into the back of the car, pissed. No. He was down the local with his buddies.

When the room is decorated and the table set, I leave the house to find a cake I can stick a toy on top of and call a Thomas the Tank Engine masterpiece.

Last night I woke up a hundred times worrying about the photo on Charlie's cell phone. In fact, I'm not sure I got any sleep at all. My imagination held me hostage as the possibilities circled my mind, keeping me from getting any worthy sleep. Was it Tom? Was it not Tom? If it is Tom's kid, what will I do?

The night was endless. At one point I stretched my leg to Tom's side and realized he wasn't there. Thinking he'd gone to the loo I waited for him to return. After a while, when there was no sign of him, I decided to go and see if he was okay.

The landing was dark as I tiptoed past the boys' room, certain I could hear Tom talking to someone – and wondering who the hell it could be in the middle of the night.

'Tom,' I whispered loudly. My initial reaction: something is wrong. 'Tom.' I arrived at the bottom of the stairs and Tom stuck his head around the kitchen door.

'Are you on the phone, Tom?'

'No. Just getting some water. Go back to bed.'

I turned like a good girl and did as I was told.

–

I park in the Tesco car park and make my way to the cake aisle. Lo and behold, what do I see but a big cake adorned with a picture of Thomas the Tank Engine! Not the three-dimensional showstopper I had ordered from Thunder's Bakery but it would do fine.

Thanking God for the small things, I place the cake on the back seat of the car between the toddler seats and a clatter of toys when a thought zips across my mind like fire. I brought the water up to the room like I do every night. I left one on Tom's bedside locker. Twenty bottles for two euros in Lidl. Tom's bottle was still there this morning unopened. He didn't go to the kitchen looking for water. He lied.

Chapter Seven

I manage to drive the car home without killing someone or hitting a tree. To add to my stress levels, Tom's mother, Ellen, is standing at my front door waiting for it to open when I pull up into the drive. I distinctly said 'No need' when she offered to come over and help with the preparations. 'Everything is under control. Just arrive at two.' Sweet Jesus, the woman is about two hours too early. It's not that I don't like Ellen, I do, I'm just not in the habit of small talk. I need to focus on making this party as good as it should be for the boys.

With my nervous breakdown put on hold, I take a deep breath, look up to the sky and exhale. Now is not the time, Sally. Hold it together until this evening when everyone has gone home. When the kids are asleep and Tom is opening a beer, expressing his delight at how great things went while I celebrate the fact that we don't have to go through it again for another year. Usually I clink glasses with him. Not sure I will tonight.

'Thought I'd lend a hand.' Ellen approaches me, speaking in her usual happy-go-lucky voice. I'm lifting the cake from the back seat of the car, trying to ignore the fact that I did hear Tom secretly speaking to someone on the phone in the middle of the night.

'Thanks, Ellen,' I say, closing the door with my foot and carrying the cake up to the house where Amber is standing.

'Is that the cake?' Ellen says, her tone unable to hide how unimpressed she is.

'She forgot to pick up the real one,' Amber says.

'Who's she?' Ellen says. 'The cat's mother?'

'Oh!' Amber doesn't like being chastised by Granny Ellen.

'If your mother forgot to pick up the cake, she must have been very busy.' Ellen takes the cake from my hand and winks at me. 'This one looks great.'

Inside, Cian and Aaron are running around, kicking balloons and mashing Rice Krispie cakes into the carpet. They've managed to make the place look like the party is over before it's even begun.

'What the hell, Amber?'

'I didn't know. I couldn't hear them with my earphones on.'

'Where's your father?'

'He had to go out. He said someone's car broke down or something – I can't remember who. He had to drop them to the golf or something. He said he wouldn't be long.'

Ellen knows I want to scream, but I can't do it in front of her. Does Tom think I'm a fool? Someone's car broke down! I hope he hasn't gone playing golf, leaving me here for the day to suffer this party on my own. Maybe he asked Ellen to come over early, knowing he wouldn't be here. He wouldn't. Would he pretend he wasn't going to play golf and then go and play it? He has become something of a stranger to me in the past twenty-four hours.

Ellen opens the press and takes out the vacuum cleaner.

'Amber,' she calls out. 'Take the boys to their room and stay with them. We'll have this fixed up in no time.'

With the mop taking the brunt of my anger we get the room back in shape with little or no conversation.

Ellen is not the type of woman to make excuses for her son. Since the day we got married I've always felt she supported me – always showing empathy for my dilemmas, offering to help when she can. Maybe she was grateful I'd taken Tom off her hands. Or maybe she just liked me, saw I was doing my best. With my own mom dying so young, it was good to know she was there if I needed her.

Taking the band from her long, dark hair that she gets coloured on my staff discount every six weeks, Ellen shakes her head and looks around the room.

At the centre of the table rests the cake; Thomas the Tank Engines at both ends. Percy and Gordon leading the convoy of sponge and icing, James and Edward securing it from the rear. All is saved. Ellen smiles across the table at me.

'Wonderful, Sally,' she says. 'Everything looks lovely. Well done. Have you got any candles?'

'Shit.'

'Don't worry, I'll pop down to the shop and get some.'

'No, I'll get Amber to go, you don't have to.' But Ellen insists, says she could do with the walk.

There's still over an hour before the crowd arrives. Taking my phone from my bag I check to see if Tom has tried to make contact. Nothing. Just a message from one of the school parents telling me her son won't be able to make it. Great. There are too many coming anyway. Refusals are very welcome.

I prepare some snacks for the adults – cheese, crackers, pate, hummus, dips – before heading to the boys' bedroom where I find Amber sitting on the bed reading them a story. Cian and Aaron sit either side of her looking at the pages as she turns them. My heart warms. This is their day. Cian and Aaron's. Their memories. Nothing should spoil it for them.

Amber lifts her eyes from the book when she sees me. She's waiting to see what humour I'm in; will I have a go at her for letting the boys wreck the room? I won't let Tom's disappearing act ruin everything. *Turn it on, Sally. Turn it on.*

'Okay,' I say in a bright happy voice. 'Who's ready to get dressed for the party?'

Amber drops the book, pulls herself off the bed and hurries out of the room. The boys run towards me. 'Me, me, me, me, me.'

–

There is still no sign, or word, from Tom when the first guests arrive. His phone is going straight to voice message each time I call. He may have decided to let the party commence without him knowing I won't say anything in front of our guests when he walks in. He'll be all smiles and hellos, playing with the kids, flirting with the mothers and joking with the fathers. He's always the same, life of the party, entertaining the masses while I rush around tripping over myself making sure everyone has what they need. Earlier on in the week, I'd asked him to look after the drinks this year, pour the odd glass of wine for someone, keep the bottle opener on hand but it doesn't look like that's going to happen.

'Are you all right, Ellen?' I say.

Ellen has arrived at the door looking the worse for her little piece of exercise.

'Yes, I'm fine, thanks.' She hands me the box of candles before going to a bottle of wine on the counter top and pouring a glass which she drinks rather quickly for her.

–

The party is well underway. Laughter, music, chatter, but all I hear is noise. I'm getting worried. People have been asking where Tom is. 'He should be here shortly,' I tell them. 'He just had to pop out, a friend's car broke down.' At least it's something to say. An excuse for Daddy not being here for his kids' birthday party.

I try to ring him again. Beep, beep, beep, beep, then straight to the answer machine. 'Tom, ring me ASAP,' I say. Like that's going to make a difference. If he's on the golf course he can't take a call. But if he isn't... I'm not sure what to think. Why is he not here? Part of me hopes he is on the golf course otherwise something bad has happened.

A thought crosses my mind. If he is playing, his golf bag will be gone from the shed. I'll slip out and have a look.

The kitchen is bursting with parents, laughing, chewing on nibbles and sipping drinks when I push through. Their kids are in the playroom being supervised by two mothers, Jen and Gillian, members of the 'can't drink in front of the kids brigade'. Thank God for them, they come in very handy at a time like this.

Outside the damp air cools my face. The tree at the back of the garden stands motionless beside the old wooden shed that's struggling to stay standing. Before the adjustment, we were meant to have it replaced with one of those all new weather sheds that last forever according to the advertisement. But nothing lasts forever, not even a shed.

The door is locked. Reaching up onto the tip of my toes I stretch to look in the small plastic window that's about as useless as an umbrella in a storm. It's covered in dirt and blocked by a load of storage boxes. There is no way of telling whether Tom's golf bag is in there or not.

Back inside the house I mingle with the laughing crowd while my heart beats a completely different rhythm to theirs. If Tom is not on the golf course where is he?

Amber looks over at me. She can sense something is wrong. Above her head her image hangs, all smiles and innocence. It was taken the day she started secondary school. Her hair short, cut in a bob. There's a gap between her teeth. Four thousand euros later and the gap is gone.

I can still remember how excited she was to be starting secondary school. The extra freedom she thought she was going to get. The extra-curricular activities. The extra friends. Always extra, more, more, more, but never enough.

'What exactly did your father say?' I whisper in her ear while taking paper plates from the table by her side.

Amber is worried. This is not normal for Tom. Amber knows it. He was more excited about the kids' party than the kids themselves. Planning, preparing, suggesting. If it was left to Tom there'd be bouncy castles, magicians, clowns, a hundred balloons. I had to show him the bank balance, remind him he was clown enough. So not being here for Cian and Aaron's birthday party is worrying. Luckily the boys are so busy opening presents and playing with their friends they haven't noticed yet.

'I hope he hasn't had an accident, Mom,' Amber says, tears glinting like jewels amongst a field of mascara.

'Don't worry, darling. He'll be back shortly.' I try to console her but my words do nothing to wash the worry from her face. She knows I'm just saying this, that I don't know if he'll be back shortly.

'Ellen, I'm popping out for a few minutes, will you hold the fort?'

'Everything okay?'

'No. Amber is up the wall over her daddy, I want to see if he's playing golf. Put Amber's mind at rest… and my own.'

'Will you be long?'

'Half an hour at the most. No one will even miss me.'

The tall shape of a man is standing on the opposite side of the stained-glass door when I walk out to the hallway. For a moment my heart lifts. He's here. Tom is back. But then I realize it can't be Tom. He wouldn't be waiting for someone to answer the door when he has a key. With my hand on the lock, presuming it to be one of the kid's daddies arriving, I open the door. Shock.

'Dad!'

'Sally.' He smiles at me.

'What are you doing here?'

'Just thought I'd call in and say happy birthday to the boys.'

His hair has a little extra grey, sprinkled among the dark strands, wrinkles jut out from his dark brown eyes. But other than that, nothing much has changed. He still stands tall and straight like he'd spent time in the army, which he hasn't. My father's wars were all fought at home.

He bends forward, his broad shoulders leaning in to hug me. As a kid I would sit on those shoulders for hours, my rest from a long walk, my outpost from which to view a game or the parade on Paddy's Day. But as I got older, the view became tainted, the shoulders of my giant slowly becoming those of a coward's.

'Are you not going to invite me in?'

I step back from the doorway allowing him to enter. Everything is dancing around in my brain. The last time I laid eyes on my father was over a year ago. And now here he is. All six feet two of him strolling down my hallway like he is doing someone a favour.

Releasing my tight grip from the door handle I close my gaping mouth and follow him into the front room.

His size reflects his presence. Intrusive. Amber is standing by the table about to lift a bowl full of jelly sweets when she looks over at him. Wow, I'm not sure if she wants to laugh or cry, her face is desperately trying to hold back some kind of explosion.

'Amber,' I call out, attempting to break her trance. 'Say hello to your granddad.' There are two other parents in the room helping to clear up the table now the kids have all retired to the playroom. Thankfully they are not aware of how fucking mad this is.

Amber steps forward, looking slightly awkward but when my father puts his arms out she steps into his embrace and hugs him.

'My, you are such a pretty girl, Amber!' he says before embarrassing himself by asking her what age she is now.

'Fifteen.' She smiles, all fears for her missing daddy gone out the window. No one expected this distraction.

The noise from the kitchen reminds me there's a party going on so I inhale deeply and head back to the crowd, leaving Amber to chat to her grandfather. My head does not know which dilemma to concentrate on but I can't sneak out now, not with my father in the next room. I reach for my phone. No messages. Jesus, Tom, where are you?

The noise has reached a new level of annoyance. I want all these people to leave. Pack up their kids and party bags and make their way to the door. Ellen must sense my wishes. She's busy tidying up, subtly suggesting they've all had enough. Asking them if they've had a nice time and what their plans are for the rest of the day. Nice work, Ellen.

All that effort and now we're practically pushing the guests out the door because Tom isn't here and no one knows why.

Deirdre from three doors up seems most upset at the suggestion the party is ending. Watching her fill her glass, I'm guessing she had plans to stay here for as long as she could. If I had to go home to her house, to that donkey of a man she married, I'd be filling my glass too. And Donna, flirty Donna. I'm pretty sure she's not impressed she didn't get a chance to flaunt her stuff at 'Big Bad Tom'. That's what she calls my husband, for some reason. It bugs me. But I have bigger things to worry about. My husband is missing and my father has arrived.

'How's it going?' His voice always has that same hushed tone like everything he says is a secret.

'What?'

'Where's Tom?'

'Oh, he had to go and help a friend who was in a spot of trouble, I'm expecting him back very soon.'

'That's a bit strange – was there no one else who could—'

43

Shooting a stare straight into my father's eyes, I stop him mid-sentence. There is no way I'm going to listen to my father criticize Tom, no way.

I walk away from his words to where Amber is standing in the bustling hallway. My dad follows, walks past me. 'I'll be in touch, call me if you need me,' he says, before kissing Amber on the head and muttering a few words to her before walking out the door.

Chapter Eight

The children are delighted with the goodie bags Amber hands them as they leave. My heart is thumping in my chest, my legs barely strong enough to hold me up. The possibility that something dreadful has happened to Tom won't leave my head.

Waving goodbye with the little energy I can pull from my exhausted body, I thank everyone for their lovely presents and wish them safe home. The smile on my face is forced, which hurts.

My dad didn't stay long, just long enough to unsettle me. Why did he call today? He's never come to any other birthday parties. I'm surprised he even remembered it was the boys' birthday. But he handed them a card each. Money, his answer to everything.

When the last of the crowd have finally gone and the door is firmly closed, Ellen asks if I want her to stay until I hear from Tom.

'No thanks, Ellen, you've been a great help; go home, Jack is waiting outside for you. I'll call as soon as I hear from Tom.'

Jack is Ellen's new man. Well, maybe not new, she's been with him almost six years but that's what he's still known as. Ellen's new man. Her first husband Thomas, Tom's dad, died fourteen years ago when Amber was a one-year-old. It took a lot out of Tom, especially the two years of suffering his father went through. In and out of hospitals. The treatment is working. The treatment isn't working. Hope given. Hope taken away until eventually there's no hope at all.

'Be sure to call,' Ellen says, giving me a hug, which I find unusual. 'I'm sure he's okay, Sally,' she whispers in my ear.

Pulling a twenty from her purse, Ellen hands it to Amber whose face lightens momentarily.

'Do what your mother says, young woman.'

'I will, Nan, I always do.' A puff of laughter leaves my mouth. Pulling Amber closer to me I hug her arm. 'Well, I *do*.'

'I know you do, sweetie,' I say, pushing a stray hair from her face. 'Most of the time.'

Amber's phone beeps sending her hurtling towards the table where it lights up. Ellen's hand waves in the air as she walks down the pathway towards Jack who nods when he sees me. He's a quiet man, doesn't like to come into the house or join any family events. He's an outsider and wants to keep it that way. Wise man.

When I close the door Amber is already halfway up the stairs. Cian and Aaron are in the playroom tearing toys out of bullet-proof packaging. I'm tearing my hair out.

I need to contact Tom. I'm really worried now. Should I call the police? How long do I have to wait before I can call them? A grown man gone missing for six hours is not going to cause much concern to the force. Especially on a Sunday afternoon when half the pubs in the country are pulling pints to the anthems of whatever football teams are playing.

With the phone in my hand I decide to ring one of Tom's golf buddy's wife. Sinead, I like her. I'll ask her if she heard anything about the lad's car breaking down. Tell her Tom went to help and hasn't been back since. My finger is swiping through my contacts when Amber comes thundering down the stairs.

'I have to go, Mom.'

Before I know it she's out the hall door.

'What the hell?' I rush out after her. 'Where are you going? Get back here now.'

'I'm going to Sarah's, she needs me, I have to go now.'

'I need you,' I shout but she's already halfway down the road.

Sarah, Amber's friend, thrives on drama and Amber thrives on consoling her. Not a good mix, if you ask me. But there's nothing I can do about it. According to Amber I should have more sympathy for her. I don't. There are too many kids starving in the world for me to lose sleep if Sarah only manages silver when she was expecting gold at the Irish World Dancing Championship. Or if her boyfriend misspelled her name on her birthday card. I admire Amber's caring and comforting nature, even if it is only for her peers. But I think Sarah takes advantage of her.

Before making the call to Sinead, I check in on Cian and Aaron who are still mesmerized by the amount of new toys they have. Hopefully it won't be long now before the day catches up with them and I can take them to bed.

'Where's Daddy?' Cian says, looking up from a plastic fire engine he pushes across the floor. Aaron looks up too.

'He should be here shortly. His friend's car broke down.'

'But he didn't get any cake,' Cian says.

47

'He can have some when he gets back.' Their little faces stare at me for answers, waiting for me to say something they understand. Why was their daddy not at their party?

'Wow, you got loads of toys!' Immediately I move their attention back to the pile of presents surrounding them. Aaron is handing me a green tractor which I smile at and admire. Cian jumps to his feet.

'He's here, he's here. Daddy's home.'

Cian rushes past to where Tom is arriving at my back. 'Daddy, Daddy.'

Aaron doesn't move from his spot, lifting a toy and holding it out for his daddy to see. I want to take the green tractor in my hand and smash it on Tom's head. But when I turn around, the face I see is completely altered to the one I left behind this morning. Ashen, the haunted expression making it clear that he wasn't on the golf course. I take a deep breath and brace myself for what I'm about to hear.

Chapter Nine

'Where have you been, I was worried sick?' I find myself speaking with concern and smoothing Tom's ruffled hair instead of shouting at him. His face is white, his breathing shallow. I look into his eyes, heavy with worry. And still he says nothing.

'What's wrong, Tom, what happened?'

He pushes past me, lifting Cian in his arms before kneeling on the ground in front of Aaron.

'I'm sorry, boys,' he says. 'Daddy had to help a friend. Look at all these lovely toys.'

'We got lots and lots and lots.' Cian runs from Tom's grip to gather as many presents in his hands as possible. Aaron stands watching Cian, then runs at him pushing Cian to the ground and grabbing a train from his hand. 'Mine, mine, mine.'

'There's enough here for everyone, Aaron,' I say. 'You have to learn to share.' Lifting Cian in my arms, I hug him tightly, kissing his forehead and sniffing his hair.

'Say sorry to your brother, Aaron,' I say.

Aaron turns his back on us and pushes the train along the ground. He's a couple of inches shorter than Cian, the first to be dragged out of my womb. He's also a lot thinner than his brother, which considering how much he eats surprises me. Aaron can finish a whole plate of dinner while Cian is still dipping his first chip into the ketchup.

'Aaron, Aaron,' I say, but he doesn't answer.

'Leave it out.' Tom shuffles over beside Aaron. Cian wiggles from my grip to join them. They have forgiven Tom already. Somehow, I have become the bad person in the room.

Standing by the doorway, arms crossed, I watch Tom playing with the boys and wonder about the man. What is going on? Is he planning on explaining where he was or does he think I'm going to accept the silly explanation he gave the kids? If he is, he can think again.

'Tom, can I see you outside, please?'

He acts like he doesn't hear me, like a teenager being asked to do a chore.

'Tom.'

'What?' he grunts, turning abruptly to look at me. There's something different in his eyes. Is he trying to hide something?

'Tom, I want to talk to you.'

'I'm playing with the boys, Sally. Can't it wait until they go to bed?'

'I guess it can… Right, boys… time for bed.'

–

With Cian and Aaron fast asleep, Tom then decides to take a shower. Anything to delay his big confession. I'm sitting at the breakfast bar in the kitchen, drinking a glass of leftover wine from the party when he walks in.

'What a day,' he says attempting to lighten the seriousness of his absence. I don't engage. 'How did the party go?'

Lifting a glass to my mouth, I stare at him without answering.

'Look, Sally, I'm really sorry, I tried to get here, I promise, but things just went from bad to worse.'

'I'm all ears,' I say, showing little empathy.

'Eamon called, his car broke down. I went to pick him up and bring him to the golf club. I would have been back in time. But...' Pushing his hand through wet hair, Tom sighs. He turns his head away from me and wipes his eyes. Shit. Is he going to cry?

'What happened, Tom?' Moving off the stool to the other side of the kitchen island I notice he is shaking.

'I hit someone with the car.'

'You what?'

'Someone on a bike.' Tom sees the alarm on my face. 'Look, they're fine... it's nothing serious... they got discharged from the hospital... but—'

'But what, Tom?'

'The police took me to the station and breathalyzed me, it took them forever. Right bastards. I told them it was my kids' birthdays but they didn't seem to give a toss. Eventually they did the breath test, which I passed. The problem is...' Taking a deep breath he pauses for a moment then, gripping my arms, he looks into my eyes, preparing me for something bad. 'I went through a red light. I wasn't concentrating, Sal, I was rushing back to the party... They have a witness.'

My heart is in my mouth. The idiot. What is going to happen?

'You're sure that cyclist is okay? Was it a man or a woman?'

'The cyclist is fine, Sally, she only had a scratch on her wrist.'

'So why did she go to the hospital if she only had a scratch on her wrist?'

Pulling away from his grip I move a few steps away.

'I don't know, Sal, she just did.' He rubs his hand into his hair and sighs. I can tell he's playing it down, no one volunteers to spend a day in A and E over a scratch. She must have needed stitches or something. And how did he hit her? In all the years I've known Tom he has never had an accident in the car, never even scratched it. Something was distracting him.

Tired of confrontation, I drop the subject, he's clearly not in the humour of discussing the implications at the moment, the trouble he could be in. Jesus, I hope he doesn't end up in jail, that's all I'd need. I'm about to leave the room when I hear the front door opening.

'Here's Amber… don't mention the accident.' Moving to the sink I turn on the tap and try to act like everything is great. Amber opens the door and glances in at us briefly.

'I'm heading to bed. Night.'

This day is getting weirder by the minute. Why didn't Amber come in to us, ask her daddy where he was or what happened to him? She seemed mightily concerned earlier. Sarah's newest dilemma must be absorbing her thoughts. Still, I'm surprised. I would have thought she'd at least ask him if he was okay. I guess she presumes everything is because he's home now.

'That's strange,' I say, switching off the tap and lifting my glass.

'What's strange?'

'Amber. She never asked what happened and she was very concerned earlier.'

Tom says nothing. The light from the fridge brightens his face when he opens the door. Taking a beer, he walks towards the front room asking how things went for the boys.

'Fine, I think, I was so distracted I… Oh I forgot to tell you, my father showed up.'

Tom stops in his tracks and turns to look at me. 'What?'

'I know – I couldn't believe it either.'

'Did he say why?'

'What do you mean, it was the boys' birthday party?'

'But how did he know we were having a party. Did you tell him?'

'No, sure I haven't heard from him for months.' Tom turns to go into the other room. But doesn't enter. He stops then turns his head slightly.

'Was Amber talking to him?'

'Yes, she seemed quite happy to see him.'

'My mom.'

'What about your mom?'

'Was she talking to him?'

'Christ, Tom, I don't know, I don't remember seeing them talking but the place was very busy so… she could have been… why?'

'Just wondering.' Taking a swig from his can of beer, he continues into the other room.

My phone beeps. It's Ellen.

Any sign of him?

'What do you want me to tell your mother?' I say through the double doors.

'Just tell her my car broke down or something.'

Well, that came easy to him. Lying to his mother. I'm not doing that. Especially when she already knows the one about the friend's car breaking down.

I reply to the message.

He's home safe, bit of a saga, can't talk now,
I'll ring you tomorrow.

I don't know what is going on with Tom. But some-thing definitely is. Should I go in and question him more? Ask him who he was talking to on the phone in the middle of the night. The way he is at the moment, stressed, distracted, I don't think I'd get the truth. He's been acting strange ever since I mentioned the photo, which worries me. Does this mean that Charlie is right? Or is something else going on? With my palm on the door handle I'm about to go in to him when Amber sticks her head over the bannisters.

'Is everything okay, Mom?' Her voice a whisper.

'Yes, everything's fine.' I move my hand from the door and walk up the stairs. I'm not about to start arguing with Tom while Amber is still awake and listening.

Chapter Ten

Lying in bed, I stare at the ceiling, then my phone, then the sheep who just won't jump the fence. Two hours twisting and turning. This is going nowhere. My mind is making a horror movie out of my thoughts. Reading doesn't help. Five pages in and I realize not one word has registered. I fling the book onto the floor by the side of the bed and slip out from under the duvet. The sound of Tom's snoring echoes through the eerie silence. Whatever is going on, it's not disturbing his sleep.

The room is completely dark. Rummaging on the back of the door, I locate my dressing gown and wrap it around me. Gently I close the door behind, walk down the stairs and hope my midnight wander doesn't waken any of the kids.

When I get to the kitchen I look out the window and see the night's stars twinkle in the sky. Their mere existence eases my stress. Moving up close to the pane of glass I stare at the sky wondering, wishing, praying. Hoping that Tom is not lying to me.

My mind becomes completely hypnotized by the beauty on show above my head and I feel a peace surround me, holding me tightly. Helping me consider that maybe things will turn out okay. Hugging my dressing gown close around me I open the back door and step out into the calm night. Into the still painting.

Inhaling the cool air, I allow myself to relax, enjoy this moment. No one is hanging on me, calling me, asking me where stuff is. I try to forget that soon I will once again be lost amongst the shuffle of life. For now, this peace brings a sense of freedom, and it's all mine. My head is tilted towards the heavens when suddenly I feel like I'm not alone. There is someone watching me. Am I imagining it?

A wave of cool air blows across my face dragging me from my peaceful world back into this mess. Who's that? I see a body attempting to pull itself over the back wall. Someone was in the garden.

'Tom, Tom,' I scream, rushing to the bottom of the garden and triggering the security light when I step off the patio.

Not considering what I would actually do if I caught the intruder, I continue to run. But I'm too late. They've scaled the wall, I can see them heading out to the laneway but not before they turn and look at me.

Dark, wild eyes open wide, staring straight into mine. With my heart racing I continue to call out Tom's name but instead of waking him, Rena from next door opens her bedroom window.

'Are you all right, Sal?' I have to drag on the air to breathe and find it hard to answer her. With one hand across my heart I raise the other one to let her know I'm all right.

'Hang on, I'll come down.'

'No… No,' I say continuing to gasp for air. 'It's okay, Rena. They're gone.'

Eventually I convince Rena that all is well, she doesn't have to call the police. My heart is still thumping in my chest as I scale the stairs to alert Tom, who has managed to sleep through the whole drama.

The light from the landing is casting a shadow over Tom who hasn't yet stirred so I shake his shoulders. 'Tom, wake up, Tom.'

'What?' His eyes flicker into consciousness. 'What's going on?'

'There was someone in the garden.'

'What?' He sits up, rubs his hand over his face. 'Why didn't you call me?'

'I did fucking call you. You didn't hear me, Rena heard me, she came to my rescue.'

Tom moves his legs from under the duvet and sits at the side of the bed, his hand brushing through his hair as he bends over considering what I've just told him. I know what he's thinking. He's worried now.

'Did you see who it was?'

'I got a glimpse of their face, just for a second and the hair. I can still see the eyes staring at me.'

Tom turns and looks straight at me for the first time since I woke him. 'Did you know them?'

I shake my head.

'What age were they?'

'I don't know, Tom, I didn't ask.'

Moving over to the window Tom pulls back the curtain and scans the garden.

'There's no one out there now, Tom, I chased them off.'

'What the hell was someone doing in our garden?'

The house is positioned at the end of the road so it's the last one in the laneway. If they came to rob us, there are a lot easier options when considering a quick escape. The Murphys at the top of the laneway don't even have a gate at the rear, it's been broken for almost a year now and they've never had any hassle with intruders, that I know of.

Tom drops his grip on the curtain and turns to look at me again. 'You're sure you didn't know who it was?'

'Positive… Should I ring the police?'

Stepping away from the window he sits down on the bed. 'I don't think they'd be of much use now… they're gone.'

'I hope it's nothing to do with that cyclist you hit.'

'Jesus, Sal, stop being ridiculous.'

A moment of silence envelops us. Both of us nervous, neither of us knowing what to do next.

'But what if they come back, Tom?'

I wonder why they were in our garden? I'm wide awake, the peace the night sky had offered me earlier, now replaced with fear. Tom eventually speaks.

'Maybe it was just some drifter, Sal, I'll go out and check.'

Tom goes to leave the room so I follow him. He turns around. 'You stay here, Sal, get back into bed. I'll make sure the door is locked.'

'But…'

'Just go back to bed. I'll take care of it now.'

The words hang in the air as I get back into bed. *I'll take care of it now*, Big Bad Tom coming to save the day. Well, it's a bit late. What if the intruder had a knife? I could have been killed. Stabbed to death in my own back garden with Tom sleeping through my cries for help.

The night continues to tease. More twisting and turning beneath the sheets. Until eventually I hear the pitter patter of tiny feet cross the wooden floorboards. Aaron is the first to rise every morning. Since the boys moved into their own beds, Aaron makes his way into our room the moment the sun threatens to rise. He can sense the world stirring.

His little face arrives into view, moving close to mine to see if I'm awake. Then he reaches his warm hand out and places it on my face. What a lovely way to wake up, if only it was two hours later.

'Hi, baby,' I whisper, reaching out and lifting him in between myself and Tom. Tom is blissfully unaware of the extra person in the bed. The rhythm of his breathing doesn't alter and his body doesn't move. My near-death experience didn't shave any slumber from his sleep.

Praying Aaron falls back asleep, I wrap my arms around the small bundle. Sometimes I'm lucky and he drops back off, giving me another hour of rest under the duvet. But other times he just lies there, wide awake, staring into my eyes, pulling them open if I dare close them.

Thankfully, this time Aaron turns away from me, allowing me to pull him close to my body. Within a few minutes I hear his resting breath take him off to sleep. But I'm unable to join him. My mind works hard flicking through the events of the past two days. The photograph. Tom's denial. The accident. My dad showing up out of the blue.

Come to think about it, Tom never actually denied having another child. He just kept calling me crazy, suggested I was drinking too much wine. He never said the words, *No, Sally, I do not have another child*. And then there was that phone call in the middle of the night. I shouldn't have called out to him. It alerted him that I was coming down the stairs. Rookie mistake. The next time I'll sneak down and listen at the kitchen door. I'm going to have to become craftier if I'm to unravel the truth.

Careful not to wake Aaron, I lie like a corpse in the bed, not a stir, not a sniffle. Then beep, beep, beep. Tom's alarm goes off. His flapping arm moves out from under the duvet and eventually ends the disturbance. The noise hasn't woken Aaron and yet the first glimpse of the sun rising behind what I was told were the best blackout curtains available and he's up like an army soldier on dawn duty.

Dragging himself out of the bed, Tom stretches his body then pulls the curtain back on the window to peek outside. He says nothing, dropping his head before walking into the bathroom. I pretend I'm still sleeping.

–

A couple of hours later I have the house to myself. Oh bliss. Monday morning is the only time during the whole week that I get to be on my own.

Amber's in school. The twins are in pre-school and Tom has gone to one of the big glass buildings in the shiny financial centre, to see if he can earn back some of my money he lost two years ago on his big elaborate fail-proof scheme, that failed. It was going to be epic. They were his words. Epic. Well, it was Epic. An Epic flipping disaster.

Tom had already decided on his fancy car, the all-inclusive, five-star holiday and membership to some exclusive golf club, everything he didn't need. I was more pessimistic, or realistic. I didn't expect immediate results, knew it would take time for the portfolio to grow and there were two other members who had to get their share of the profits.

I was out in the garden trying to convince Aaron that leaves falling from trees was normal and he didn't have to cry each time it happened, when Tom walked out on to the deck. His face was white, green, grey. I can still see it changing. Words wouldn't leave his gaping mouth. He stood there trying to say my name. He told me the portfolio had collapsed, the money was all gone. I wanted to hit him with the hurley stick lying by the wall, but as usual, the kids were there; cushions for his fall. I had to hide my true feelings and walk away.

Every penny of that money had been hard earned. Ten years of tips stashed away in a post office account waiting for the day I would have enough to put a deposit on a small space. *Sally's Styles*. I had everything picked. The layout, the colours, the brochures. I'd sourced the suppliers, planned the advertising and designed the logo. When the right premises came on to the market at the right price, I'd be ready to pounce.

There will be no pouncing. Tom took it all. Convinced me we'd be mad to let the opportunity pass. Himself and two of his hair-gel buddies had secured a portfolio of apartments in countries whose names were unfamiliar to me. The only way the value could possibly go was up. I would have my thirteen thousand euros back, accompanied by a further thirteen thousand euros at the end of one year. I felt pressurised, told it would set the family up for life. 'It's a no brainer,' he said. Turns out, they were the ones missing the brains.

Looking out the kitchen window, I sip my coffee and notice the last of the leaves have surrendered to the winds. The trees at the bottom of the garden are finally bare. I'm not sweeping them up. Tom can. My time will be better spent trying to figure out if there's any truth in what I thought I saw in the photograph.

Confusion is circling my brain. I take the laptop off the counter top and open it. I'll check his email account first. Tom and I have never had separate passwords. Never had a need to hide anything. I thought.

Bogstandard.

'Nothing we'll find difficult to remember, just something bog-standard,' Tom had said, when I asked him what we should use as the password.

Flicking down the emails, I see nothing to alarm me. There are the usual advertisements: Hotels.com, Amazon, a few bill reminders and of course golf updates. No 'Your loving son, Kenny'.

I'm about to make my way up the stairs to have another poke around when the doorbell rings. Who the hell is that?

'Hi, hun.' Donna steps into the hallway without waiting for an invitation. 'Hope I'm not disturbing anything saucy.' She giggles. 'I'm just here to pick up my navy cardigan that I left behind yesterday.'

'Nothing saucy going on here,' I say. 'Tom's not even here, he's gone to work.'

'Ooh. What makes you think I was talking about Tom?'

Donna walks past me into the hallway and I follow. I'm confused by her comment and trying to pull my hair into some kind of shape. Donna is groomed to perfection, red hair tied up in a loose bun on the top of her happy head. Diamond earrings, dangling at both sides of her flawlessly made up face. YSL Opium, blazing a trail as she walks into the kitchen.

'What are you implying, Donna? I can assure you I...'

'Lighten up, woman. I was just joking.'

Suddenly I feel bad, I should have got that joke. Answered it with something witty. What is happening to me? 'I'm sorry, Donna, I'm just a bit tired today.'

'You were a bit tired yesterday too. What's up, girl?' Donna pulls a stool out, sits down and rests her arms on the island counter. Her eyes look straight into mine like she's planning on going nowhere until I answer.

Should I tell her? Should I make Donna my confidante in this, my latest saga? One half of me wants to blurt it out. 'I think Tom has a secret child.' But the other half of me says, no. Say nothing. You can't trust Donna. You don't know her well enough to share your paranoia with her. Especially when you doubt it yourself.

'I think Tom might have a child that he's not telling me about.' It's out of my mouth before I have time to stop it.

'What?'

Donna pulls the stool in closer to the counter top, her eyes unable to hide the shock, her head shaking in disbelief. Immediately I regret saying anything. This is just gossip to her. Why did I tell her? Donna must see the regret written all over my face because she stands up from the stool, walks over and hugs me close, squashing her ample boobs into my deflated ones.

'If it is true, Sally, you will survive it. It's not the worst thing in the world.'

I hold onto her hug, let some of my pain seep into her. Tears wet my face and I feel the burden of the last two days ease.

After a second cup of coffee, I find Donna's cardigan, hand it to her and thank her for calling over.

'We all have our troubles,' she says. 'It was my turn last year.' Taking her cardigan, she walks out to the hallway.

'He thought he could get away with it but I caught him, some girl in his office. Anyway, it's over now. I hope.'

I'm shocked to hear this. I always thought the grass was at its greenest in Donna's garden. 'Jesus, Donna, I'm sorry, I don't know what to say.'

'There is nothing to say, Sal.' She opens the door to leave, reminding me I'm a strong woman and I will get through this.

The door closes. I stand in the silence of my house and pray to God that Donna is right.

Chapter Eleven

Cian and Aaron are standing at the crèche door, hats, jackets and bags in hand when I arrive. I'm late, only by a few minutes but the look on Laura, their playschool teacher's face, does little to hide her annoyance. After apologizing one, two, three, maybe four times, I strap the boys into their car seats and drive out of the car park. A couple of minutes down the main road, I arrive at the Tesco car park. This is my life now. A series of chores made easier by strategically located car parks.

Today I'm wearing lipstick. Something I don't often do on my day off but Donna encouraged me. Do whatever it takes, hun, to make yourself feel better. *Don't be sitting around looking like your life depends on what your man does. Because let me tell you, it doesn't. It depends on what you do, babe.* Donna's all cheap lingo and expensive advice. But I like her.

Leaving the vegetable section behind I push the trolley down the first aisle, Aaron twisting from left to right in the seat in front of me. Cian shuffles by my side. Then I see her. At least I think it's her. Her blonde hair tied back, that cheeky face, confident strut and the jacket that looks the same as the one she had on in the salon. White. It had an embroidered tiger on the back. It has to be her.

Grabbing Cian with both hands I lift him in the air and drop him into the trolley to stand. Aaron turns his head in amusement but Cian is not happy about it.

'Let me out,' he says, looking down at the fruit and veg gathered around his feet.

'It's just for one minute.' I push the trolley to the end of the aisle where I initially saw her passing by.

'No, I want to get out now.' He's threatening to cry. I ignore him, continuing to push the trolley as fast as I can without knocking into someone.

At the end of the aisle I look left, then right and down the next aisle. Where's she gone.

'Let me out.' Cian continues to object much to Aaron's amusement. The speedy rush past the other customers is more to Aaron's taste. Where is she?

I travel the length of the store looking up and down each aisle, thinking Charlie must have left, when I see her again. She's not pushing a trolley full of vegetables and kids so she has an advantage over me. Swinging the trolley around to face where I last saw her, I push my load. I must look like a mad woman running down the aisle with two kids in a trolley, one laughing his head off, the other screaming at me. Thankfully, being Monday, the shop is not too busy. When we get to the checkouts, I see the white jacket again, leaving already. She mustn't have bought anything.

'Charlie. Charlie,' I call after her and she turns to see who it is. Pushing past the tills my hands grip tightly to the trolley.

'Charlie,' I call out again but this time she quickens her step, to get away from me. Why the hell won't she stop? I arrive at the exit still calling her name and push the trolley outside. Where has she gone? I need to ask her about that photograph. I need to see it again.

My eyes search through the faces walking up and down the pathway but I can't see the white jacket with the embroidered tiger. I can hear a voice though... and something bleeping.

'Going somewhere?'

'What?' I turn to see a tall security guard standing beside me. His hand is on the trolley. Cian is staring at him with his mouth open. 'Oh sorry, I was trying to catch someone.' I take one more glance across the car park. 'There was a young girl with the white jacket, she just walked out of here, did you see where she went to?'

'Could you come back inside, please?' the tall man says.

'Yes... I was just trying to...'

'Inside, please.'

This guy is not at all friendly, avoiding eye contact as his left arm directs me. Keeping his focus on the door he turns the trolley around and pulls it.

'I'm sorry, sir. I didn't realize I...'

'Can you come over here, please?'

'Shit.'

Trying to explain that I had no intention of stealing two bags of lettuce, a bunch of bananas and a bag of apples took almost twenty minutes. Two more judges joined the court. The manager and a second security person. Aaron looked mesmerized by the commotion. Cian looked scared. I had to keep reassuring him that everything was okay.

Thankfully the second security person was a woman around the same age as myself, with an understanding of the days that feel like your train is pulling away from the station just as you arrive on the platform. She hurried proceedings along, releasing me with a wink and a caution. My nerves are shattered. I could not imagine going home and saying I'd been arrested for shop lifting. It was bad enough having one criminal in the house. I lift the kids out of the trolley and leave the shop. A quick lap of Lidl, and I have everything I need to paddle through the next few days. My anxiety levels are on a high. It was Charlie. I know it but why didn't she stop? Why did she run away from me? That's very strange. Well, she's gone now and so are my plans for ever shopping in that branch of Tesco again.

--

The boys are perched in front of the TV, eating chopped banana, when the phone rings. Shit – Ellen. I forgot to ring her. I'm in no mood now to go through her son's encounter with the law, so I let it ring out, then send her a text saying I'm busy. That I'll ring her when I can speak. It's not really a lie. I am busy. Busy screwing the top off a bottle of merlot.

Amber will arrive home from school just after four so I've made sure to brush my teeth three times since having the glass of wine. If she found out I was drinking during the day, I'd never hear the end of it. She's worse than Tom when making a point. Amber quotes statistics.

I needn't have bothered. Dropping her bag in the hallway, she shouts out that she's home then heads straight to her room. I'm beginning to worry that her distancing herself from me so much in the past few months has become a bit more than just a teenage thing. I have enough on my plate but I'd better keep my eye on her. Check her room from time to time, try to get my hands on her phone.

With the boys still navigating the world of animation and Amber pretending to do homework upstairs, I finally ring Ellen and fill her in on what her son was up to yesterday. She doesn't say much about it, just listens and asks are we all okay.

I get off the phone, prepare the dinner and wait for Tom. Big Bad Tom. He'll probably come through the door all cheery and smiley. Joking with the kids and making out we haven't got a problem in the world.

It's six o'clock when the key turns in the door. *Wrong again, Sal?*

Chapter Twelve

Tom said nothing, barely acknowledged the kids before he went to bed feigning some sort of tummy bug. I didn't believe him, it's too coincidental. Anything not to talk. Even when he was dying with shingles he was able to finish off his dinner. But tonight, no. He moved a few meatballs around the plate, rearranged strands of spaghetti then stood up and left the room. I'm beginning to think he may have played down the events of yesterday.

Any other time I would have told Tom about my saga at Tesco, how I walked out of the shop with the trolley. But at the moment, I don't feel like sharing anything with Tom, especially when it happened over the photo and makes me look like I'm losing it. God, I hope I'm not losing it?

–

The boys are safely tucked into bed when I check in with Amber. Immediately she lifts her head from her phone. Soft pink pyjamas, no make-up hiding her beauty, Amber looks about twelve years old. Her big green eyes open wide when I sit at the end of the bed. Brushing my hand over her bare foot, I look at her. This angel. This gift. When did she stop being a little girl? What day was it? I can't remember. I certainly wasn't given any warning. There was no graduation ceremony. It just happened.

Amber went from being by my side every moment of every day to barely being there at all.

Amber is the reason I put up with so much shit on the quiet. I want her to be happy. She doesn't need to know it was her dad who ruined her mom's chances of owning her own salon. There are times I wish I could tell her, wipe the look of admiration from her face when Daddy arrives on the scene. But what good would it do? She would just end up disappointed in both of us.

'Amber honey.'

'What?' she answers abruptly, sitting up and wrapping her arms around her folded legs. Is she expecting bad news or something?

'Nothing, nothing, I was just wondering if everything is all right?'

'Yeah, why wouldn't it be?'

'It's just… you seem a bit distracted lately, like something is bothering you and I don't think we spend enough time together anymore.'

Amber pulls her feet away from my hand. 'Well, that's your fault, you're in work all the time.'

'I have to work, sweetie, bills have to be paid.'

I don't want to tell her Tom's debts have to be paid too. That not only did Tom lose my thirteen thousand euros but he also managed to extort ten thousand from an acquaintance of his who is threatening to take him to court if he doesn't get it back at one thousand euros a month.

'I'm going to cut my hours as soon as I can, Amber, I want to spend more time with you. There's nothing I want more.'

'Except money.'

'Now, don't be so smart, you know I'm doing my best here.'

Amber's face softens. Her lips close into a gentle smile and she lifts her eyes to look at me. Releasing the phone from her grip she places it on the bed beside her and reaches out to me with both hands.

'I know you are, Mom. I love you.' Moving closer, she hugs me like she did when she was a little girl. But instead of embracing the moment, I end up feeling sick. Now I'm sure there is something going on with her.

The scent of coconut wafts from her hair, I inhale it, not knowing what I should do. Continue to question her? Ask her what the hell is going on? Or should I tread gently? Little steps. Let her know I'm here when she's ready to talk. I don't want to scare her off by pushing it. Christ, I wish there was a manual.

A few more precious moments pass before Amber pulls away from our embrace.

'Is there anything you want to tell me, Amber?' I say, stroking her long shiny hair before she moves out of reach.

'No. I'm fine, Mom, really. Don't be worrying, you're always worrying.' And there she goes. Taking the phone in her hand she pulls the duvet up over her body. Well, that precious moment didn't outlast its welcome. She's back judging me in no time.

'Someone has to do the worrying around here,' I say, leaning over to kiss her on the head. 'Don't stay on that phone too long, you've school tomorrow.'

–

Back downstairs and eventually I have a bit of peace. Tom's not here flicking through the stations until he finds whatever he wants. The remote is all mine. I switch on the TV in the hope of finding something easy to watch. Something to distract me from my life and something I don't need to use any brain power to watch.

The news is airing on RTE1. I'm about to switch the station over when I hear the reporter announce the body of a woman has been found in suspicious circumstances at her home in Sycamore, Dublin 15.

Sycamore?

The woman, late thirties, is the mother of one son. The police are asking anyone with information to contact them.

The report shows the media stationed outside the dead woman's house. Red brick walls, a big tree in the middle of the garden and beautiful plant pots decorating the porch entrance. The blinds on the windows are closed and there's crime scene tape across the driveway. Late thirties. Poor woman. That could have been me. Well, except for the lovely pot plants, I don't have time for that sort of thing.

Shit, that actually could have been me. The person in the garden. This happened yesterday, the same day I saw the intruder. Dublin 15... which means it's not far from here.

'Tom.' Adrenaline pushes me up the stairs to where Tom is lying fully clothed on the top of the bed. 'Tom, a woman was killed yesterday.' He turns on his side facing away from me. 'Tom, the same day someone came into our garden. I'm calling the police.'

Rushing back down the stairs I grab my phone about to ring 999 when Tom follows me into the room.

'What are you doing?'

'I'm calling the police, Tom, I'm going to tell them about the person who came into the garden – they could have something to do with the murder. The police should know about them.'

'Don't be so silly, Sally, the cops will think you're mad. They get all sorts of weirdos ringing them with suggestions, and sightings and whatnot. Do you really want to go there?'

'But Tom…'

'It's up to you, Sal, but you're gonna look like a fool.'

'They said Dublin 15.'

Walking over to my side, Tom puts his hand on my phone, pushing it away from my ear, sniggering. 'Why don't you wait and see what happens? They probably have their suspect already, Sal. Just wait and see.'

Tom has a special way of making me feel small when he wants to. That smarmy look on his face like he's dealing with an idiot.

'I thought you were sick,' I say, but he doesn't answer me.

When Tom goes back upstairs I dial the emergency services and get directed to the cops. A woman answers, takes the details and thanks me for notifying them.

'It's just with the murder in the area, I thought it was best to call it in.'

'You did the right thing,' she says, telling me she'll pass it on to the relevant section.

So I did the right thing. I'm not even going to tell Tom I called them. He'll probably say I was being stupid, panicking, making a big deal out of it. All the things I'm quite prepared to do to keep my family safe.

Returning my attention to the TV, I hope to get some more information about the murder but the news has moved on to some story about a footballer who was killed in a car crash. I've never heard of him. I scan social media, but there's nothing more there either.

For the third time tonight, I find myself checking the back garden. Everything is still and peaceful. A half-moon hangs sideways in the night sky. There are no clouds to block the beauty and no strange person hanging around my garden. I think of the dead woman. A shiver runs down my spine sending me back into the safety of my house. What could have happened? Drugs? Domestic? They say most people know their killer. I wonder, did she? Was it her husband?

Chapter Thirteen

There's no husband, according to this morning's news, the dead woman was single. Holding the steering wheel, I shuffle through the heavy traffic that comes with travelling into work at the same time as half the city, not to mention the school drop-offs. I'm looking forward to getting into work. Hopefully it'll be so busy I won't find the time to worry.

Tom was up, showered, infused with coffee before I even got out of the bed. I asked him if he would drop the boys to the crèche, give me a few extra minutes to sort out the washing. He said he would but not with his usual gusto, his hugs, his 'anything for my lovely wife' attitude. I'm worried. Worried for the two of us.

The drive into the city is the only time of the day I'm on my own. The radio presenter has moved on from the murder and is now talking to someone who wants to cycle in every country in the world for some charity, something to do with saving the earth... all I can think about is saving my marriage.

In my head I go through my to-do list for today. Not too bad. A trip to the bank to top up Tom's account for the monthly transfer to his debt buddy. Penny's for Amber's fake tan and while I'm there, some new clothes for Cian and Aaron. They're growing up so fast. Some days I drop them to the crèche and when I pick them up that evening, they look older. Like they've sprouted in the space of ten hours.

Ouch – the guilt. It hits me right in the stomach. Ten hours. It's a long time to be away from the boys and certainly wasn't my plan. But what can I do? Life has to go on. I have to adapt to the new script, the one I was handed. It's not like I got to write much of it.

Maybe someday when they're older and we're all sitting around the dinner table for the kids' annual visit home, I'll tell them. And Amber. She needs to hear it too. I'll tell them it was their precious Daddy who fucked everything up. Not Mommy, Mommy was great.

Oh God, what's happening to me? Why am I thinking like that? The last thing I want is for my marriage to end. For Amber, Cian and Aaron to have to deal with the pain of a broken home. I cried almost every night for three years after my own mother died. Staying in my room so I couldn't see what was going on. Blasting the music so I couldn't hear what was going on. But I couldn't keep the reality away. It always found me. I will not be the reason any of my children shed a tear.

The car park is almost empty. I pick a spot near the exit on the first floor and step out into the city. Now I'm Sally the hairdresser. A strong breeze attempts to slow my pace but I push on past the stalls and scents, grab a coffee and croissant for Elsie, then cross the road.

'How are you today, Elsie?' Handing her the bag, I step into the porch area, Elsie's bedroom. I wonder what she'd make of my problems. Swap?

'Good, good.' She opens the bag. 'Thanks, Sally.'

'You're very welcome.' And she is. Always has been. And when I'm not in work I make sure one of the other staff members grabs her a breakfast.

77

'See you later, Elsie.'

Inside the salon my mood lightens.

'Morning, Sal.'

'Morning, Meg.'

'How'd the weekend go – oh, you had the party, how was that?'

Disastrous, bloody disastrous. 'Fine, it went well. Glad it's over for another year though.'

Walking past the reception desk and down to the staffroom, I sing along to Rihanna, happy that she managed to find love in a hopeless place.

The staffroom is empty when I enter. I hang up my coat, fix my hair and top up my lipstick. Just as I'm about to open the door, Anna comes bursting in from the other side almost knocking me out in the process.

'What the—' I say, watching her slam open the door to one of the cubicles, her head tilted, trying to hold the puke down before releasing it like an explosion into the bowl.

'Sweet Jesus, Anna, are you all right?' I rush towards her. Anna is on her knees with her head stuck in the toilet bowl. Her hair threatens to land in the mess so I hold it out of the way while she continues to vomit. After a few more minutes and with little chance of anything being left in her stomach Anna lifts her head and takes some deep breaths.

'What the hell did you drink last night?' I ask, wetting some tissues and handing them to her. She shakes her head from side to side, eyes red, face green. An alien on the floor of the staffroom toilet.

My heart goes out to her. I have been here, sitting on this floor, apologizing to my helpful crew who tried to pull me back on board. The words, *sorry, sorry, sorry* uttered a hundred times. I always promised myself I'd never ever drink again. It's been a while since I felt like that, too long maybe. But I was that soldier. So I won't judge Anna. She is my colleague who needs my help keeping her hair away from the puke.

'Is there anything I can get you?' I hand her a bottle of water from my bag. The thoughts of drinking it make her gag. 'Take a few deep breaths, Anna, you'll be fine in about three days.'

'Fuck off,' she manages to mutter.

'Ah, feeling better already?' I giggle, trying to coax her back to normal, to bring a bit of that gothic pale back to her face. 'Late night?'

Without answering, she pulls herself upright and drags herself to the mirror on the far wall. Eyes open wide, Anna stares into the glass.

'Am I going to die?' she says.

'I don't think so, Anna, but I wouldn't bet on it, it's only Tuesday.'

A sarcastic smile creeps onto her face. She turns away from the mirror and rests her hands on the counter behind her. Her face is snow white now, more familiar.

'What do you mean by that?'

'Nothing,' I say. 'I mean nothing, I'm just joking.' Anna can be so moody, it's impossible to know how she'll take anything you say. But she's no pushover. If she doesn't agree with you or like what you're saying, she'll pull you up on it. She's never trying to keep anyone happy, not even herself.

I didn't mean to give Anna the impression I was judging her. Anna can do what she likes. In fact, at the moment I wish I was her, twenty-one again. No obligations to anyone but myself. Hangovers on a

Tuesday… bring them on. No major money worries or a teenager who might be hiding something, a husband who definitely is. Then, an irrational thought crashes into my brain. *Christ, I hope Tom's not having an affair.*

Believing Anna to be capable of looking after herself from here on out I head for the door to begin my day, cutting, curling, colouring – whatever the client wants, the client gets.

Anna splashes water on her face then wipes it dry with a tissue. When she turns to lift her head, I see it.

My stomach lurches. Suddenly I'm dragged back to that moment all those years ago. The first time I saw the bruise on Mam's face. A dark circle of hatred, right above her eye. I didn't know what to do. Mom was cowered on the floor in the corner of the bedroom, tears flowing down her ashen face. There had been arguing, shouting – I did what I had learned to do. Grab my headphones and drown out reality. After a while, I finished nodding my head to the rhythm of Take That making all sorts of promises and lifted the earpiece. Silence. It was over. My cue to go back asleep. But this time I heard the front door banging closed, I was scared. I went in to see if Mom was crying again, she did a lot of crying. When I saw the bruise, a part of my childhood flew away.

'Anna.' I move towards her and lift her hair back. The water had removed her make-up revealing a bruise at the top of her cheek. 'What happened?' Anna pulls away lowering her head. 'Anna?'

'It was just an accident. I opened a door and whacked my face.' Ah, the door, the broken step, the falling box, the ice, I'd heard them all. Something in my face must have given my thoughts away because Anna says, 'Jesus, Sal, don't be such a drama queen. It was the door, I was getting into Gary's car, the door flew open into my face, it hurt like fuck.'

'Is it okay now?' Moving closer I inspect her face. Anna is right, I am being a drama queen. It probably was just an accident, I know I shouldn't be jumping to conclusions but it's hard, experience has hardwired my reaction.

'You'll be fine… in a couple of days you'll be as ugly as ever.'

'Bitch.'

Leaving the staffroom, still not convinced that Anna is telling the truth I tell myself I have enough problems to be dealing with, no need to invent more.

Out on the floor people are chatting; one common theme floating through the air. The dead woman. Everyone is shocked. Domestic murder holds so much more intrigue than the everyday gangland murders that plague our city – live and die by the sword and all that but an innocent woman in her own home, well, that's a different story and one everyone wants to hear.

So far the information filtering through suggests the body was found with stab wounds to the chest in the kitchen of the house. The police aren't saying much but the neighbours are. They're saying what a lovely quiet lady she was. Kept to herself. A great mother.

'They always say that.'

'What?' Amy is putting rollers into a woman's hair at the next station.

'They always say they were nice… quiet… minded their own business.'

The brush in my hand dabs red liquid onto Shirley Dunne's head. I laugh.

Amy continues. 'Why do nosy bitches never get killed? I'd love to hear the neighbour's comments then. "Oh she was a right old cow... Glad to see the back of her... Couldn't keep her nose out of other people's business... Never cleaned her bins.'"

I'm trying not to laugh too loud when Shirley Dunne comments.

'Maybe there's a lesson in that... Stay alive... Be a nosy bitch.'

Amy throws her head back laughing. 'I can't see myself peering into my neighbour's garden to see what they're up to.'

Suddenly my mind jumps to the intruder in my garden. Who was it? What were they doing there? Rummaging in the bins? I don't think so. Not the furthest house in the laneway. There are plenty of bins in the area a lot easier to get at. Scaling a six-foot wall seems a little extreme for the remains of a ham sandwich. Unless of course they were hoping to find the dregs of wine in the bottles lined up for the recycling bin at the bottom of the garden.

The voices around me fade. What will I do? Why was Tom so against me ringing the police? I'm guessing he probably had enough drama after Sunday's accident, but still, this could be important.

Chapter Fourteen

If there's one thing that will frighten the living crap out of someone it's seeing cops outside their house. Which is what I'm looking at now. Two of them getting into their car having just walked out of my garden. What the hell is going on? Did Tom contact them about the intruder in the garden? I doubt it. He was too against me doing it. Or maybe they're following up my call. They didn't seem that interested. Still, my chest tightens.

Breathe, Sally, breathe. Cian and Aaron, strapped into their car seats, watch the big police car driving on down the road around the corner and out of sight. I want to run after them, flag them down and ask them but then I remember Sunday, Tom's accident. The cops must have called to clarify some information he'd given them or something like that. But do they do that? Knock on your front door without any warning and drag your good name to the attention and judgement of the neighbours? Maybe they do. I'm not familiar with their routines. All I know is my heart is beating a lot faster than it was five minutes ago.

Eventually I park the car into a tight spot in front of the house and release the boys from their seats. They both jump out of the car and race towards the door.

'Daddy's home,' Cian calls out when he spots Tom's car in the driveway.

The weight of the crèche bag drags on my shoulder, getting heavier and heavier as the years go by. I thought when the nappy stage ended things would get a lot easier. But no. Now they have to have a change of clothes for this, a T-shirt for that, a pair of slippers for something else. Ensuring they get full marks from their minders takes a lot of organization.

I follow the boys, rummaging in my handbag for the key. Before locating it, the door opens. Taking both boys under his arms, Tom swings them down the hallway into the kitchen.

'What's for dinner?' he asks, placing Cian and Aaron down, so they can scurry off into the playroom.

What's for dinner? Is the man gone mad? What about the cops, Tom? Is he going to continue like nothing has happened? Pretend two policemen didn't just walk out of the house. Maybe he thinks I didn't see them. That's it, he thinks they were gone before I pulled up in the car. I'll say nothing, give him the benefit of the doubt, he might be waiting for me to take my coat off before he drops the bomb.

–

I'm wrong again. Two hours have passed and he still hasn't mentioned the fact that the police were at the house. With the boys fast asleep in bed and Amber at Sarah's, he's had ample opportunity. I even tried to introduce the subject, asking how his day went? Was he feeling okay after the accident on Sunday? But Tom just gave the usual information-free replies. At one point he seemed a little jittery, like he wanted to say something but couldn't. Maybe he just doesn't want to bother me if it's not impor-tant. Maybe he's mad that I went ahead and phoned in about the intruder. Shit, I don't know what to think, but I'll wait until Amber is home and in bed before mentioning it.

I don't have to. He brings the topic to the table and in a tone that makes me nervous. Tom is holding my hand, sitting beside me on the sofa, looking into my eyes. His expression is unfamiliar: concern? Fear? I'm not sure, but the man is definitely about to tell me something I don't want to hear and I'm worried. Amber had no sooner closed the bedroom door when he asked me to sit down.

'There's something I have to tell you,' he says.

So here I am, sitting, waiting for my world to be turned upside down. There is no other explanation for the scene setting. This is serious. Losing all my money was serious too, but that bombshell was disclosed in front of the kids, out in the garden like he was commenting on the disappointing results of a football match. This, I'm afraid, is a lot more critical.

'Sally,' he starts. I nod, holding my breath, my past, my future, huddling them all into a safe place in the corner of my mind before he destroys them. 'I don't know how to say this.'

I pull my hand from his grip. 'Just say it, Tom.'

'Before I say anything, I need you to know that I've only just found out about this myself.'

Here we go, exonerating himself before he even tells me what's going on.

'I hate having to tell you like this… but…' Tom stands up and walks over to the wall, leaning with one hand against it, the other on his face. The fucker *has* got another child.

That's what he's unable to say. I know it.

'Sally, there is another child, a boy, Kenny...' I let the pain sting me. Ouch. Sitting silent on the sofa my insides somersault and blood rushes to my head. My body feels weak, my mind, not so much. Part of me wants to jump up out of this chair and hit him, scream at him, shove him out the front door. Tell him never to come back, that it's over, I hate him. Another part of me wants to cry. I do neither.

Tom continues. 'He contacted me two months ago... I promise you, I knew nothing up to that moment.'

Two months ago! I thought he was going to say last week. He's been lying to me for two months! Kissing me, making love to me, though I think that might have just been the once. Our sex life has taken a battering since the boys arrived. I shake my head in despair as tears start to fall down my cheeks.

Tom moves away from the wall, slowly turning to look at me. Feeling braver, now that he's told me and I haven't hit him over the head with the nearest suitable object. I quickly brush my tears away, unsure if they are tears of hurt or anger. I don't speak, I want to hear his whole lame story about why he kept it from me. Why he didn't admit it when I questioned him on Saturday? Why did he hide it from me then? Why did he have to lie?

I've spent a lot of time thinking about it, what would happen to us, how I would react, since the possibility was put in my head. Since seeing the photograph. And now, here I am trying my best to stay calm on the outside while I'm burning on the inside. *Say nothing Sal, wait until he tells you everything.*

His voice becomes less wimpy. 'I had to wait for the DNA results. I didn't want to upset you if it wasn't true.'

'What fucking DNA results?' I hear myself scream at him.

'Let me finish. Please, Sal.' He's searching to make contact with my eyes but I turn my head away. 'Sal, you have to understand, I was under fierce pressure, I didn't know what to do. I planned to tell you as soon as the time was right... as soon as the moment was right and then, when you mentioned it on Saturday you... you caught me off guard, I wasn't prepared and I... I just panicked.'

It didn't look like panic to me. In fact, he was pretty relaxed as far as I can remember. If I was asked for my honest opinion in a court of law, I would say Tom thought the problem would go away. That this boy would be happy to have a distant relationship with him and Sally Cooper wouldn't have to know a thing about it.

So what has gone wrong? Why is Tom telling me now? And why were the cops here? Maybe it's time for me to ask a few questions.

'Were you with me at the time this *son* was conceived?' I can't hide my bitterness.

'No, Sal, it happened before I met you.'

'What age is he?'

'Sixteen.'

I want to vomit. My heart is about to explode. If the kid is sixteen, which ties in with what Charlie said: Tom *was* with me; Amber is fifteen. Does he think I'm a fucking idiot, that I can't do the maths?

'Tom, you were with me,' I say, working hard to keep my voice even.

He's taking deep breaths now.

'Not really, Sal, I'd met you but we weren't going steady or married so...' He takes a few steps closer to me. 'We weren't together, Sal, I was never unfaithful to you.'

Standing to avoid any pathetic attempt he might be dreaming up to soothe me, my face creases with anger. He steps closer, I can smell the woody scent of his aftershave and it turns my stomach even more. Lifting both my hands in the air I take a step backwards to warn him off. I will need the exact dates to work out if Tom and I were going steady at the time: if we were, it changes everything; if we weren't, he's a liar and a dickhead.

'When were you planning on telling me all this? If I hadn't seen that photo would I ever have known?' And then I remember what started this all off. 'Why were the police here today, Tom?'

Tom rubs his chin looking up at the ceiling and letting out what I can only describe as a sound an animal might make, a squeaky groan. Something tells me this is going to get worse.

'Well… that's the thing,' he says.

Chapter Fifteen

I have a choice. Drive to work, or drive myself mad. I choose work, for now, mad might come later. I'm still trying to digest what Tom told me last night. The pure unadulterated mess of it all. It turns out this Kenny kid, who half belongs to my husband, is the surviving child of the dead woman whose body was found in Sycamore. The woman whose plants I was admiring on the TV... whose neighbours think she was a lovely woman.

For most of the night I sat on the sofa staring into the darkness, trying to come to terms with what Tom had told me.

The one-night stand had taken place when Tom had started going out with me, but we weren't going serious and definitely not engaged. It happened the night his team won the championship final and everyone was in Copper's nightclub celebrating and getting bombed out of their minds. I got the exact date from the championship medal he keeps propped in between his two golf trophies.

Tom kept apologizing, going on and on about how he was pissed and how he never meant it to happen. That it only ever happened the once. He only ever loved me, blah, blah, blah, blah and he never saw the girl again. He didn't even remember her name. My guess is he never knew her name. Copper's nightclub has a way of blowing the base off people's standards.

There's a part of me feels slightly sorry for Tom, the fool. I still love him despite all his faults. Nothing ever goes right for him. Even a one-night stand seventeen years ago has come back to bite him. Now he's the sole guardian to a kid he doesn't even know. And the worst part about all of this is the police want Tom to take care of Kenny, to bring him to our house. *To live with us.* Such madness.

This is where I will have to put my foot down. A sixteen-year-old boy that we've never met moving in on top of us would not work. What are the police thinking? Jesus, Amber would have a fit. She already thinks the house is too small and that we should be moving to one of the big houses they're building on the old hospital grounds down the road. *Dream on, Amber.*

So that's where we left it, after talking for less than half an hour and not talking for a further two. Tom squeezed me tightly, asked me to forgive him for not telling me earlier and promised me he would sort the whole mess out so that it would not affect our family. Tom is going to tell the cops that we will not be taking Kenny to live with us, that we feel the kid would be better off with people he actually knows at this sad time.

Of course there are a lot more questions to be asked, a lot more consequences to deal with, but for the moment, I've enough barbed wire to suck on. I need a break, so I'm heading in to my girls.

-

The salon is extra busy when I arrive. Walking through the door I notice the waiting area is full of clients. I'd almost forgotten about the big awards ceremony taking place in the Morrison Hotel later on today. It's just as well

I didn't pull the sickie I was intending until the reality of staying at home played out in my mind. At least in the salon I might get to laugh at some point, have my mind transported away from the unfolding drama at home for a brief moment.

'Morning, Sal.'

'Morning, Meg. Sorry I'm running a bit late. Is my first client here yet?'

'Yes, she's at the basins.'

The basins are situated at the back of the shop near the towel library and beside the staffroom. I glance around to see if I recognize anyone, always on the alert for Charlie's return. But not today, there are no teenage heads being soaked. These are all mature ladies, in need of special products to disguise their ageing.

Sienna moves her attention from her suds-covered hands and smiles over at me. Suddenly I feel vulnerable, like the whole world knows the shit I'm in. I know they don't – I've only just discovered it myself, so how could they? Yet every gentle hello or smile feels like a gesture of pity. Paranoia is a terrible thing. The weakening of confidence that comes with a life-changing scenario. That's what I'm suffering from now.

The morning flies past with little thought for Tom or Kenny or Tom and Kenny. I'm too busy. No sooner is one head prepped for the ceremony than another bum lands on the seat. I haven't even had time for a coffee and I really could do with one.

In the mirror I see Anna working away on the opposite side of the floor. I hope she doesn't notice me checking her out. Her hair is tied up revealing a tattoo of I-don't-know-what across the back of her neck. It's got twists and turns and letters that don't spell out anything in particular.

No bruises, though. Her arms are covered in black lace which is pretty normal for Anna. A long skirt finishes the ensemble and she appears happy enough chatting away to a fellow goth in the seat.

One last blow-dry to complete and then it's time for my break. But before that much-needed moment arrives, my phone beeps. This time I don't care if Meg pulls me up. I'm not waiting until I've finished with my client to find out who it is. I'm too anxious, which is another side effect of the world being pulled out from under you. Anxiety.

Making my apologies to the woman who's flicking through the pages of *Hello!* magazine in the seat in front of me, I head to the toilet. It's Tom, texting me to ring him ASAP. My heart starts that overexcited beat again, thumping in my chest like the tribal dance of worry. Well, it's going to have to keep playing – I can't reply now. I can't leave a client with her hair dripping at my station any longer. I text him back.

I'll be free to ring in twenty

The fact that Christina Murray's dress is not what she intended to wear to the awards ceremony – her first choice having been ruined in the dry cleaners – is of absolutely no interest to me. But I can't tell her that. I must listen and where possible nod in agreement. If my mind was not obsessed with finding out what Tom is about to tell me I would do a lot better. Relay some similar disastrous experience of my own or that of a client, family member, neighbour, friend. Anything or anyone to keep her thinking I'm totally involved in her story. That's what I do, what we all do. Make the clients feel like they matter. Being able to style hair is just one of the skills needed for the job.

Christina Murray has become sidetracked by a woman, a competitor, sitting at the other end of the salon. Apparently both ladies are up for the same award. Bereft of curiosity, I don't ask her what the award is for but I do remark on how Christina's hair is definitely the better of the two. She laughs at my confidence, placing a fiver tip on the shelf before leaving to pay at the reception. Without bothering with coffee, I head out of the salon to the anonymity of the busy street.

Tom answers before the second ring.

'They're not buying it, Sal.'

'Not buying what?'

'Kenny.'

'What about Kenny?' Mentioning his name is like drinking poison. I want to gag after saying it. I know it's wrong, this is not the kid's fault, but he should not be my problem.

'They're saying he has no other next of kin, that I'm the only family. His grandparents are both dead and the mother has no siblings that anyone knows of.'

'Well, did *you* tell them we're not taking him, that I won't have it, that we have a fifteen-year-old girl in the house and I'm not allowing some strange teenage boy we don't know to live under the same roof as her. *Did* you? Did you tell them *that*, Tom?'

I must be shouting now because I seem to be attracting the attention of passers-by. Every second person is turning to look at me. Hiding my face to the wall I listen to Tom's voice moaning at the far end of the phone.

'I told them all that, they said there would be a social worker coming out to talk to us this evening. How quickly can you get home?'

'Tom, you can tell the cops to shove their social worker up their uniformed arses. I'm not taking that boy into our house and that's final.'

My shaking hand struggles to end the call.

'You tell 'em,' a passer-by shouts as I turn around, tears streaming down my face. This is unbelievable. Tom is beginning to sound like he's prepared to entertain the idea. Does he not hear me? Can he not see the madness of it all? I know the kid needs somewhere to go, I get that and I really feel sorry for the boy. His mom is dead, he only recently found out who his father is. He must feel like his whole world is collapsing around him and as much as I'd love to be able to help him I have my own kids to think about. What would it do to them having a stranger living under the same roof? There has to be a better way, there has to be someone else. We're probably just the first and easiest option. Then again Tom is his dad. Oh, I don't know what to think.

Wiping the tears on the sleeve of my shirt I walk towards the salon door just as Megan steps outside.

'Here.' She pulls me to the side of the entrance and hands me a tissue. 'Girl, you're going to have to tell someone what's going on. I'm not suggesting me but there has to be someone you can share your problem with, Sal. You've been in bits since Saturday and I'm guessing it's something to do with that teenage kid whose hair you were doing when you collapsed.'

'I'm okay, Megan. Thanks.'

Deep breaths, pink lipstick and I'm walking back into the salon. Megan is right, I do need to talk to someone, but not her. This is my work place, my sanctuary: if I drag my problem in here where can I escape to?

My phone rings. It's Tom again. What does he want now? Anger seeps through the cracks in my tolerance. I want to tell him to go away and leave me out of it. *Sort out the problem, Tom.* He promised he would not let the situation damage our family but here he is having difficulty getting his horse over the first hurdle.

When the ringing stops, it's replaced with the beep of a message.

She'll be here at five this evening.

The social worker. Does he think I'm going to sit in the room with him while he explains that the kid is not coming to live with us? *No. You're on your own, Tom. Just like you were the night you shagged his mommy.*

-

By three o'clock my head feels like it belongs to Anna. Thumping. My mind is going backwards and forwards. It's not like I can ask anyone else. *Hey, what did you do when you found out your husband had a secret child and the child's mother was murdered?* I'm pretty sure even if I put it on one of those Google chat forums I wouldn't find one other person in the whole world to share the experience with.

-

Two hours of utter stress pass, my mind imagining all sorts of scenarios, none of them good. Was it just a coincidence that person came into our garden the same night the mother of Tom's other child was killed? Or were they there for a reason? What if it was the killer? What if they had got into the house? What if they come back?

When the clock allows it, I grab my bag and coat from the staffroom. Time to collect the boys and head home. The fiver tip that Christina Murray gave me falls from my pocket so I hand it to Louise, the new trainee, who is also getting ready to go home. Her eyes light up like she's never had a fiver before. She's probably broke. First-year trainees don't get enough to pay for their bus fare never mind have a lunch. But that's the hair game, that's how we all trained. Gradually increasing our income, increasing our skills, until eventually qualifying and ending up with lots of money for our husbands to lose. *Don't be so cynical, Sally, not everyone is married to a fucking idiot.*

With Cian and Aaron in the back of the car, I head for home praying that the social worker has left before I get there. I text Tom to make sure the coast is clear. I'm not allowing myself to be judged by some do-gooder who wants to pump me with guilt for not opening my arms wide enough to welcome a stranger into my life.

Tom texts back telling me that she has left. Nothing else, no comment on how the meeting unfolded. I guess he's keeping that to tell me when I get home. God, I could do with some good news.

Chapter Sixteen

Once again, Sally, you are wrong.

Dinner is on the table when I walk through the door. Well… what passes for dinner on a weekday. Frozen pizza and chips. Thank God for the crèche, making sure the kids get all their fruit and veg during the day. Tom whispers that he'll fill me in when the boys are out of the way. I try to appear nonchalant but I'm dying to find out what's going on, what plans are being made for my life.

Amber walks into the kitchen and lifts a slice of pizza in her hand while reading her phone at the same time. Is there no end to her talents?

'Hi, Ma,' she mumbles through the mush in her mouth before taking her attention away from the screen long enough to give Cian and Aaron a kiss. I don't get one.

'What about me?' I say.

'What about you?' she laughs before blowing me a kiss across the table.

I move around to where she is standing, squeeze her tightly and kiss her on the head. 'I want a real one.'

'Ask him.' Amber points at Tom. He looks at me, poor neglected Tom and in that moment I see the man I love, the man I married. Not the man who lied to me.

'Okay.'

There's extra heat in his body. Extra power in his hug. Lifting my face, I kiss his lips. Tom clings tighter. He doesn't want to let me go.

-

Eat, clean up, get the boys' bags ready for tomorrow, put in a wash, take out a wash. Suddenly it's eight o'clock. The boys are in bed and Amber is in her room. I feel like I'm going through the motions when I should really be having a mental breakdown. It reminds me of when I heard my mother was dead. The sudden jolt, like I'd been transported to a different dimension. I was only fourteen at the time.

My dad called the school to say I was to come home straight away. Mam was sick. It was news to me, she was perfectly well when I'd left the house that morning. Mam had handed me my lunch which she made fresh every morning, I put it in my bag and unknowingly listened to her voice for the last time.

'You should do something with your hair.' Pushing my fringe out of my eyes, she kissed me on the forehead. Sometimes I kiss my fingers and place them on the same spot.

The ambulance was already at the house when I got home but it was too late. Mam was already gone. A brain haemorrhage. And just like that I had to adapt. The days passed like it was all happening to someone else, the wake, the funeral. How did we pull that out of the bag with no notice and no experience? Numbness, shock, accepting help; the realization that the practical things are all we can control, making the arrangements, choosing readings, picking songs, buying flowers. Crying. From that day on, I never felt like a child again.

I won't be picking songs for this latest shock. There is no tune to suit the sudden realization that everything around me, everything I've built, worked hard to save, is at risk.

Tom is standing in front of the fireplace. I'm sitting on the sofa. His eyes are darting from the floor to the ceiling to the window to the anything but me. He lifts his hand to pull at the collar of his shirt. *Pull harder, Tom.*

'Go on,' I coax him. 'Tell me what happened? What did she say?' I want to get this over with as soon as possible. Return to normality. Boring and all as that normal is, it's mine.

'There's a problem, Sally.' I shuffle forward in my seat, my eyes glued to Tom's lips.

'The social worker, Saoirse, she wants to meet you, Sal, to explain what's happening.'

'What do you mean to explain what's happening?'

'Well… It's… there's no other family Sally, I'm all he has.'

'Did you tell that woman what I said, that we can't have a stranger in the house? It's not going to happen. You did tell her, didn't you?'

Tom rubs his hands into his face like it's cleaning off a layer of skin.

'You told her, didn't you?'

'I told her how you feel. I did… but—'

'But what, Tom?'

'She just said it's what she'd expect your initial reaction to be.' Tom moves his head to the side like a dog being scolded.

'It's not *initial*, Tom. It's final.'

He's looking at his feet now, anywhere but at me.

'Is that not what you think, too? I thought we were of the same opinion, that housing a complete stranger is not an option.'

I can sense a shift in his attitude. Tom is no longer with me on this. The social worker has guilted him into caring about this boy. She got to him. She won't get to me.

'Tom you're not suggesting we take this kid into our house to live with our children, this stranger that we know nothing about… Are you?'

My heart pounds in my chest, tears blur my vision. I move closer to him to take his hand. He pulls away from me.

'I don't know what to think, this is all just a bloody mess. I've a son I didn't know existed up to a few months ago. He's been living without a father and now he needs me I… I—'

'Look at me, Tom.'

Slowly his head turns to face me. Tears gathering in his eyes.

'This cannot happen. You will find a way to help the boy but he is not coming to live in this house. Do you understand?' Placing my hands on his cheeks I rub Tom's face and look into his eyes. A little boy stares back at me. He does not know what to do.

'We're not going to ruin this family, we need to be strong here, we need to tell that social worker we cannot have that kid in this house. There has to be another option, Tom. What if he'd never discovered you were his father, they'd look after him then, wouldn't they? They'd have to find another alternative then.'

Lifting my hands from his face, he stares at me.

'But I *am* his father, Sally. He did find me.' Tom walks out the door.

There's a tightness across my chest that the doctor called anxiety, my gift from Tom. *When it happens, Sally, take a few deep breaths and try to relax.* The first time it paid me a visit was two days after Tom lost all our money. I went to the A and E believing I was having a heart attack. We might lose the house, be out on the street, or living with Ellen. Even worse, my father. It was just too much for me to bear. All I could feel was terror. All I could see was clouded in darkness. I panicked. My body panicked. It felt like someone was tightening a vice around my chest. When the ECG came back clear, I felt like a fool because I was a fool. I was diagnosed a fool.

Tom's footsteps pace the floorboards in the bedroom above my head. He's on the phone to someone, probably the social worker, filling her in on how the little wife took the news or maybe it's him, the boy. I wonder does Tom want the boy to come and live here? How close has he become to the kid in the past two months? If it is only two months. He could be lying about that too.

The following minutes are spent sitting on the sofa waiting for my body to relax. When I finally have control over my breathing, I go to the kitchen to get a glass of cold water. If Tom wants the boy to live here with us, what will I do? Do I have any rights?

I'm about to refill a glass with more cold water when Tom arrives into the kitchen. His face is grey, his hair standing on end.

'We need to talk, Sally.'

'I thought we did talk. I've made myself very clear. I've nothing more to say about it.'

'What if I don't have a choice?'

'Why? Did she say that? Did the social worker say we don't have a choice?'

'No, but she did say the court will rule on it.'

The court? Oh my God, this could go to court.

'Are you sure… Court… should we get a solicitor?'

One step, two steps. Tom is pacing the floor of the kitchen, one hand rubbing his hair the other clenched tightly against his chest.

'Who was on the phone?'

'Ah… just someone from work.'

Anger shoots through me like someone just opened a dam. Three steps and I'm standing right in front of him. My eyes staring him out. Tom flinches.

'If you think I'm listening to one more of your bloody lies you can think again, who was on the phone?'

'It was just—'

'Give it to me.'

'What?' Tom's eyes open wide, his eyelids flicker. I think he's scared. I hope he is. Holding my hand out, I say, 'Your phone, give it to me.'

He reaches for his back pocket and hands me the phone, dropping it into my hand likes it's dirty before stepping back. Turning away from him, I scroll to the recent calls. Kenny's Golf Supplies. His last phone call was to, Kenny's Golf Supplies?

'You were ordering fucking golf stuff in the middle of all this?' I say, turning to look at him. His face turns from grey to a bright flushing red, this isn't the case. It dawns on me. 'Kenny's Golf Supplies.' A decoy, so I wouldn't be suspicious if I saw the contact. *Kenny's Golf Supplies* is Kenny.

'You bastard,' I say, realizing the contact Kenny's Golf Supplies has been on Tom's phone for sometime now. I remember it ringing when we were over at his mother's house for dinner at Easter. The name came up on his phone and I joked about the shop ringing him on Easter Sunday. Tom had brushed it off, saying he was supposed to pick up prizes for the following week's tournament but had forgotten. That was in March. Over six months ago.

Seething with anger and punctured by his lies, I throw the phone at Tom and walk out of the kitchen slamming the door behind me. Amber is standing at the top of the stairs. Her worried face is looking down at me.

'What's going on, Ma?' she says, squashing a small cushion in her grip.

'Nothing, Amber, myself and your father just had a little row but it's sorted now.'

'Are you okay?' she says, stepping slowly down the stairs.

'I'm fine now.' But I'm not fine. I want to scream and shout at Tom, tell him what I think about his deception. He's obviously been in contact with this kid for a lot longer than he admitted so what else is he lying about?

The front door is two feet away from me. I want to open it and run out. Leave this lying man behind me, but I can't, I have two little boys asleep in bed, dreaming good dreams, I hope. And Amber walking past me in her fluffy slippers heading towards her dad in the kitchen.

All these chains holding me here, forcing me to deal with this disaster when all I want to do is run. But from what? What else is Tom hiding from me? I cannot trust this man. Maybe he's known about his son all along. I shouldn't have thrown the phone at him. I should have held on to it and searched to see how long that contact number has been in his phone. When Amber goes to bed I'll make sure he tells me the truth.

Standing in the hallway I hear Amber and Tom talking. The door is closed so I don't know what they're talking about. Probably me, how unstable I am. At fifteen she doesn't realize women don't slam doors for nothing in their own home, they are driven to it. But if I know Amber, she'll be comforting Tom. Telling him everything will be okay while I stand here feeling like an outsider. Amber might not be so willing to comfort her daddy when she hears the truth. Which she is going to have to now. Anything could leak into the papers. Oh Christ. I never thought of that. We'll be bait for the media if they get wind of Tom being Kenny's dad. This weekend I'll find an opportunity to sit her down and tell her what's going on. It will be hard but it will be harder if I don't. I have to deal with this.

And then there's Tom's mother, Ellen. What will she think when she hears she has another grandchild? I'll leave that for Tom to deal with. I'm not going there.

–

Cian and Aaron are both asleep when I open the bedroom door, their little bodies straddled across the beds, duvets hanging to the floor. Tiptoeing over to their bedsides, I pull the duvets over their innocent bodies, kissing them at the same time. Cian's mouth is wide open, his breath puffing like the engine on his favourite toy. Aaron's is closed in a smile. I put my face close to his and feel the heat of his soft breath caress my skin. My heart tugs watching my two boys sleep and I worry what all this could do to them. How they would feel if a stranger came to live in their house. Sit at their table when they're having breakfast. Set up house in their playroom.

What we have is perfect compared to the pain and sadness I grew up with. I've spent far too long building this beautiful family, put up with all Tom's mistakes, put my own dreams on the back burner. Making sure the kids have everything they need. No one is going to destroy that. I kiss Aaron one last time and whisper that I will take care of him and his brother.

Chapter Seventeen

'How did he contact you?'

Tom jumps with fright when I walk into the room. He must be so on edge. *Anxiety, Tom, welcome to my world.* Stirring milk into his coffee before turning around he takes the mug and moves away from the counter.

'Sal, it was earlier in the year, I'm sorry, I just… like I told you, I only got the DNA results two months ago, so technically I've only known for sure since then.' My God, bullshit knows no boundaries when it's oozing from Tom's lips.

'I know he rang you at Easter. I remember the call coming in from Kenny's Golf Supplies when we were sitting having dinner. How did he first contact you? Was it her, the mother? The woman you said you never spoke to since the night you had sex with her. Did you even know her name, Tom?

He shakes his head.

'Well, how did he track you down?'

'I don't know, I never asked him, it was all such a shock.' He sits down at the table, nodding his head at the chair by my side, inviting me to sit. I don't.

'It was the boy himself who made contact. He made an appointment to see me in work, said he wanted to talk about insurance.'

'A kid?'

'I didn't know how young he was, Sally, not until he arrived. It was arranged through the company's contact email.'

'Where did you meet him?'

'He came into the office... I thought it was just a regular enquiry until I saw him.'

'How did you react?'

'I can't remember, Sal, shock, I guess... actually, at first I thought it was one of the lads playing a joke... but then... he had information. He knew about the night I met his mother, so... but I still didn't believe it, which is why I asked for the DNA test... which is why I didn't mention it to you.'

If Tom squeezes that mug any tighter it will break.

'Why did she wait so long to tell him?'

'I don't know, Sal, I never asked her... maybe his age or something. I don't know.'

Tom looks exhausted from answering questions. God love him. I'm exhausted from asking them. Every day there's something new, some little piece of this sour apple that gets peeled away. Maybe one day we'll get to the core.

–

I didn't intend going to bed so early but when I rested my head on the pillow; bam, I was gone.

The next thing I know, Aaron is tapping me on the face trying to wake me up. Beside me the thunderous grunt of Tom's snoring echoes through the room. Daylight is creeping through the cracks in the curtain. I decide not to take Aaron into the bed beside me, instead I lift him in my arms and go downstairs.

The silence is beautiful, the haze of mist covering the back garden mystical. Aaron sits on my hip looking out the window with me. He doesn't ask any questions, just stares at the morning melting into the day in front of his wide-open eyes. His tiny hand wraps around my neck holding on. Reminding me to hold on. The clock says six thirty, we have an hour before all hell breaks loose.

'What would you like to do, Aaron? Would you like to play with Mammy?'

'Trains.' Aaron points to the playroom.

So I swing him up in the air and say, 'Trains it is.'

I'm sitting on the floor with Aaron pushing his Thomas the Tank collection in every direction, paying no attention to me. I've noticed that about him, the way he gets locked into his own world, ignores everything around him until someone comes along and breaks in. It used to send him crazy. There was a time he wouldn't even let Cian play alongside him but thankfully, thanks to his time in the crèche, that's changed.

'Choo-choo, Aaron,' I say, trying to join in, pushing a train across the carpet but he grabs it off me and holds it close to his chest. I decide to leave Aaron on his own, the way he likes it and go have a shower.

Within the hour everyone is up and eating breakfast somewhere in the house. Amber took her bowl of muesli to her room, Cian is sitting with Tom at the table and I'm putting a bowl of Cheerios into the middle of Tidmouth the fictional town where Aaron currently believes he is living with Thomas and his friends.

I won't get a chance to talk to Tom with the kids around so I'll have to ring him on my way to work or maybe arrange to meet him for lunch where we might be able to have a civil conversation about Saoirse, the social worker who is trying to break into my world. Maybe I should throw a tantrum like Aaron used to. Maybe I'll get used to it like Aaron did.

'I can't,' he says, fixing his tie in the hall mirror. 'It's Friday, I always go to the Mayor Inn with the lads for lunch.'

'Do you not think this is more important, Tom?'

'I do, Sal, I think it's a lot more important. But Graham Scholtz is joining us for lunch today and he's the one who hands out the leads. You know I need some good leads, Sal, especially now.'

What does he mean by 'especially now'? Kenny? Is he suggesting he didn't need them before all this? *What about when you lost all my money, Tom?* I decide not to get into a row with him at this hour of the morning and not in front of the boys.

'Tonight then, as soon as the boys are asleep.'

'Grand, do you want me to pick up some wine?'

'We're not having a party, Tom.'

Amber comes down the stairs putting an end to our conversation.

'Who's taking me today?' she asks, checking herself in the mirror.

'Your mother,' Tom says. 'I'm taking the boys to the crèche.'

The words send a shiver down my spine. 'Your mother.' In one second I imagine the horror of our family broken up. Every chore being divided out. Your mother will be… Your father is… Mom and Dad no longer words we use to refer to one another. For some reason I feel the need to hug everyone; a family hug, but we never do that and it would just feel weird. Instead I go to Amber and pull her hair out from inside the jacket she's putting on. 'I love you.'

Amber leans in and hugs me. 'Love you too, Mom.'

Tom turns and looks at me. Is he waiting? What will I do? Amber stills, her eyes flicking from me to Tom, last night's row eliciting her interest. I have to hug him now.

Getting into the car Amber says hello to Rena next door who's coming out of her house with her little boy Owen.

'What time do you need me to call in tonight?'

'Seven o'clock?'

'No probs.' Amber sits in the passenger seat.

'She asked me to babysit again.'

'Well, that's great, it's good money too.'

'It's slave labour but I've no choice, you won't let me get a proper job.'

'I'm not going through this again, Amber. You're too young, you'll be working all your life, you don't…' The headphones are already in place, her head nodding to the beat of some coked-up rapper.

The engine purrs. In the mirror I see Tom putting the boys into the back of his car. To look at the man, you would not believe he had a care in the world. He's laughing at something one of the boys has said or done. The suit on his back impeccably crisp, the shirt snow white. Shaved and polished he sits in the front of the car and waves at me like there's nothing going on. Like our whole world is not about to be crushed by his past. I wave back.

Chapter Eighteen

Time of death, Sunday afternoon. Place of death, the kitchen. The woman lived with her son in the Sycamore estate. Apparently she was killed with a knife, stabbed in the heart and left bleeding to death. Everyone in the salon is talking about it.

Amy is like the 'go to' person for information on the murder, following the news like she committed it.

'I don't know, I think's it's cause she's the same age as me ma.'

Anna tells her she's a weirdo, which is strange to hear. Anna is usually the one we refer to as the weirdo. White make-up, black clothes and dark eyes all warning us to keep our distance.

'It's just fascinating; are you not fascinated by it, Sal?'

More than you fucking know.

'Not really, Amy.'

'They found the kid's da.' Her fingers are sliding through the latest comments on social media.

My heart skips a beat. 'Did they name him?'

'Nnnnope… I bet he killed her… Oh look, there's a picture on Facebook of the dead woman.' Blood rushes to my head. I have to see it.

'Where?' Moving to Amy's side I take her phone to have a look. The woman is smiling. Oh my God, I can't believe this woman was murdered. She looks completely harmless. Her hair is brown, hanging down both sides of her face like curtains. She's older than I imagined... but then I'm still picturing a girl in Copper's nightclub. I wonder what Tom saw in her back then, when she was young and beautiful, before time and raising a child on her own added those wrinkles to her face.

Lifting my eyes from the screen to the mirror in front of me I consider how my own face has changed, aged, when Sienna bursts into the room.

'Sal, there's someone on the phone for you.'

'What?' I check my cell. Two missed calls from an unknown number.

'The landline.'

The landline? Why is someone ringing me on the salon landline? Swallowing down the last of my coffee, I leave the table and walk out to the shop floor.

Elsie is tapping on the window, warning Meg of impending trouble. She's like our personal security system, alerting us when any of the well-known bag snatchers are passing by the shop or something unusual is happening.

Meg nods at her, peering out the window at the two female suspects before handing me the phone.

'Sally Cooper,' the voice says.

'Yes.'

'I tried your mobile twice but didn't get an answer.'

'Who is this?'

'Saoirse O'Neill. I'm Kenny's social worker.'

I don't know how they do it, specially trained in subliminal bullying. The one thing I promised myself I wasn't going to do was meet that social worker. After two minutes on the phone with her, I'm suggesting venues.

Saoirse O'Neill is standing and waving at me from the last booth in the corner of the café when I arrive. She's younger than I expected with blonde hair and a pretty face. The blue jacket with the white furry collar that she has resting on the seat beside her is similar to one I picked up for Amber in Penny's last week. It's hard to take someone half my age with a tattoo on their neck seriously. But seriously I must because this young woman is about to cast judgement on the rest of my life whether I like it or not.

I sit facing her, opening the buttons on my jacket but not removing it. I don't want her to think I'm staying here long.

She beckons at a waiter who is standing in the corner.

'Coffee?' she says to me, watching every step the young man makes. His lack of speed must be irritating her. Her own mug is almost empty. She must have been here early, making sure she could seat us discreetly, so she can bully me without the other customers in the café hearing.

I nod at her and immediately explain that I can't stay long. I have to pick the boys up from the crèche. It's a lie. Tom is picking them up, but I need to be able to take myself out of this situation the minute it gets too much for me. My plan is to listen to what she has to say, tell her that I don't think it's right to ask us to take a young man into our home who we know nothing about. I'll say 'man', it sounds more dangerous than 'kid'.

'Saoirse O'Neill...' Holding out her hand she takes mine. 'It's terrible, isn't it?' she says. 'The poor child, imagine losing your mother at such a young age and in such horrific circumstances.'

'It is,' I say, wondering is this a tactic. Does she know I lost my mother at a young age? If Tom has told her anything about me I will kill him.

'Tom tells me you're not too happy about helping Kenny out for a while.' So Tom has decided to put all this on me. What happened to us both agreeing it was a bad idea?

'No, I'm not, I don't think it's a good idea.' The waiter arrives and puts the two cups down on the table. Saoirse lifts her hand almost shooing him away.

'Thanks,' I say as he walks away.

'I totally understand your concerns, Sally, it's a very hard thing Tom is asking you to do.' What does she mean Tom is asking me to do? *She* is asking me to do it. Tom was on my side until she got her hands on him.

'Sorry – eh, Saoirse, is it? Are you saying Tom wants to take Kenny to live with us, because that's not what he told me?'

'I did get the impression he would like to help his son, yes.'

'There's helping and there's helping. Uprooting our whole family life is not an option – we don't even know this young man. Sure, for all I know he could have killed his mother.'

'There's no need for that, Sally?'

'Why… do *you* know who did it?'

'Kenny is in a terrible state over the murder of his mother, Sally. He is helping the police with their enquiries but he is not a suspect.' She's talking in a soft tone and staring at me with a gentle smile on her face like she feels sorry for me, like I'm a fool who just said the worst thing in the world. I'm not listening to any more of this crap.

'Saoirse, it's been lovely to meet you but I have to go now. The children I am responsible for are waiting for me.' I stand up and button my coat, the coffee hasn't been touched.

'I'll make arrangements for you to meet Kenny as soon as possible. You can see for yourself what a lovely boy he is?'

'I have to go, have to pick up the kids, goodbye.'

Heading for the exit, I try to ignore her voice calling after me. 'I'll be in touch with the details.'

My heart is pumping. Out on the street the Friday night suits and skirts head for the bars. My head is lifting and I really don't feel like going home. It was a bad idea meeting her, I knew it was but Tom insisted, said it would be for the best for me to express my opinion but I think he thought the pretty social worker would be able to convince me to give it a try.

The noise from the bars spills out on to the street. Laughter, music, fun. I wish I could join them, get drunk, forget this unfolding disaster for a while. But I can't. I have to drive home to where Tom is probably waiting for me to say, 'Fine, I'll do it.' He can think again.

Chapter Nineteen

Click clack, click clack. Donna's heels pound the tiled floor inside. When she opens the door, she's holding a glass of wine in her hand. Her hair looks like she just left my salon, puffed and perfect framing a beautifully made-up face. Donna is dressed in a tight pair of white jeans with a royal blue T-shirt hugging her chest. Her hand stretches out to pull me inside.

'Delighted you called, darling,' she says, closing the door behind me.

I wasn't sure whether I should call or not but I thought Donna might be a better option than going home. I sent Donna a text to see if she was busy. Her reply:

I'm never too busy for a friend.

'Here.' She hands me a glass of red wine.

'But I have the car, Donna, I can't...'

She puts her finger over my lips quietening my plea and bends forward looking into my eyes. 'Leave the car, Sal. Walk. You're under a lot of pressure, one glass won't do any harm.'

I'm not sure what I should do. I only planned on popping in for a quick chat but then I think, why not? Tom never worries about leaving me alone on a Friday night, why should I worry about him? The kids will be asleep shortly. Amber is next door so she won't even know I'm not home. I'll have two glasses, no more, leave the car and walk around the corner to my house. We can talk then.

'Thanks, Donna,' I say, swallowing down half a glass in one gulp.

Donna laughs. 'I'm guessing there's more you want to tell me.' She tops up my glass.

'There is.'

When Donna is updated she assures me that I am doing the right thing. This should be between Tom and me, she says, devaluing any interference from the social worker. Donna also suggests that Tom and I should sit down and talk about it, that we both need to know each other's feelings. Shouting things out during a row doesn't count. I can tell the woman has probably indulged in a bit of counselling herself.

Donna surprises me when she asks me to be understanding of Tom's situation. Even though he lied to me about how long he has known about Kenny, he probably only lied because he's a man and in Donna's opinion men never know what to do. 'Always kicking the can down the road,' she says. Thankfully the red wine is dulling my senses. At this stage I'm just listening to her words.

After what felt like an hour but the clock on the wall confirms to be two, I begin to wonder why Tom hasn't rung looking for me. Does he not care where I am? Lifting the phone from my handbag my breathing stops. Endless missed calls and messages. Shit, I'd forgotten to take it off silent when I left the social worker.

'I better ring him.' But the phone goes straight to voicemail – and shit, some of these calls are from Amber's phone.

'Something's up, Donna.' Standing up quickly, the room spins, so I hold on tightly to the corner of the counter. 'Everyone's looking for me.'

'Now don't panic.' She gets me a glass with water. 'Everyone is always looking for Mammy when she disappears for a few hours.'

'No, something's up, I know it, Amber should not be ringing me, she's supposed to be next door babysitting and Tom's phone is going to voicemail.'

'Here, drink this.' Donna hands me the glass of cold water. It slips down my throat like a shot of reality. She takes the empty glass and goes back to the sink to fill it up again. I'm hitting Amber's contact with my shaky finger.

'Where the fuck are you?' she yells down the phone. I'm shocked by her language but even more shocked by the fear in her voice.

'Amber, what's going on?'

'We were looking everywhere for you, ringing you, ringing the salon.'

'What is it, Amber?' My heart beats faster, something bad has happened.

'Come home, Ma, please, come home now.'

'I'm on my way, Amber. I'll be there in two minutes. What's going on? What happened?' My mind races, I picture an accident, Cian, Aaron, blood, I see tears, I see frightened little faces. Taking a deep breath, I try not to show Amber how panicked I am.

'Are the boys okay?'

'Yes, Cian and Aaron are fine, they're in bed asleep. It's Da.' Amber is scared, her voice rising with every word.

'Tom? What happened to him?'

'The police were here, Ma.'

My legs buckle beneath me. Donna moves the stool for me to sit down. 'The police? What the hell did they want?'

'I don't know.' Amber is crying, panicking at the far end of the phone.

'It's going to be okay, Amber, it was just a silly car accident. He knocked down someone on a bike, they're…'

'They took him to the station, Mam.' Oh God, poor Amber. Donna is telling me to relax.

'*What?* The station?' I end the call and run.

Ellen is standing at the door. Amber's face is red from crying. A shudder runs down my back when I see Amber holding Rena's baby on her hip. I don't know why but I don't like the picture.

'What's going on?' I say, panting my way to the front door.

'They took Dad away in the car,' Amber cries. I pull her close and hug her and the baby in her arms tightly.

'I know all about it, Amber. It was just an accident with a cyclist, Dad will be fine.'

Tom called Ellen to come over to sit with the boys because he couldn't get me on the phone. Amber saw it all from the next-door neighbour's window. If I'd have been here the cops wouldn't have had to stay so long. Amber might have missed it. But apparently it took half an hour for Ellen to arrive and the lights were flashing outside the house. But why did they take Tom to the station? The accident, the cyclist? Or, please don't let it be something to do with the dead woman?

'Dad couldn't get you on the phone, so he had to ring Nan and I had to come in with Owen because I was too scared to stay next door on my own when I didn't know where you were.'

'I'm sorry, I was at a friend's house and my phone was on silent.'

Ellen is saying nothing with words, it's all written on her face. She shakes her head at me then winks a nod to get rid of Amber.

'Go back inside, Amber, put Owen in his bed, everything is okay, your dad was in an accident the other day. They just want to clarify some details. It's nothing serious, so don't worry, sweetie. Would you like me to ring Rena to come home early?'

Taking a deep breath, Amber leans in for me to hug her. 'No, it's okay.' Owen whimpers in Amber's arms. Cuddling him, she walks away, turning when she gets to the end of the garden. 'Call me if anyone else breaks the law.'

My head is thumping, my mouth, dry as burnt toast. When Amber is safely inside Rena's house, Ellen closes the door and we both walk into the kitchen. She reaches for the painkillers while I pour myself a glass of water.

'The police weren't here over the cyclist's accident, Sally.'

No, please no, don't say what I think you're going to say.

'If they weren't here over the accident, why were they here? Do you know?' Ellen's face is white with worry, her eyes sad, her breathing laboured.

'They wanted to ask him questions about some woman. Claire McCarthy.'

'Claire McCarthy? Who the hell is Claire McCarthy.'

'She's the woman who was murdered in Sycamore last week.'

Ellen stares at me, unable to disguise the fear in her eyes. Her stare lingers, as if she's searching my face for answers. Answers that I don't have.

Chapter Twenty

Tom is still at the station and I'm sitting here in my kitchen about to explain to Ellen that she has another grandson. I wish I didn't have to do this. I wanted Tom to tell her, to look her in the eye and tell her he has been lying to her for the past six months at least, possibly even more. Just like he's been lying to me.

I almost collapsed with the shock when Ellen told me the reason the police wanted to talk to Tom. But I realize it makes sense. He's the boy's father, naturally they would have to speak to him, but did they have to call to the house? Surely they could have rung him, asked him to go down to the station. Couldn't they?

Ellen pours milk into her tea. I'm leaning against the counter top sipping strength from a strong cup of coffee.

'I was hoping Tom would be the one to tell you this, Ellen.'

She shuffles closer to the table putting her elbows down and hugging the cup. Her focus is completely on me, waiting, wanting to know how I can be so calm about her son being questioned about a dead woman.

'That woman who died has a son, Ellen.'

Ellen nods without moving her stare.

'Turns out Tom is the father of that boy.'

I let it lie there between us, dangling like a piñata in the air. This massive revelation. Ellen's mouth slowly opens but nothing comes out. It's the first time I've seen Ellen speechless.

'Congratulations, Ellen, you're a granny again.' I turn away from Ellen's stunned gaze and pour the remaining coffee down the sink. How do I continue? What do I say next? It's not up to me to be ruining everyone's life, that's supposed to be Tom's job. Big Bad Tom.

Tears fall down my cheek and splash one by one into the sink but they're not taking the pain with them. The warmth of Ellen's arms wrap around my shoulders. The scent of worry and White Linen filling the air between us. I hug her back.

'How long have you known?' she whispers. Turning around I see her face age in front of me. Her eyelids sag over dark blue circles, freshly carved wrinkles stretch out like winged emotions. Until now, Ellen has always looked younger than her years.

'I've only known a couple of days but apparently Tom has known for the last six months, at least, I don't know for sure, I know nothing for sure. Tom has been lying to me.'

Ellen lets out a sigh before releasing her hold on me. When she walks towards the table I notice a slight stoop creeping into her gait.

'I don't really want to go into the details, Ellen, I'll let Tom fill you in on all that.' Nodding her head repeatedly she sits back down on the chair.

'So that's why they're questioning Tom, Ellen, nothing else.'

Ellen nods her head again. It all makes sense now.

'You knew nothing about this… did you?' Her silence overpowers. Why is she not answering me? 'Well, *did* you, Ellen?'

'Sorry, Sally, what did you say? My mind is racing here, I can't keep up with myself, I'm…'

'Did you know anything about this, did Tom ever mention anything about this boy to you?'

'No, Sal, of course not, Tom told me nothing about the boy.' Moving her gaze to the table, her fingers trace the table top. 'I would have made him tell you straight away if he had.' I continue to look at her, waiting for her to lift her head, to see her eyes. I will go mad if he told his mother before telling me. She stands and walks to the kettle, nothing more to say.

—

Ellen stays while I ring the station. The woman on the other end of the phone tells me Tom is in a room talking to the detectives, helping them with their enquiries. She knows nothing else and is not the slightest bit interested in the fact that I'm his wife, sitting at home worried sick. I feel desperate. Helpless. Poor Tom stuck in that stuffy room with some stranger dragging up his past. He's been there for almost three hours now. That's a long time if you know nothing.

With little chance of getting any further information, I insist Ellen go home, promising to ring her as soon as I hear from Tom. I'm not in the humour for answering her questions. Though, to be fair, she hasn't really asked any; strange, that.

The following hours pass like a bad movie, I need this to end. For Tom to come home and tell me everything is okay. I check on the boys, kiss their foreheads, but even the scent of innocence does little to relax me.

Once again, I look out through the curtains onto the quiet street. Light shines from the windows opposite.

Most of my neighbours work during the day, then pick up their young children from the crèche, dream about weekends. Friday night is takeaway, beer and wine night. Tom and I were once that couple. Before Tom's job got too important for him to miss the Friday after-work sessions. It all stopped. The sofa nights. The chats, the falling up the stairs legless, laughing with one another. I didn't really notice them coming to an end, they just seemed to fizzle out.

When we first got our own place we lived for Friday night so much, we often planned it on the Monday. What we would order in, what movie we would watch. It was so, so long ago now, and more than time has passed.

–

A noise interrupts my thoughts. My heart leaps. It's coming from outside the house. Could it be the intruder coming back? Jumping out of the chair I rush to the window, the thoughts of a murderer at large filling me with fear as I pull back the curtain. A shadow moves in the dark. It's Rena from next door. Shit, that means Amber will be home on top of me any minute. What will I tell her? I better stick with the story of the accident and the bicycle. I have no intentions of telling her about her new brother. Tom will have to be beside me when we release that monster.

Chapter Twenty-One

Amber has been crying, I can tell. Her skin is blotchy and her eyes are stinging red. My heart bleeds for her as she tries to carry on like nothing is wrong. Which is not like Amber, she usually faces things straight on with a shot gun.

'There's no need for you to worry, Amber.'

Taking a can of Sprite out of the fridge, Amber yawns. 'I'm so tired, Mom.'

'I know, sweetheart, you go to bed. I promise, nothing's wrong.'

I'm not sure she bought the story about the accident, saying it was a bit of a big deal to drag her dad down the station especially on a Friday night when the cops should be busy dealing with drunk Dublin. I explained to her the officer on the case was only back on duty tonight and that's why they called now. Tuts, huffs, then finally a kiss on the cheek.

'Did you make much money?' I ask her, trying to lighten the atmosphere as she walks out of the room.

'Slave labour,' she replies, lifting my spirits ever so slightly. At least this nightmare hasn't erased Amber's sense of humour.

There's still no news from Tom and now my body is aching all over so I'm going to lie down on the bed. If I can read, it will drag my thoughts somewhere else for a while. I take one last look out the window. The night is still. Fewer lights shining from the opposite side of the street.

Tom must be exhausted down there at this hour of the night. What could he be telling them that would take this long? They must be finished with him soon. Lifting my cell, I decide to ring the station again. A male voice answers this time but he can't tell me anything except that Tom is still there. I try to engage him in conversation, ask him if he had any idea when Tom would be home but he knows nothing.

Anxiety is lying in the bed with me. Holding me hostage. Reading doesn't help. The words on the page are blocked from entering my head by the big question that has now set up camp there. What if Tom *has* got something to do with the woman's murder?

Don't be silly, I tell myself, *Tom wouldn't hurt a fly*. I know this. I love him and I've been married to him fifteen years. He's never once raised a hand to me. He rarely even raised his voice to me. His idea of being angry is to say nothing and head to the pub. He hasn't got a violent gene flowing through his blood. I know, I've seen what that gene looks like.

So why is he still down there?

Moments later I get my answer. Tom pushes open the bedroom door and walks over to my side of the bed.

'You're back!' Dragging a misplaced smile across my face I sit up straight.

He rushes over to me, his hug almost crushing me. 'I'm so sorry, Sal, you must have been up the wall but they wouldn't let me ring you.'

'What's going on?'

'Did Ma tell you?'

'Yes, she said they wanted to ask you questions about the dead woman.'

Tom stands and walks towards the en suite. I wonder why he asked that? Was he checking to see if I already knew why he was brought in, was he planning to spin me the line about the bicycle accident like I did to Amber?

He opens the door of the en suite, about to walk inside when I say, 'What happened, Tom?'

Turning to face me, a shadow in the low light cast from the bedside lamp, Tom stretches both arms out to the frame of the door.

'Nothing much, they just want to speak to anyone who knew the woman, nothing for you to worry about, Sal.' He walks into the en suite and closes the door.

I'm confused – is his casual, just-another-day-at-the-office voice an attempt to keep me calm or confuse me? Pulling back the duvet, I move to the en suite door.

'Tom,' I call after him. 'You didn't know her, did you?'

My stomach hurts, acid leaks into my mouth. *Surely* Tom didn't know the woman. Did he? Suddenly I have this picture in my head of him sitting having lunch with his 'other' family. The woman, the kid, Tom at the top of the table laughing out loud with them. The waiter comes along, Tom rushes to pull out his wallet. Hugs and kisses all round, plans for next week.

I rush to the closed door and push it open. With one hand leaning against the wall Tom stands peeing into the toilet.

'You didn't know her, Tom, did you?'

'I wouldn't say I knew her… as such.'

'Did you ever meet her, Tom, did you? Did you ever see her since that one night seventeen years ago when that thing in your hand got us all into this trouble?'

I want to push him, knock his head off the tiled wall in front of him, the lovely shimmery silver tiled wall. I picture his blood dripping down it.

'No, not like you think.'

Unable to stay in the same room, lie in the same bed, I take my pillow and drag the duvet with me. I was hoping he would come home and tell me the police just wanted to know about the kid. What he was like? Did Tom think the boy could have killed his mother? And all those types of question. I didn't count on Tom knowing the dead woman. What if he did meet her and they rekindled their love from that one night of passion?

Shit, *were* they having an affair? *No, don't go there, Sally. Because if you do go there, you might never come back.*

Lying between the folded duvet I rest my head on the pillow, hoping to fall asleep, but my mind is racing. If the newspapers said she was murdered sometime on Sunday afternoon, why were they questioning Tom? He was with them Sunday afternoon at the station, when the accident with the bicycle happened, when he was given the test to see if there was any alcohol in his blood. At least that's what he told me.

I'm too warm. Kicking my legs out from under the cover the thought suddenly crashes into my mind. What if there was no accident, no bicycle, no alcohol testing. What if Tom made it all up to keep me from going berserk on him for not showing up to the birthday party? No, he wouldn't, would he? Or worse still. What if he killed the woman? It's not in his nature, I know, he's not violent. But accidents can happen when knives and angry people hang around in the same space. Maybe he killed her by mistake. Got angry, lifted the knife to enforce his demands. She could have slipped. He could have slipped. We're all slipping now.

Chapter Twenty-Two

I hear crying. *Who's that?* My eyes open and I realize I'm not in my bed. It must be Aaron. He's on the landing looking for me. His tiny pleas echo down the stairs. Poor kid, he doesn't know where I am. I rush to the hallway up the stairs and grab him in my arms.

'It's okay, baby, Mammy is here.'

Aaron is holding a scraggly teddy bear in his hand and wiping his nose on it. His dark hair is stuck to his head like he's been rained on and his feet are bare. Lifting him in my arms I hug him gently.

'Mammy is here, mammy is here.'

His little arm wraps around my neck as he holds me tightly. He's different to Cian, any break in his routine sets him off. The poor child must have got the fright of his life when he came into the room and I wasn't there. That's Tom's fault.

Warmed by his embrace I lift Aaron down the stairs and sit him on the duvet. His face brightens, he thinks we're going to play, he doesn't know his Mammy only slept for about an hour last night and it's not even 6 a.m. yet.

'Let's go back to sleep, Aaron, Mammy's tired,' I say, pulling his cosy body close to me.

Within ten minutes I hear the soft pant of his snore and feel his breath brushing off my face. I close my eyes, hoping to get another hour or two sleep but my mind won't let me. Today is the day. Today we tell Amber.

–

'What did I do now?' Amber is sitting at the kitchen table.

'You've done nothing, Amber,' I say. 'Your father and I need to talk to you about something.' Amber looks at Tom who is taking the seat beside her.

'Dad, what's wrong?' She knows something is up when both of us want to talk to her together. It hasn't happened since she 'experimented,' as she describes it, with the vodka last year. Tom had sat beside her on that occasion, talking to her like she was a victim. 'Who gave it to you, princess?' 'Did you feel pressured into taking it?' etc., etc. There was something about the way he said it that made me laugh out loud, so loud that both of them turned and stared at me. I tried to stop but I couldn't. I laughed and laughed and laughed even more at their still faces, mouths open with shock. Tom asked what I was laughing at but I couldn't stop to tell him. All I could see was sneaky little Amber, who finally admitted to me that she had robbed the vodka from the cupboard in our kitchen, hid it at the bottom of her bag, then took it to her friend's house where she disguised it in a bottle of Coke. Then she had the audacity to drink it in front of her friend's mother while she drove them to the venue. Poor Amber my arse. And there's Tom talking to her like she was kidnapped and held down while someone poured vodka down her throat. I got up from the table leaving the two of them staring at me as I left the room. 'You're grounded for a month,' I said, then closed the door behind me.

Before sitting down I check that Cian and Aaron are still engrossed with Peppa Pig while munching on their

Rice Krispies. Leaving the door slightly ajar in case either of them calls me, I return to my seat at the table.

I don't think Tom will be laughing this time. Looking at Amber's pale face bracing herself for what she presumes is bad news, I want to cry. The poor kid shouldn't have to deal with this. What's she going to think? Amber has always looked up to Tom, respected him, trusted him. I don't want her to think less of him, I'm doing enough of that for both of us. It could knock her self-confidence, one of Amber's greatest assets.

Her belief in herself impresses me. I never had that kind of self-belief at her age. I could never argue a topic with someone older than me, especially not my dad. He scared me. Mom was already gone. *Please God, do not let this crazy situation put a crack in Amber's armour.*

'Hurry up, Ma, I haven't all day,' she says. 'I'm supposed to be meeting Sarah at eleven.' Her phone sits on the table in front of her, upside down of course. God forbid anyone else looked at it. Tom is rubbing his hands on his jeans, looking at me nervously as I sit opposite them.

'So what is it?' she says, looking at me. 'Are you getting divorced?'

'What? No, Amber… why would you think we were getting divorced?' I look from her to Tom and a little part of me wonders if I've just been given a portal into the future.

'What is it then?'

My hands lie intertwined on the table as if in prayer. Tom looks nervous.

'Amber, there is something I have to tell you.'

When Amber realizes that I'm not the messenger, she shuffles in closer to the table, a serious look dropping over her face as she turns her attention to Tom.

'Amber.' Cough, splutter, finally eye contact. 'A short while ago, I discovered I have a son…' Pause… Silence… Action. 'He's sixteen, just a year older than you and his name is Kenny.' Tom's eyes are fixed on Amber's. She swings herself around in the chair to face him. Finally, we have news big enough to hold our daughter's complete attention.

My fingers are pressing so hard into my hands I think I'll be bruised by the end of this. What will she do? What will she say?

'The thing is, Amber, Kenny's mom has died and he has no other family.'

Amber remains silent, her eyes still glued to her Daddy's, hanging on to his every word.

'I'm sure you have a lot of questions, pet. You will want to think about it, then ask me whatever you want. I will tell you anything you want to know.'

'When can I meet him?' she says forcing me to fall backwards into my chair. *What are you saying, Amber?* I'd better say something quick.

'Amber, sweetie, this is all new to us, we haven't decided what we're going to do about it yet. We're telling you now because we didn't want you finding out from someone else.'

Turning around to face me she sits up straight. 'But he's my brother, I have to meet him.'

'And you will, Amber, you will meet him but there's a lot going on at the moment and we have to do what's best for the family.'

Moving her attention back to Tom, she says, 'Have you met him?' Tom nods a yes. 'What's he like?'

'He's…' I interrupt Tom, this is not going how I expected it to. *Where's your tantrum, Amber, why don't you shout at him, ask him why he lied, was he dating me when he got the kid's mother pregnant?* No, nothing. No criticism whatsoever. I can't believe this Amber is only interested in knowing when she can meet her half-brother.

'Amber, that's all we have to tell you for the moment. Go and meet Sarah now and we will have another chat later on.'

'But…'

'But nothing, Amber, your father and I need to talk.'

'It will be okay, Dad,' she says, kissing him on the cheek before leaving the table. I'm sitting here with my mouth open. A fucking kiss on the fucking cheek and all I get is a shrug of the shoulders.

Tom's like the cat that got the milk. 'Well, that wasn't too bad,' he says. 'She seems to have taken it well.' Standing up from the table he walks over to the fridge, opens the door and looks inside. I'm left feeling confused and slightly angry. I didn't want Amber to be upset but I was expecting a bigger reaction from her. More shock, drama, more when, how, where. But nothing, just, when can I meet him?

'She's only just heard… I'm sure she'll be back with plenty of questions, Tom.'

'Yeah, I'd say so. Still, I'm glad she wants to meet him.'

With a heavy heart, I push open the door to where the two boys still sit tuned in to the TV. I know I shouldn't feel hard done by. Amber's reaction is a good thing. I don't want her to think bad about her father because it doesn't feel good. I know.

'More Krispies,' Aaron says, holding out his bowl for me to fill. Tossing his hair, I take the bowl from his tiny grip and return to the kitchen to where Tom is now filling the kettle.

'Aaron wants more Krispies… I'm going out.'

'I thought you'd be here today, I've to—'

I cut him off mid-sentence. 'I'm going out.'

Grabbing my bag from the table, I walk to the front door. I need some time to think, time on my own. I'm sick of running and racing after everyone, being taken for granted by my own family. Let's see how they get on fending for themselves. Doormat Sally has had enough.

Chapter Twenty-Three

I'm not going to work. I just want to be on my own, all day, all week if I could. I need a break from this life that has happened to me while I was planning the real one. Taking my disappointment with me, I get into my car to drive somewhere, anywhere. Somewhere no one can find me.

And now I've to meet the boy. The social worker rang Tom with the arrangements. I wanted to say no, I'm not going but my heart wouldn't let me. The poor boy has been cast in his worst nightmare. He certainly didn't ask for his mother to be killed and replaced with some stranger, me. I do feel sorry for him, just not enough to adopt him. I'm sure if I was standing on the outside of this drama, listening to someone relaying the story, I'd be all 'of course the father should take him, it's the least he can do, sure what harm could the youngster be? He could do with a break he's been through so much.' But I'm not standing on the outside with my opinion the only thing involved. I'm stuck right in the centre. This is my life, my family's future, no one else could possibly understand what it's like to be put on the spot like this. Driving past the house, I remind myself not to get carried away. With a bit of luck the kid will not want to live with us. After all he doesn't know us from Eve.

She's arranged for us to meet tomorrow. I'm nervous; afraid I won't like him. *Remember, Sal, he's only a kid, if it was Amber in this situation I'd want someone to help her.*

Phone, make sure you have your phone, Sally. Checking my bag the idea suddenly hits me. If Tom won't tell me anything more about what is going on or why he was questioned by the police, I'll do my own investigating. I'll drive to her house, the dead woman's house. There's bound to be some neighbours hanging around with gossip they're dying to unload, hoping for some casual passer-by to ask the question. *What happened?*

According to Journal.ie. Sycamore Gardens is the name of the street where Claire McCarthy lived. I put the address into Google Maps and follow the directions. *Why does that street name sound familiar?*

The traffic is less busy at this hour on a Saturday morning: car loads of kids in jerseys heading off to play matches but none of the usual mid-week jams. I get to Sycamore in a few minutes. It's not far from my own house. If I'd walked across the fields at the back of my estate, I'd arrive at the back of the Sycamore Estate.

When I get to the entrance, Google sends me through two large pillars that lead into a small community of red brick houses. I read the plaques on the walls at the top of each street until I find Sycamore Gardens. Eight semi-detached houses line both sides of the narrow road and I wonder will I be able to tell which one it is? They all look the same.

It doesn't take long for me to spot the house. There's no crime scene tape, or cop standing outside anymore but I remember the fabulous flower pots lined up across the front. Reds, yellow, blues, purples, whites. They look out of place, glowing in front of the house where death has so violently paid a visit.

I slow my car down to have a good gawk. A young boy walks out of a house a couple of doors to the left catching my attention. He's carrying a sports bag and wearing football shorts and a T-shirt. Could that be Kenny? Is that the family friend's house who took him in while his long-term care is being arranged? The kid's hair is black but other than that I don't see any features that resemble his daddy's. I wish I had paid more attention to the picture of him in the photograph. But I was so busy staring in disbelief at my husband smiling back at me that the kid's features never really registered. I think he was a bit fuller than the skinny little rake who is now walking out of the garden with his bag threatening to pull him to the ground.

'Hello,' I say with my head out the window. The young boy is now swiping through something on his phone and he can't hear me with the headphones in his ears. 'Hello,' I shout louder this time but I don't get any response.

He walks past immersed in his music unaware that there's a mad woman calling out to him. Continuing my slow progress down the road, I watch each house with interest, wondering if Kenny is behind one of those doors.

Reversing in the small cul-de-sac at the top of the road I drive back down the street and see a woman walking out of her garden. She's making sure to pull the latch on the iron gate at the bottom of her yard before walking down the road. I guess people around here will be nervous for a while, while the killer is still at large. Wondering if he will want to kill again. Or she.

My plan was to ask one of the neighbours for the local take on the murder but considering they may all be living on their nerves at the moment, a stranger pulling up alongside them in a car may not be a good idea.

When I drive out of the estate I see a Costa coffee shop on the opposite side of the road so I park my car outside. I'm about to get out when the phone rings. It's Amber.

'Where are you?' she says. I want to say 'Mind your own business' but instead I say, 'I'm going to visit someone, Amber. Why?'

'Dad didn't know where you'd gone.'

'Oh, I'm so sorry I didn't tell you where I was going, Amber… after all, you or your father would never leave the house without telling me where you were, now would you?' Silence at the far end of the phone. Amber does not expect sarcasm from her Mammy, that's *her* job. Oh God, I shouldn't have done that. Upsetting her. She has enough to deal with without her mother turning on her.

'Are you there, sweetie?' I ask, picturing her at the far end of the phone calculating her next move.

'What time will you be back?' Her voice is softer now, weaker, showing her disappointment in me for being smart with her. I can't let that happen again. Amber needs to know how much she means to me, that I'll always be there for her. Especially now with all that's happening.

'I'll be home as soon as possible, Amber, hopefully an hour or two.'

–

The coffee shop is busy when I step inside. Which is good, it means I'll have to share a table and might get to talk to someone. Taking my place in the queue I notice the man in front of me being very friendly to the young woman behind the counter. He knows her name and she knows his, which means he must be a regular. With my eyes ignoring the rows of delicious cakes and treats behind the glass barrier in front of me, I eventually arrive at the order station.

'One skinny latte,' I say to the girl who immediately goes to the barista machine and begins to prepare it. The man has paid at the till and is taking a seat on a table close by the wall. There's an empty chair facing him, I'll head for that.

With the cup rattling on the saucer, I make my way to the chair but just as I'm about to reach it, a young girl rushes in from the door and plonks herself down. 'Thanks, Dad,' she says, picking up the mug of coffee.

'There's a chair free here,' a voice says when I'm left standing looking around for somewhere to sit. Turning to find the face behind the voice I see an older woman, late sixties, I'd guess, pointing at a chair opposite hers.

'Thanks,' I say, sitting down in front of her. 'It's very busy today, isn't it?'

'Always the same on a Saturday morning, it's a lot quieter during the week.'

So she's a regular too. I know I can't just jump in and ask her if she knew the dead woman. I'll have to be discreet. Open with something general. The weather.

'Not a bad day out there,' I say glancing out and noticing the rain beginning to pour down. 'Oops, think I spoke too soon.' The woman also looks towards the window to see the change in the weather. She's not taking the bait though. Her words have dried up and now she seems to be turning her attention to her handbag.

'Are you using that sugar?' I ask her, pointing at the two sachets in the middle of the table. I don't even like sugar in my coffee but I need to engage this woman.

'No, you fire away, love, I'm not using it.'

'I shouldn't really,' I say opening the sachet. 'They say too much sugar can shorten your life.'

She pushes the second sachet in my direction saying, 'Sure everything nowadays can shorten your life.'

Watching the grains of sugar fall into the coffee, I say, 'It's not up to us, it's up to the man above.'

'Or the devil below,' she says. Lifting my stare from the spoon I'm circling around in my mug, I look up at her.

'Yes,' she says, unable to maintain her polite façade any longer. 'That poor woman.'

I lean forward slightly, all ears.

'A neighbour of a friend of mine, young woman, killed in her own home last week.'

'Oh, was that around here... I heard something about it on the news... did the police find out what happened?'

'No, not yet.'

'I'm sure they will, was she married?'

'No, had a boy though, poor kid, left without a mother at such a young age.'

'And without a father too.' I sigh.

'Oh no, he has a father, they just don't live together.'

'Well, that's something.'

'It is, if he's not the one who killed her.'

My hand grips the handle of the mug tightly. Too tight. 'Why? Do you think he killed her?'

'No, but you know gossip, people always say it's someone close to the victim.'

'And was he close to the victim?' The woman pauses momentarily like she's wondering whether to say any more. Maybe she thinks I'm a journalist I'm beginning to sound like one.

'I don't know much about them, I feel sorry for the kid, and the woman of course. A life cut short.' I decide not to push my luck, so I turn my attention back to the rain pouring down outside the window and sip my coffee.

'I'm sure the boy will be all right, they give them all sorts of counselling now. It wasn't like that in my day, you had to swallow your bad luck without any help.'

I turn and nod at her before returning my gaze to the window.

'He visits him every week, apparently. So he can't be too bad a man.' Her words thump me in the heart. Tom has been visiting this kid every week and I knew nothing about it. Lifting my coffee to my lips I watch my hand shaking.

'Jane told me.'

'Jane.'

'Yes, my friend, she lives on the same road as the woman – in number seventeen – the murder was in number twelve.'

My hand shakes, the coffee spills. That's where I saw it. On the envelope in the suitcase under the bed.

Tom Cooper
c/o 12 Sycamore Gardens

Without saying another word. I jump up from the table and run for the door, pressure pushing down on my chest. My head is spinning.

Tom visited that boy every week.

Chapter Twenty-Four

I sit in the car for a while, forcing myself to relax. Deep breaths, like the doctor told me. I rummage for something to breathe into. I find an empty crisp bag and breathe in and out until I eventually calm my lungs and get the strength to drive home.

Amber is sitting on the sofa when I go inside. Her head bent over, reading the phone glued to her hand. Cian and Aaron are on the floor by her feet, eyes staring at the TV that's blasting out a song from a Disney movie. They scrabble to stand when they see me.

'Mammy, Mammy.'

'Where's your father?' I say, hugging the boys before pulling Amber's earphones from her ears.

'What did you do that for?' she groans.

'I was asking you a question. Where's your father?'

'How the hell do I know? He said he had to go out, I didn't ask him where he was going, I'm not his fucking mother.'

'Amber! Don't you ever swear like that again and especially not in front of the boys.' Bending down, I pull Cian and Aaron into my grasp. 'Mammy's missed her best boys,' I say kissing them both on the head. 'Did they eat since breakfast?'

'They had a sandwich.' Dragging her feet off the sofa, Amber gets up to leave.

'Did you go into Eason's to see the...'

'No.' Amber plugs her ears again and walks out the door. Her face looks sad and I don't blame her. She's been looking forward to going in to meet her favourite boy band who were signing their book today. Their book has been sitting on her bedside locker for the past few weeks in anticipation. More and more she's being called on to look after Cian and Aaron when she really should be out enjoying herself with her own friends. Tom should not have asked her to mind the boys today after what she heard this morning. I want to hug her, to comfort her, but she's already traipsing up the stairs to her own space. If I get a chance later on I will try to have a gentle word in her ear. Reassure her that she is the most important person to me and to Tom. Tell her that things will settle down. That this trouble will soon pass. I don't know if it will, but I'll tell her anyway.

—

The suitcase lies open on the floor in front of me. The white envelope sticks out from amidst the bundle of brown ones. My nerves are getting the better of me. If I'm right, Tom was getting post sent to that dead woman's address. But why? What is in it? Pulling on the envelope I read the address to confirm what I thought. I'm right. *12 Sycamore Gardens*. My hand shakes as I pull out the letter inside. It's the DNA report.

Holding the letter, I read the truth. My eyes fill with water. It's true, I knew it was true but seeing the words on the page confirming it turns the knife a little deeper into my wound. I'm crying. I want to cry more but I have to keep it together. The kids can't see me like this. Why did he not just tell me when he found out? We could have dealt with it together, introduced the boy to the family on our own terms. Got to know him, got to like him. *Why this mess, Tom?*

Folding the report I put it back in the envelope. I'm about to return it to where I found it when I notice the postmark on the envelope. Sixteenth of March, the day before Paddy's Day, the day before we took the boys to the parade, held them on our shoulders, laughed like a normal family and all the time Tom was keeping this secret. How did he do that? And why did he tell me he only found out two months ago in August? I'm convinced now that Tom had no intention of telling me about Kenny… unless he had to. How will I ever be able to trust him again?

'Ma, the cops are here again… are you crying?' Amber sticks her head in the door.

'What?' Jumping to my feet I shove the case back under the bed and follow Amber out of the room.

'They're downstairs, they want to talk to you.'

Taking a deep breath, I drag my sleeve across my eyes. Amber puts her two hands around my shoulders and hugs me.

At the bottom of the stairs a woman and a man stand, nodding when they see me.

My arms are wrapped across my chest, my whole body shaking. 'Tom's not here.'

'That's okay, Sally, I was hoping to have a word with you.'

'Sure, sure.'

Amber pushes open the door where the boys are watching TV. 'I'll mind the boys.'

'Thanks, love.'

'Will this take long? Do you want to go into the kitchen or—'

'Yes, the kitchen will do fine.'

My blood pressure is shooting through the roof. What do they want with me?

'Sally, my name is Detective Angela Burke. This is Detective Michael Dunne.'

I nod at them, my heart dancing in my chest.

'Sally, can I ask when you found out about Kenny being Tom's son?'

'Eh… a few days ago, last week, I'm not sure what day it was.'

'Okay, but you didn't know before his mother was killed.'

'No… well, yes, actually.' What am I to say? There have been so many lies, I believe I must tell the truth. 'The day before she was killed, I was shown a photograph of Tom with the boy.' My breath is catching in my throat.

'Oh… by…?'

'I don't know who by, some stranger in the salon, a young girl called Charlie.' Burke looks at her partner then back to me.

'That must have been a huge shock to your system.'

'It was, but…'

'The day Claire McCarthy was killed, Tom told us you were having a party. Did you leave the house at any time?'

Am I a suspect now? Does she think I left my kids' party to go and kill that woman?

'No, well, that morning I went to Tesco to pick up the cake but after that, no, I was here all the time.' Michael Dunne is jotting down notes. 'Why are you asking?'

'I just need to know, Sally.' What is she implying?

'But why?'

'Someone was seen crossing the fields from this estate to the victim's estate around the time of the murder.'

I'm listening to her talk, and I know she's not telling me everything.

'Can you tell me which adults were at the party?'

'What? Do you think someone from the party killed that woman... seriously?' My look expresses how mad I think she is, coming up with that scenario but she doesn't comment.

'Names, please.'

'Well, I...' Moving over to the press I pull open a drawer. 'I think I have the list here somewhere.' I rummage through all the crap and surprise myself by finding it. Holding it out I tell her they were the people invited, but not all arrived.

'Can you tick off family members for me?'

Well, that won't take long, I have the smallest family in Dublin.

My hand shakes as I go through the list: Tom, myself, Ellen, Amber, the boys. Tom's cousin Mick who always brings his kids along without the wife, and that's it.

'Why do you need that?' She ignores my question, handing the list to her partner.

'That's all for now, Sally, thank you for your time.'

When the detectives leave the house, Amber rushes out to the hallway. 'Well, what did they want?' I'm not comfortable with Amber seeing all this.

'Ah, they were just asking about the day of the party, who was here, stuff like that.'

'Why?'

'I wish I knew, Amber.' Lifting her face in my hands I look her in the eye. 'There's nothing to worry about.'

Amber wraps her arms around me and hugs me. 'I hope so, Mam, I really do.'

–

When Cian and Aaron are finally in bed and Amber has gone around to Sarah's place, I give in and ring Tom. It's hard to believe a man who spent the previous night being questioned in the local police station is probably now swallowing pints with his mates, like nothing happened.

I was right, he is in the pub, said he had to get out and clear his head. I didn't bother asking him where he went today, why he left Amber with the boys. Deep down I know what his answer is and I don't want to have to deal with it. He went to see Kenny. Can't stay and mind his own two boys.

Maybe I'm being unreasonable. Naturally he has to go and see the boy. The kid is probably in a terrible state over his mother's murder. But he didn't have to go to the pub, we're all feeling the pressure. He should have come straight home afterwards, spent time with Cian, Aaron, Amber.

Tom says he won't be long, that he'll be home after the match. Like I know about 'the match,' care about the match. I couldn't give a bloody damn about a match. Will he ever grow up?

'I want you home now, Tom, your real family needs you too, the cops were here asking questions.' The anger in my voice must have frightened him, for a moment he doesn't answer. I can hear him taking a deep breath.

'What did they want?'

'Just get home, I'll tell you then.'

With the phone in my hand, I lift my feet up on to the sofa and prepare to download my misery on Donna when the hall door opens. Gosh that was quick. But instead of Tom, Amber walks into the room. The poor kid looks confused.

'Do you want something to eat, Amber?'

Removing her jacket, she tosses it on the sofa. 'Erm, maybe a cheese toastie?'

'I think I'll have one myself.'

'Is Dad back?'

'He'll be here shortly, he's in the pub watching the match.'

'Oh.' Even Amber finds that a bit much.

She follows me into the kitchen. Maybe she'll talk to me now. Tell me how she's really feeling about what's going on without the usual smartass answers. To my surprise she must have been thinking the same.

'Are you okay, Ma? Like… you must be in shock with all that's going on.'

My heart lifts, my little girl is concerned about me.

'I'm more worried about you, Amber,' I say, opening the press and taking out a few slices of bread. 'How do you feel about it, having a half-brother you knew nothing about until this morning?'

Amber doesn't answer at first, opening the fridge door she takes out the cheese slices. 'Well… actually…' But before she can finish her sentence the front door opens and in walks Tom. The smell of beer arrives into the kitchen alongside him. He walks over to Amber and kisses her on the head. 'Da, the smell off you' – she pushes him away – 'you're pissed.'

'I'm not pissed, Amber, I just had a few pints with the lads.' Tom sounds like he used to when I first met him, 'a few with the lads'. This man is going backwards. I'm raging that he walked in on us just as Amber was about to express her emotions to me. With his swaying body dominating the room I feel anger rising inside me. Why is he the one who gets to go out and forget about it all with the lads? This mess is his fault and here he is carrying on as if he's a victim, feeling sorry for himself.

'What did the police want?' he slurs.

'They wanted to know who was at the party.' The smell from his breath makes me want to throw up.

'Why did they want to know that?'

'I don't fucking know. Why weren't you here? You could have asked them yourself.' *Don't lose it, Sal, not in front of Amber.*

With the bread in the toaster I tell Amber to pull the plug when it's done and walk out of the room. There's no way I'm going to have this conversation or confront Tom over the date on the DNA result, when he's half cut.

Chapter Twenty-Five

The boy stands almost as tall as Tom. Dark hair falls in a thick shiny fringe down one side of his face. His skin is glowing red with embarrassment. He must be nervous, he looks nervous, fidgeting with his hands as he walks over to the table. Tom smiles at me when they get closer, introducing me to Kenny who holds out his hand like I'm about to interview him. It probably feels like that to him. That I'm the one who'll decide if he stays or if he goes. Kenny is finding it hard to look at me, his eyes darting all over the place before eventually settling on mine. And then I see it. The similarity. Tom's smile, his blue eyes, the jutting chin and square forehead. It might have taken a DNA test to convince Tom but I see it the moment my eyes land on the boy. He even stands like Tom: straight back, chest out like a peacock. Getting up from the table I take Kenny's hand and shake it. His palms are sweaty like mine. This is not a natural introduction. It feels weird, like none of us should be here.

'This is Sally, my wife,' Tom says as Kenny and I shake hands.

'Sal, this is Kenny.'

The whole thing feels so strange my instinct is to laugh out loud, bring the house down. But I don't, instead I chew on the inside of my lip trying to hold a serious face. Am I really sitting in McDonald's being introduced to Tom's secret child?

Saoirse the social worker suggested McDonald's, said it would be a good spot to meet as Kenny and Tom have been here many times. Saoirse seems to know a lot more about Tom's relationship with Kenny than I do. I wonder what else he's told her?

She said it would be less intimidating than some formal restaurant or even our house where Kenny would feel like a stranger. So here we are, two big Macs and a chicken wrap away from forming our judgements.

The thing is, I don't care what Kenny thinks of me. I'm not the one trying to impress, even though I'm pretty sure Tom cares what I think of Kenny. He shouldn't, my opinion on the matter is nothing to do with Kenny himself, I don't want any stranger moving in with us.

'What would you like to eat?' Tom asks Kenny as he shuffles into the seat on the opposite side of the table to me.

'Eh, just a drink, thanks.'

'Ah, eat something. Will I get you the usual?'

'Okay.' Kenny mumbles, shifting slightly in the chair while I let Tom's words unsettle me. The usual. Does he know Amber's usual? Or Cian and Aaron's usual? I'm beginning to realize the new kid on the block has been getting most of Tom's attention.

'What about you?' He turns to ask me. His nerves showing all over his fidgeting hands and unsteady gait.

'Oh, I'll have the usual too,' I say.

The sarcasm removes Tom's smile, replacing it with a look that says, *Not now, please*.

'A skinny latte.'

Tapping his pockets like he's hoping he remembered his wallet Tom hurries to join one of the three queues growing at the counter.

'I'm so sorry about what happened to your mother, Kenny,' I say, trying to remember this kid is grieving. 'I'm sure she was a lovely lady.'

'Yeah,' he says, turning away to look for Tom. He looks so fragile, his sad baby face searching out his daddy. Then it hits me, like a bus. It's something I've been ignoring or pushing away since I heard the news about Kenny. Tom is his daddy, they have a relationship and at this particular moment in Kenny's life, Tom is probably the only one he feels safe with. The only one he trusts. I'm not sure how that makes me feel.

I don't know what I'm supposed to say to this kid. I didn't think I'd be left on my own with him. With both of us avoiding eye contact, we wait for Tom to arrive back to the table and defuse the atmosphere.

I turn around and see Tom is only arriving at the top of the queue. *Say something, Sally, you're the adult here.*

'Do you play any sports, Kenny?' I ask in a gentle voice.

'Football.' Kenny's voice is barely audible. He's afraid to look at me, choosing the table top instead. I'm trying to sound interested but the truth is I'm as nervous as he looks.

'What club do you play for?'

'The school.' Still just a murmur. The poor fella is probably wishing he could disappear into thin air.

'What school's that?'

'St Vincent's.' Finally he lifts his head and looks at me.

'Oh. That's a nice school.' I don't know what else to say. I've run out of questions. At least he doesn't go to Amber's school and I can't help feeling relieved.

I look around and see Tom lifting the tray from the counter. Thank Christ. Talking to this kid is like trying to draw blood from a stone. Kenny's face relaxes when he notices Tom on his way back to the table and I realize he probably feels a hell of a lot more uncomfortable than I do. Putting my arm out, I place my hand on top of his trembling fingers.

'Kenny, it's going to get better.' He looks at me and nods and that's when I notice the tears in his eyes.

Tom arrives and plonks the tray on the table, handing Kenny his food and drink before I get mine. It's pretty clear Kenny is Tom's priority. The young boy's mother was violently murdered only a week ago, but I can't forgive Tom that easily. He lied and deceived me. That has consequences.

Suddenly I feel the weight of someone else's actions landing on my shoulders. Pushing me down, holding me hostage until I realize that this boy needs my help. How can I say no. What if it was Amber? Wouldn't I want someone to help her? Taking the lid off the coffee I add some milk and stir it. Tom bites into his burger and Kenny lifts a chip from the bag on the table. The tension has us all performing like robots.

'Is the burger nice?' I say to Tom hoping to melt the edgy atmosphere. He nods his head because his mouth is full. Across the table Kenny is playing with his food, pushing the chips into his mouth taking little bites like he's wondering if they're poisonous. Is his new mammy trying to poison him?

I'm beginning to question the sense of this meeting. What was the social worker thinking getting us to meet like this? Surely there must be a better way. I won't be having any of this tension when Amber is dragged into the fold. That's what I'll do. I'll mention Amber. Tell him about his wonderful half-sister, that should move the situation on a bit.

'Did Tom tell you about Amber, Kenny?'

Kenny lifts his head to look at me and nods, he's still looking at me when I say, 'I guess you'll have to meet her someday.'

'I've already met her,' Kenny says.

Immediately, I sense the ground shifting. Tom stops chewing and drops his hands, holding the dregs of the burger over the table.

Kenny's words crash through my head. What is he saying? How can this be? How can he have met Amber? What is going on? I look at Tom who has tomato ketchup dripping from the side of his mouth. His face is frozen like he's just witnessed a shooting. When I turn to look at Kenny, he's staring at Tom, his breath still. It's clear from the shock on his face that Kenny knows he has said something wrong.

'Where… when, when did you meet her?'

'I…' The kid is too nervous to answer, so I turn to Tom.

'Tom, when did Kenny meet Amber?'

'Erm… I don't know… I?'

'You don't know or you don't remember?' I stand up suddenly aware everyone around me can hear my raised voice. I think about yesterday morning, sitting down telling Amber about her new half-brother. Why did Tom let me do that? Make a fool of me in front of her. Allow her to make a fool of me too.

'Why didn't you tell me, Tom?' My voice doesn't even sound like my own.

Kenny sits like a scolded child, head bent, staring at the table top again. Tom puts his arm out and asks me to sit back down, which I do. Suddenly it all becomes clear why the social worker suggested a big busy public space to wash the linen in. So Sally can't make a show of herself, won't lose her head in public when the truth is revealed.

Taking my bag from under the table, I turn and walk towards the door. Amber has been lying to me. Was that what she wanted to tell me when Tom disturbed us last night? Was she about to say she has already met Kenny? How long ago? And why did she keep that from me? God, I don't know my own family any more. I open the door as I fight back the tears.

When the door swings closed behind me, I find a spot to lean against the wall of the building. Dragging in deep breaths I look up at the sky and find myself questioning everything I thought I knew. If Amber knows, who else knows? And why did nobody tell me?

With shaking hands, I open the car door. I'm getting good at this, operating under immense pressure. Ever since seeing that photo I've been living an emotional nightmare. Nothing is making sense and I'm trying to put all the pieces of the jigsaw together only to be handed more pieces with every passing day.

Without even glancing behind to see if Tom has followed me I drive out of the car park. Amber is at home now minding Cian and Aaron again. Was it her idea not to tell me? Or did Tom put her under pressure? If he did that, then Amber must be so confused. I need to talk to her, find out when and where she met Kenny and tell her she was wrong to hide it from me. But that doesn't add up. I'm missing something. Amber would not do that. I need to talk to her. Now.

Chapter Twenty-Six

Fifteen minutes later, I'm sitting in the car outside my house with my nerves pushing the boundaries of my breaking point. Tom has sent me a text.

I didn't know Amber met Kenny.

If Tom wasn't aware that Amber had met Kenny, that means the sweet little Kenny chap with the salty tears and quivering lip contacted Amber behind Tom's back. I was right. I didn't trust him from the minute I saw him. Hitting the dial button I wait for Tom to answer.

'Jesus, Tom. What the fuck is going on?'

'Sally, I swear to you I did not know Kenny contacted Amber.' His voice is trembling on the far end.

'I believe you, Tom, but what does this all mean, how long has Amber known?'

'That's the thing, Sal. She doesn't know... I questioned Kenny and he said he contacted her on Facebook and met with her and her pals but he never told her who he was.'

'The little shit, I'm damned if he's coming anywhere near this house now.'

Tom falls silent at the far end of the phone.

'He's been stalking Amber, Tom, you can tell that to the social worker. She's asking us to take a stalker in to live with us.'

'Sal, relax for a minute, he's just a kid, he was curious, I'd hardly call it stalking.' Blood boils through my veins, hot enough to melt metal. Is this man for real? That young fella has lured Amber to meet him under false pretences, God knows what he told her.

'Tom, you do what you want. I'm going to tell Amber.'

When the door opens, Amber is standing in the hallway waiting for all the news.

'Well, what's he like?' Amber says the minute I step inside.

Amber was aware I was going to meet Kenny today and wanted to come along protesting when I told her she couldn't. I wonder what she'll say when I tell her she's already met him.

'I'll tell you in a minute. Where are the boys?'

'They're in the playroom, what's he like… did you get my McDonald's?'

Shit, I was supposed to bring Amber and the boys back a takeaway but I completely forgot about it. Maybe Tom will have remembered.

'And where's Dad?'

I'm not about to tell her that I abandoned him in McDonalds, walked out and left him with his new son, the stalker.

'He's following, he had something to do.'

'Is he bringing the food?'

'I don't know, Amber. Look, sit down, love, something has come up. I need to talk to you. I just need to check on the boys first.'

I'm all jittery walking in to where Cian and Aaron are engrossed in their play. Their little faces light up on seeing me and they run to hug me, then immediately return to their toys.

Hoping I might get at least five minutes with Amber before the boys interrupt us, I return to the kitchen to where Amber is sitting on the counter top.

'What happened?' Her eyes are wide with interest.

'It's about Kenny.'

She moves forward slightly, swinging her skinny legs. 'What about him?'

'Well, apparently you have already met him.'

'No, I haven't,' she shouts, jumping off the counter and heading for the door.

'Amber, wait, listen to me, this is important.'

She stops, turning to look at me with tears in her eyes. 'But you said I met him and I...'

'You did meet him, Amber, you just didn't know it was him.'

'What—' she breaks off. Amber is digesting what I've told her.

'Yes, he says he met you and your friends. He didn't tell you who he was. Your dad knows more. He'll be here soon.'

'But—'

'I know, love... it's unbelievable.'

Amber's mouth is open and I can see her trying to compute what has happened. Suddenly she pulls the phone from her pocket and swipes down the screen.

'Is that him?' she says showing me a picture of Kenny.

'Yes—'

'I just thought there was something funny about him, he kept asking me questions, not like normal questions about me, he seemed more interested in my family...' She looks back at the screen. 'Fucking hell, is he my brother?'

'Half-brother, Amber, half-brother.'

'Oh God, this is shit.'

I can think of a lot of worse things to call the situation. 'How did he contact you?'

'Facebook.'

When her initial shock subsides, Amber tells me how she received a message on Facebook from Kenny asking her to friend him. Nothing unusual there, especially as he played rugby for St Vincent's, which is the same team that Sarah's unreliable boyfriend plays for. They met at one of the matches that Sarah dragged her along to. Kenny messaged her a few times on Facebook and Amber thought maybe he fancied her. She cringes when she says this. 'Uh, my brother.'

When I point out how serious it is, Amber laughs, saying she'd have done the same thing if she was him. It worries me, how easily she accepts his deceit. How he managed to enter her world unnoticed. Who else could do that? My mind doesn't want to go there.

'Don't make a big deal of it, Ma,' she says leaving the room, her face glued to the picture of her half-brother.

Tom comes through the front door at the same time as the boys run out from the playroom. His face looks as flustered as I feel.

'I've told her,' I say pulling open the press door in the hope I might find a tin of spaghetti or something to put on toast for Cian and Aaron. Amber can go to the chipper.

'What did she say?'

'Like you, she doesn't seem to give a shit that she was stalked by him. She's back in her room, probably messaging him as we speak.'

'Maybe that's a good thing.'

'Tom, are you out of your fucking mind? We know nothing about this young man who – by the way – lied to you about contacting your daughter. Or so you say, I'm not sure what to believe anymore.'

'You have to believe me, Sal, I didn't know, I would not have allowed him do that.'

'Well, there you go, Tom. Like father like son.'

'For fuck's sake, Sal, you're being totally unreasonable.'

'Daddy said *fuck*!' Cian exclaims, bringing both boys to a halt staring up at their father.

'I'm sorry, it just slipped out,' Tom says kneeling down to talk to the two boys.

'Silly Daddy,' I say sternly, putting two plastic beakers full of juice on the table. The boys are far too old for beakers, but Aaron still has too many accidents with regular cups, so sometimes I take the easy option and give them beakers. It won't kill them.

'Silly Daddy,' Aaron laughs as they both take their place at the table.

Two plates of toast and spaghetti later and the boys are rendered silent.

'What do we do now?' Tom says. 'I'm supposed to report to the social worker how the meeting went.'

My head is banging with pain. Pulling open a drawer I search and find a packet of paracetamol then fill a glass of water and swallow two down.

'Tell her what you want, Tom, we need to talk about all this but I haven't the energy now.' He makes to leave the room like a kid having been told 'yes you can go to the movies with your pals,' when I add, 'And make sure you tell her about your son stalking our daughter.'

Chapter Twenty-Seven

It's been nine days since I saw that photo. Nine days, since the world I thought I was living in began to unravel. One small image. That's all it took.

Donna is preened to perfection when I walk through the door on my day off. A pale blue blouse. White trousers hanging loosely over blue heels and her hair curled up into a bun.

'What did the police say?' Her voice echoes as we proceed down the hollow hallway before arriving into the kitchen. I'd already given a short version of events to Donna over the phone when I rang to see if she was open to having a visitor.

'Oh, by the way, I met the boy yesterday.'

Turning her head, Donna looks at me, her eyes open wide. 'You what?' I nod. 'Tell me all.'

When I'd conveyed the details of the meeting to Donna, she wraps her hands around her mug of coffee and leans over the island facing me.

'Sal, can I ask you something?'

'Of course.'

'Do you think Tom is telling you everything?'

I think about this, his initial denial about knowing the kid, his flip-flopping over the details of last Sunday when he told me he had rescued a friend in car trouble then ended up at the station. The idea that Tom could have been lying about that Sunday is real. Maybe he had been to the dead woman's house that day and that was why the cops interviewed him. He lied over how long he knew Kenny. The woman in the café said he visited every week. When I asked Tom about it he said he only ever picked up Kenny from outside the house. He'd never actually been inside the house or met the woman.

'I'm not sure, Donna. He seems to only disclose the information on a need-to-know basis. Or rather when he's been found out. I'm still curious as to why the cops questioned him. He says it was because he's Kenny's father and I believe that bit but is there more? I don't know. I don't think he's done anything wrong it's like he's trying to protect me from the truth.'

'Did you check?'

'Check what?'

'The friend, the guy whose car is supposed to have broken down.'

'Well...' Sitting here filing through the information I realize Donna might be onto something. Did Tom lie about why he left the house the day of the party?

'How can I check that.'

'Simple, it was Eamon Byrne's car, wasn't it?'

'Ye.'

Donna takes her phone in her hand. 'I'll ring Catherine Byrne.' My heart jumps, I don't want her dragging other people into it. They'll start asking questions and that'll only lead to...

'Hi, Catherine, Donna here.' Too late, she's already made the call. 'Quick question. I'm thinking of getting a new car and I heard Eamon just got one.'

By the end of the call, Donna has found out that Eamon never takes his car to golf because he always has a pint in the club house. Last week was no different. I feel my chest constrict and I take three deep breaths to quell the rising panic. Tom lied again.

I blankly refused Donna's suggestion that she ring the hospital about the bicycle accident pretending to be a cop looking to clarify some information. Donna didn't push it.

Through the glass wall of Donna's kitchen I watch her tropical plants sway across the bottom of the garden and try to make sense of what I've just found out. Tom needed to leave the house that day, but why, what took him away? Did the boy ring? I haven't yet told Donna that he has already made contact with Amber because my mind is in a muddle trying to digest the truth seeping through the cracks in Tom's lies. I need to talk to my husband, to tell him what I know and try to get him to open up to me.

I say my goodbyes, thanking Donna for listening to all my woes and head home. The unusually warm breeze for this time of the year caresses my face. I'm feeling uneasy with all the lies coming out of Tom's mouth. If he didn't leave to give Eamon a lift, what took him out of the house that day? It must have been something important, someone contacted him, Kenny contacted him.

–

Like nothing has happened, I collect the boys from their morning playschool session with a fake smile on my face and take them home. It's important I maintain an upbeat persona when they're in my company. Aaron in particular is very perceptive to my moods, cuddling into me whenever I'm feeling down. From the time he was a baby he seemed to nurture a sixth sense, sometimes looking at me, waiting for me to smile before his whole face would stretch with happiness.

Heading straight for the playroom when we get home, they pull the toys from the shelves. Flinging them over the floor where they believe they belong, rendering my earlier efforts at tidying invalid. At least they're happy. Which for a brief moment makes me happy. But not for long, by the time I reach the kitchen I have fallen once again into the gloom of the unfolding nightmare.

Chapter Twenty-Eight

The day passes slowly, the usual Monday chores seem so much more difficult to complete than normal. Washing clothes, vacuuming, changing the bed sheets, providing alibis and dragging the kids to Lidl, now that Tesco is a no-go area.

Ellen rings just as I'm about to prepare the dinner. Today I'm roasting a chicken, boiling fresh vegetables that I've prepared myself from scratch and making mashed potatoes the way Amber loves them. Plenty of butter and a tiny bit of white pepper. What seemed like an ordinary boring meal when I was growing up has become a treat in my busy world.

Ellen wants to know how we are all doing. She asks me about the boy and I tell her the little bit I know before cutting her short on the phone. Tom should be answering these questions, not me. As usual Tom's not around.

When Amber arrives in from school she remarks on the smell of food cooking, like she'd never smelled food cooking before. I want to ask her if she contacted Kenny but I need to be subtle. Jumping down her throat the moment I see her will make her avoid me or worse, lie to me. Like her Dad.

By six o'clock we're all sitting around the table, eating. Tom didn't have much to say for himself when he arrived home and I made no effort to engage in conversation.

What I want to say to him can't be done in front of the kids. He spoke to the boys for a bit before going to the bedroom to change into his jeans and a T-shirt. Tom has the ability of carrying on like nothing unusual is happening.

'Can I pull the bone?' Cian says, stretching his neck to look at the chicken carcass on the counter top. He's so bright that kid, he forgets nothing.

'Sure,' I say getting up from the table and pulling the wishbone from the chicken. Cian takes it from my hand and holds it out for Tom to pull on it with him.

Everyone smiles looking at Tom and Cian's hands preparing to go to battle. This little flash of excitement lifts all our hearts and for a brief moment everything seems normal.

'What are you going to wish for?' I say, gathering the plates on the table.

'He can't tell, Ma, or it won't come true,' Amber says, in her all-knowing voice.

'Oops.' Putting the dirty plates by the sink I turn on the tap and let the warm water run over my sticky fingers.

'I'm going to wish the scary woman stops looking in our window.'

Chapter Twenty-Nine

A woman with big green eyes and stringy black hair was staring in the window at my children playing. Cian describes her as looking like Coraline from some movie he saw.

We play down our reaction so as not to frighten him. The second time he saw her, which was today when I was upstairs, he told her to go away.

It's hard to get an accurate timeline from a three-year-old but he said he knows I was upstairs because when he called out to me to tell me she was there, I didn't hear him. It must have been when I was changing the bed sheets at around three this afternoon. My heart sinks, my kids were in danger while I was worrying about matching pillow cases.

'Did you ever see her anywhere else?' Tom says, pushing Cian's toy train across the kitchen table. Cian is building a track for him with the cutlery. 'No.'

Tom looks up to where I'm standing by the sink. Amber is watching both of us, wondering what's going to happen now.

'The train is running out of fuel, Cian, we need to get it to a station.' Tom pushes the train between the knives and forks as Cian moves the gravy boat to the end of the track.

'I'm not sure there's any fuel left in that, maybe we'll go into the playroom to the real station.'

Tom is doing good. Managing to keep Cian distracted while he extracts the information from him. Sliding off the chair, Cian runs towards the playroom, Aaron runs after him. Tom takes a deep breath. His eyes look worried when he nods at me. Even Amber gets involved following us into the room.

With the train full of fuel, Tom asks Cian where he saw the woman and Cian jumps to his feet and walks over to the window.

'There,' he says, pointing to the corner of the window.

'Can you remember what she was wearing, Cian?'

Gliding back into position on the floor, Cian holds the train on the track, pausing for a moment to think before saying, 'No.'

Aaron is playing alongside Cian, saying nothing, then suddenly he opens his mouth. 'Jesus,' he says.

Tom and I look at him, Amber giggles. Cian is still focused on the train's journey.

I'm about to correct Aaron, tell him he can't take the Lord's name in vain when I realize it would create friction in the room and undo Tom's work. He probably heard it from me anyway. I let it go.

'It's okay, Aaron.' Tom turns his attention to Aaron tossing his hair before pulling him in close to his body to hug him. Amber stands nervously at my side. I know she's nervous because she's not giving her opinion.

'Did you see the woman, Aaron?'

'Jesus.'

Amber giggles louder this time lifting her hand to cover her mouth.

'Well, I guess we better get these people home,' Tom says, leaning in to move one of the trains.

We put the boys to bed before Tom rings the police. It could be nothing but at the same time it could be something.

Detective Burke arrives into the house, her auburn hair tied tightly in a ponytail hanging down her back. She doesn't stand much taller than I do but her presence once again dominates the room. Detective Dunne is accompanying her.

'You can sit down,' she says. Tom and I sit side by side on the sofa. My hand is resting in his, my nerves resting on the edge of a sharp drop. I have a funny feeling this woman is about to tell me something I do not want to hear.

'So you say Cian said she had black stringy hair and big eyes.'

'That's right,' I reply.

'Is there any chance I could speak with Cian?'

Immediately I shift in the seat. 'No, he's in bed and I'd rather you didn't speak to him, he's only three. I'll ask him anything you want me to but I'm not letting him speak to a cop. It would only scare him.'

Burke is nodding her head. 'Okay,' she says, opening a file in her hand and taking out a sheet of paper.

I tell her about the night I heard a noise in the back garden at two in the morning. How I went to investigate and frightened off what I thought was an intruder. The person had green eyes. Dark hair jutting out from below the collar of the hood. It could have been a woman, I couldn't tell, it was too dark and I only saw them for a brief moment. She turns to mutter something to her colleague.

'Do you think you could describe this person?'

I thought I just did.

'Maybe this is the person who called to the murdered woman's house the day she was killed. The same person who was in my garden that same night. Maybe this is who you should be looking for.'

'Who called to the house, what's all this?' Tom stands up.

'Fuck.' I jump to my feet. 'This could be the killer, the woman who was here at my house, looking in the window at my boys playing.' My heart is bouncing in my chest and my teeth start to chatter; every bit of my body is shaking. Tom stands and puts his arm around me pulling me close to him. 'Relax, Sal. It'll be all right.'

'How can you say that?' I pull back out of his embrace. 'How do you *know* that?'

Turning my attention to Burke, I feel my whole body weakening. 'Could she be the killer?'

'I'm not saying that,' Burke says. 'We don't know that.'

'Holy fuck, Tom, there was a killer at our house, look what you've done—'

The door swings open and Amber walks in.

'What's going on?' she cries out, her face white with fear. Seeing her lips tremble, I immediately get a grip of myself.

'Nothing, sweetie, I thought you were in your bedroom.'

I knew this would happen, there was no way Amber was going to heed our request that she stay in her room until the detective left. She's probably being earwigging outside the door since the cops arrived. Wrapping my arms around her, I tell her that there's been a bit of a misunderstanding and I will explain everything when the cops have left. But I'm feigning this confidence, just like Tom was with me a few minutes ago.

'Do you want me to wait in the kitchen with you Amber?' Michael Dunne says. 'I could do with a cuppa.'

Looking to Tom before moving her vulnerable stare back to me. Amber slowly walks out the door beneath the shadow of a six-foot-tall man.

'What do we do?'

Burke is asking us to sit back down.

'It could be a coincidence, Sally, the woman in the back garden, but we'll get a drawing done from your description and show it to Cian. See if it's the same woman.'

I wonder if she thinks I've made it up. The mystery woman who appears on the scene after I'm questioned. She probably thinks it's all a sham.

'I called the police, I told them about the intruder.'

Tom looks at me. 'You what? You never told me you called the police.'

'Well, I did, and I'm glad I did, now it's on record. She could be the woman who was at the house that day, isn't that what Kenny told you, Tom, that he saw a woman? Surely he can identify who it was.'

'He never said he saw her. He said he heard her.' Tom sighs, moving to the sofa, sitting down and putting his face in his hands.

Burke whispers something to her colleague before turning her attention back to me.

'Even if this woman exists, it doesn't make her the killer, Sally. Kenny didn't see the woman do anything and she wasn't the only visitor to the house that day.' Burke slowly turns her gaze to Tom.

'Tom, were you there that day?' Tom is still holding his face in his hands. Good grief, man, grow a pair. 'Well?'

Burke breaks the silence. 'I think I'll leave you two to talk, in the meantime if you have any sightings of, or contact from this woman, get in touch with us immediately.'

'But are we safe?' I say, my voice cracking.

'I've no reason to believe you're not safe but if you have the slightest worry or concern about anything or anyone at any time, call us on this number and we will have a car out to you in a jiffy.'

Burke hands me a white card with two phone numbers and an email address.

'Either one of these numbers will be answered immediately, just be on alert.'

'But why would she want anything to do with us? Why would she come here?'

No answer.

Tom remains passive, nodding politely as he walks them out. I know now why he had to make a quick exit the day of the party. He needed to go to the dead woman's house. But what reason did he have to call there the day of his sons' birthdays. Something happened to take him there. Did he see something? Does he know something? And what about that woman, stalking our house. If it's the same person who came into our garden the night of the murder, and she did kill Claire McCarthy? Then there was a killer at my house today.

I'm finding it hard to breathe, to accept the possibility that we are in danger. That my family is in danger.

Chapter Thirty

I was up twice last night, my head lurking by the window searching for any sign of the woman returning to the garden. It's hard to sleep when the world is having a go at you.

The idea that Cian and Aaron could be in danger robs me of my ability to breathe properly. I gasp each time I think about it. They will never be left in that room on their own again. I don't care what's going on, someone will be in there with them. Until this woman is found, I won't be taking any chances.

Last night my mind was filled with images of the playroom being empty when I walked in. The window open. The boys gone. And then images of Cian and Aaron lying motionless on the floor. Imagination is midnight's curse.

Amber refused to go to bed until we did, so my questioning of Tom was brief. He told me he called to Claire McCarthy's house that day hoping to find out the reason I had been shown a photograph of him with Kenny. He thought she might have been behind it. They argued, she denied it. Tom told her he wanted nothing more to do with them, they were ruining his life. They argued more. She said she never wanted Tom in their life in the first place. It wasn't her idea for Kenny to find out who his father was.

When he left the house everyone was still alive. Tom finished off by telling me that was why the cops interviewed him at the station. He told them the same thing he was telling me. He said this like I was privileged he was sharing this information with me, which really pissed me off.

–

Thankfully, there's hair. Which is where I'm heading now. Burke said not to change any of our usual routines, to leave the boys in the crèche as normal and let the staff there know they are not to allow anyone in to visit the boys. They'd never do that anyway. My mind attempts to set to normal mode while I continue down the city street with all its urban smells. The clicking of my heels on the cobbled pathway announces my arrival.

When I reach the salon door, I hand Elsie her breakfast. A wave of warmth washes over my body. Megan is waving at me through the window before I push on the handle.

'Hi, Sal,' she says when I enter, the scent of coconut dressing the air.

Megan's face glows with a smile. 'How's things with you?'

How's things with me? If only she knew.

'Fine, all's good and yourself?'

'Grand.'

Unbuttoning my coat, I continue to walk through the salon to the staffroom at the rear of the building. Anna is inside when I open the door.

'Hi, Anna, how are you?'

'Okay,' she says, immediately leaving the room and walking out to the salon floor. Have I done something wrong? If I have, I care less, I've no room in my head for paranoia today. I came here for a break from my problems not to embrace someone else's.

Marie walks in just as Anna leaves. 'What's her problem?' she says, without expecting an answer. 'Did you have a nice weekend?'

'Quiet.'

'Me too, ate too much though.' Pulling the belt on her wrap-around skirt, Marie complains about the size she's getting. But I don't indulge her. She's about two sizes smaller than me with legs twice as long. I hate when skinny people talk like that.

'Are you going to the hair show, Saturday night?' she says, jogging my memory with a commitment I made to Megan two weeks previously, when I volunteered to look after the trainees at the event. Stop them from getting drunk too early and dragging the good name of the salon into disrepute.

'I'm supposed to be, anyway.' *If my world hasn't caved in by them.* Not surprisingly, the idea of enjoying a night out with the staff doesn't hold the usual excitement. There was a time I would prepare for weeks in advance. What will I wear? Who will do my make-up? What will I drink? Now I'm lucky if I get ten minutes to have a shower.

My first client is checking her new hairstyle in the mirror when my phone rings. The guy is ready to see me now. I tell Megan I have to leave, something important. Megan tells me to take my time; the shop is quiet today.

Crossing over the bridge I walk to the police station on Pearse Street where Burke has arranged for me to meet a sketch artist. I'm making better progress than the cars on the road that are stuck in a tailback for as far as I can see. The trucks aren't helping. Their heavy loads are making me nervous as I scurry past them as they try to manoeuvre around a tight corner. I reach the double doors of the station just as rain starts to fall. At least the clouds are on my side.

I check in at the counter and wait to be called. It doesn't take long. Not long enough for me to check my phone.

A man who introduces himself as Martin Keegan takes me through a door. The corridor we walk down looks old and in need of a paint. I thought all these places were state of the art nowadays. I was wrong. This is a tip.

As if reading my mind, the guy, who's about to draw my vision says, 'Sorry, we're stuck in the old part.'

He opens a door onto a small room. There's a table, a few chairs, bare walls. Is this an interview room where baddies get questioned? I feel like a criminal.

'Sally, we'll run through what you saw, then I'll make a few sketches.'

'I'm not sure I can remember much. I remember the eyes but…' We both sit down at the table.

'Let me worry about that. You'll be surprised what you remember when you try.'

Half an hour later I'm walking back to the salon with a sketch of the person I saw in the garden that night. Martin Keegan was right. He helped me focus on what I'd seen and I'm sure now it was a woman. Even though I only saw her image for a split second, it had been imprinted on my mind. The eyes, the hair, the bone structure. What surprised me most was the cross around her neck. The shape dangling at her bony throat was so clear and yet I hadn't remembered it until now. I'm impressed. I'm also a bit nervous. If it's the same woman that was looking in the window at the boys playing, I fear we're in danger. Hopefully it's not. I'll know soon enough.

Back in the salon, I'm blow-drying fifty strands of dry grey hair trying to make it look like a thousand. Mrs Walsh really shouldn't waste her money but she says she comes more for the experience than the hairdo. I get her. I know what she means. Her heavy blue coat hangs looser every time she leaves.

'Thank you, see you next week,' I say, wondering will I? Will next week be the week she doesn't return. It's coming soon.

I think about the young woman taken in her house that day. What could have happened, who wanted her dead. It's looking like the cops are focusing on two people, my husband Tom who has admitted he was there and a second person. A woman, who has yet to be identified. But that's just because the kid heard two arguments. It's possible it was neither of them, that there was a third person. They still haven't located the knife used to murder her. I'm hoping they do soon, take Tom out of the picture because I know he didn't kill her. He might tell lies but seventeen years in his arms and he has never lifted one of them.

My phone rings. Dad. *Why is he ringing?*

'Dad.'

'Sally, how are you?'

'I'm fine, is something up?'

'No, just calling because I was a bit worried when I didn't see Tom in the house at the party.'

'Everything's fine.' Silence, always silence. Since Mom died, myself and Dad only communicate when we have to. I lived in the house with him for five more years but we never spoke outside the necessary. Sometimes I blame myself, I should have been nicer, more considerate. But

I was young and at the back of my mind this niggling question festered that I didn't want answered. Why a brain haemorrhage?

'I have to go, Dad, there's a client waiting.'

'Okay, Sal, talk soon.'

We won't. I probably won't hear from him again for another six months.

I'm walking towards the reception area smiling at my next client when I remember the list. Dad wasn't on the list, he just arrived at the party uninvited.

Chapter Thirty-One

Later that evening I'm standing in the kitchen piercing the plastic on an Indian meal that has a very appetizing picture on the front of the box. I empty the heated contents on to a plate with a bit of lettuce on the side to make it look healthy before serving it to my husband.

I'm not hungry. I ate lunch with Meg and Marie earlier today in the café next to the salon, before my trip to the station.

The boys were fed dinner in the crèche, so I gave them spaghetti on toast when we got home. Amber said she ate at Sarah's. I wonder: did she?

'Well, did he see the picture?' Tom says, sitting down at the table looking at the plate in front of him likes it's Michelin starred.

'I didn't show him yet, I thought it would be better if you were here, bring it into their play.'

'You're right.'

Amber is in the playroom with the boys. She's not happy with the added pressure and I don't blame her but until we know that the woman Cian saw looking in the window is not the woman from the back garden, that's the way it has to be.

It's possible it was simply someone canvassing at the door, didn't get an answer and snooped in the window to see if anyone was home. I might not have heard the doorbell if I was being assaulted by a duvet cover at the time, especially with the radio on.

—

After reinforcing his inadequate dinner with two slices of bread and cheese, Tom unfolds the sheet of paper that sits like an unplayed deck of cards on the windowsill.

'I'll give it a go,' he says, stretching his back like he's preparing to go to battle.

'I'll wait here.'

Scraping the lettuce from Tom's plate my nerves start to get the better of me again. Pain pierces through my forehead. Reaching for the paracetamol on top of the shelf in front of me, I hear Amber walk into the room.

'Well, that's me off duty,' she says. 'Can I go out now?' Her tone is sarcastic, milking the situation while implying this is all my fault. She doesn't use that tone with her father.

'Of course you can, but remember what I told you to keep your phone with you at all times and don't talk to any strangers.'

'Jesus, Ma, you're watching too many movies. I'll be okay.'

I hope she's right. I know I'm probably being over-cautious but I don't care. It's better than being under-cautious.

'Nine thirty!' I shout after her but she's already gone out the door.

The boys' laughter sounds out of place when I approach the playroom. Thankfully they are totally unaware of our crumbling world that is supposed to be protecting them. Tom is sitting on the floor, holding Aaron up in the air when I walk in.

'Anything?' I say.

'Nope.' Putting Aaron down on the rug, Tom stands up taking the sheet of paper with him and walks over to me. In a low voice he says. 'He says it's not the woman, that she was real and this is only a drawing.'

'But did you ask him if the woman looked like that?'

'Yes, but he shook his head. He's not making any connection. Maybe it wasn't her, Sal.'

My tension eases. Great, it wasn't her it was just a coincidence. I guess it was just some random caller.

'I think it's time for bed.'

'C'mon, bedtime.' Tom moves towards the boys, dropping the sheet of paper on the floor.

'Two more minutes,' Cian says.

'No. Bedtime.'

Tossing Cian in his arms, Tom goes to leave the room when Aaron picks up the sheet of paper from the floor.

'Jesus,' he says pointing at the picture.

'What?' I bend down to Aaron's side and watch his little finger land on the cross around the neck of the woman in the drawing. 'Jesus.'

Tom plonks Cian down and walks over to Aaron's side. Taking the paper from his hand he looks at the picture. Then holding it in front of Aaron's face he says, 'Is that the woman that was in the window, Aaron?' Aaron nods and points. 'Jesus.'

Chapter Thirty-Two

Burke is by the table, Michael Dunne by the door. Eyes glued to her lips, Tom and I sit and wait. Within a few minutes she informs us that Joyce McCarthy, the woman in the picture is Claire McCarthy's sister. Both women grew up in Kilkenny. The cops in Kilkenny found out that Joyce, the sister, moved to the USA about fifteen years ago. They didn't discover any other family. Joyce returned to Ireland for the first time two weeks ago.

Why? They don't know. But they believe Joyce to be the woman who called to Claire's house the day of the murder. Bad of me to think it, but I do. If Kenny has an aunty, maybe he can live with her.

Sadly my moment of bliss is short-lived. The woman is now the number one suspect in the murder case and is perceived to be 'not of sound mind'. She may have been lurking around our house trying to see if Kenny was living here now.

Continuing in a low voice, Burke explains that Kenny didn't know he had an aunty. His mother never mentioned her but she could have been the woman who was arguing with his mother when he left the house that afternoon. When he returned a few hours later he found his mother's body lying in a pool of blood.

'So why haven't you arrested her?' I say.

'Currently, we don't know where she is.'

I can't believe what I'm hearing, anger rises in my voice. 'Someone must know where she's staying.'

'We're on the case, Sally. We will be releasing her photo to the public over the next couple of days and we're contacting the hotels. If she comes anywhere near the house again, call us.'

'I bloody well will call you.'

I get the feeling Burke is keeping something from us, telling us as little as possible. The fact that the woman was peering in through the window of our house and is also the woman I saw in the back garden last week is beginning to cause her concern. She repeats her request that we alert and contact her immediately if the woman shows up again.

Tom is sitting like a moron beside me. He hasn't opened his mouth to ask one question. He's probably thinking, well, that's me off the hook anyway.

'How can you be sure this woman is not a risk to us? If she's hanging around our house, there has to be a reason. Should we not have someone on duty outside protecting us until you find her?'

'I'm sorry, Sally, we don't have the resources and I really don't think it's necessary. Just keep doing what you do and remain vigilant at all times.'

I'm a bit peeved by Tom, why is he accepting this? His wife and kids could be in danger and he's just sitting here saying nothing. Nodding like a toy dog in a car window.

'Does Kenny remember what they were arguing about?'

Burke moves her eyes from Tom to me, shaking her head like I'd just asked a ridiculous question. 'Sorry?' she says.

'Did the boy hear what they were arguing about? I would have thought that was important.'

'He says he didn't hear, that he left as soon as the argument started.'

Turning her gaze back to Tom, it's clear Burke is not too interested in talking to me. Tom is the one she's directing her conversation to. I'm being treated like the interfering wife. So I will.

'I find it a bit strange that the boy didn't hear anything they were saying. Can he be trusted?'

Burke interrupts. 'Kenny is under a lot of emotional pressure. He's almost certainly still in shock. As things come back to him, he knows to tell us.'

With her gaze back on Tom, she continues. 'Which is likely to happen over time. If he's blocked out some details, they may come back to him when he's settled in your care.'

'Settled in our care?' My voice doesn't hide how I feel. Alarmed.

'Yes.' Burke flicks open the file she earlier placed on the table in front of her.

'Tomorrow, is it?' she says, reading something on the page before looking up at Tom. Big Bad Tom does not know what to do, what to say or where to look.

'What's going on, Tom?' Twisting in my seat I look at him rubbing his hand over his mouth, something he has a habit of doing when he's caught red-handed. It's like he's trying to put the words in order before they leave his lips.

'Well, Tom?'

'I was going to tell you later, Sal.'

'Tell me what, Tom?'

Burke moves towards the door. 'I'll leave you both alone. I'll be in touch.'

Pushing back the chair I jump up. 'No, don't leave us alone, tell me what is going on? Why do you think that kid is settling into our care? I never agreed to anything.'

She nods at Tom. 'Is this true, Tom, did Sally not agree?'

'I didn't have a choice, the court placed him into our care until the next hearing, which is…'

'When did all this happen?'

'Yesterday.'

'And you couldn't tell me last night?'

Burke touches her colleague on the arm and walks out into the hallway leaving Tom and I to do battle. Apparently, Tom attempted to tell me last night but everything got side-tracked when Cian mentioned the woman looking in the window. I have to hand it to Tom. He can grow excuses like no one else. The guy would attempt to dig himself out of his own grave.

There's no point arguing with him anymore. He's a coward, has been since this whole thing erupted, allowing me to discover everything before he admits to any of it. I'm liking him less and less.

'Sal…' Tom walks over and sits by my side. Putting his arm around my shoulder he starts to cry. 'I'm so sorry, Sal, sorry for this whole mess. I can't believe I brought this on the family, on you. I love you, you're my world and now look what I've done.'

I want to believe him, I do believe him, but it doesn't change anything. Before I get a chance to reply Amber enters. Her face is ashen.

'What were the cops doing here again?' she says to Tom. He releases his hold on me, wiping his eyes as he stands up to answer her.

'She called to tell us they're looking for a woman in connection with Kenny's mom's murder. And we've to be vigilant. So no going out, Amber, for the next few days. I want you here at all times unless you're in school.'

'That's not fair, what about Saturday, it's Sarah's birthday.'

'It's not about being fair it's about being safe,' Tom says, turning the tap on to fill a glass with water. His mouth must be dry from giving orders to his daughter. It's not from challenging the cop.

'But...'

Tossing his head back he swallows the water down in one go.

'We'll wait and see, Amber. Saturday is a few days away, hopefully they'll have found the woman by then.'

Amber turns to walk out the door, her feet stomping like she's only just been promoted to a teenager.

'This is all your fault,' she says, slamming the door behind her.

Tom turns to face me, his tortured eyes meeting mine, waiting for my comment.

'Well, she's right there.'

'Sal, it's only for a trial period, couple of weeks at the most, if it doesn't work out I'll tell them.' He may as well be talking to the wall because I don't want to hear. Taking my phone from the table I leave the room. No slamming doors for me, although I do feel like it. This whole nightmare is tumbling down on us because of Tom's actions and lack of them. I'm glad Amber realizes that. With Tom wallowing in his own thoughts, I head to bed. I'm not sure what I feel about him anymore. Even when he frittered away my money on a useless idea, I still loved him, felt safe with him. Now I'm not so sure.

The soft glow of moonlight creeps in through a small gap in the curtains. Listening to Tom's noisy breathing fill the silence, I consider what will happen when that Kenny chap comes here to stay. Where will he sleep?

The only good thing to come from this evening is Tom's no longer the main suspect, they have their woman. The sooner they find her the better, I'm sick of the cops in our life.

The trial. Jesus, if the kid is living with us it's bound to impact on the whole family. And what if they never find her? How long will we have to be extra vigilant for? My mind races. I can't stop worrying about how this is affecting Amber.

Cian and Aaron are too young to understand what's going on. Plenty of steam trains and ice cream and they'll be fine. But Amber, what must she think of her father? Of Kenny? How is she going to cope? I twist and turn all night without any answers making their way into my head.

Chapter Thirty-Three

Tempted as I am to stay in bed and ignore the day, I can't. I have to get up, get breakfast, take the kids to crèche, go to work, take a half day from work, come home again, because this is the day Kenny McCarthy is laying his hat under my roof.

His expected arrival is sometime between three and four when Tom and I will be here to settle him in. He's moving into the boys' playroom. Tom will spend today changing the room into a bedroom.

The boys will now have to push Thomas, James, Percy and Sam around the floor in front of the TV. I'm dying to see how that works out. It all sounded fine to Tom when he was making his plans but wait until Liverpool are about to take a penalty and Cian or Aaron jump up in front of the TV announcing the arrival of Arthur at the station. We'll see how much he likes it then.

I can't believe it's actually happening, especially after putting up such a good fight to stop it. It's not that I don't want to help the young boy. I do, but from a distance like most do-gooders.

The court says he's legally allowed to live on his own at age sixteen but Social Services say he's not capable or responsible enough at the moment. So here we are. If he calls me Mammy, I'm getting the first flight out of here.

Amber arrives home just before the social worker's car pulls up outside the house. I was hoping that wouldn't happen. That Amber would be out of the house and would not have to welcome him into the fold. I don't know why I feel this way but something is niggling at my mind telling me not to trust the boy. The way he contacted Amber unsettles me and no matter how anyone disguises it, I call it stalking.

Kenny walks up the pathway, head stooped, both arms dragging bags. He does not look happy to be doing this. Now I feel sorry for him. This is not what he planned either. Moving lock, stock and barrel into a small semi with three other kids, a dad he barely knows and a step-mother he doesn't know at all must be frightening. Oh God, did I just say that. *Am* I a stepmother now? Yikes.

Tom has spent the last half hour looking patiently out the window and now he's rushing to the door. Both of us stand inside waiting to greet him. What the hell will I say to him? Do I tell him he's welcome in our home or is that a bit formal for a teenager? I'll leave it to Tom.

'Welcome to our home, Kenny,' Tom says. I'm turning my eyes up to heaven before I realize and quickly put my smiley face back on to nod at him. The poor chap looks uncomfortable. He also looks very tall. I hadn't noticed it in McDonald's when he was sitting down in a big glass dome, but in the confines of this narrow hallway, the kid looks like a giant.

The social worker goes back out to the car with Tom to carry in the remainder of Kenny's things and I'm left standing in the hallway with him. Pushing open the door of the playroom, I invite him in to see his room.

'I know this must be putting you out something awful, Sally, but I'll be as quiet as possible.'

My heart bleeds for the boy. I know what it's like to lose your mother when you're young. The utter disbelief, the emptiness, the sadness. Turning to talk to her before realizing she's no longer there. It happened to me so many times in the first year, sometimes publicly: the day I won Student of the Month at school, I turned to my friends and said my mom was going to be thrilled. Everyone went silent.

'I can do my own washing and all that stuff. I need to learn how to take care of myself so I can be out of your way as soon as possible.'

The suitcase lands with a thud on the floor when Kenny drops it at his side. The poor kid looks lost.

'It's okay, Kenny, you're welcome for as long as it takes.' I have to do this, make him feel welcome. He's not much older than I was when my mother died but at least I got to stay in my home, with Mam's things surrounding me, keeping her memory alive. If I'd had to leave and stay in some stranger's house I don't know how I would have coped. So, for as long as he's here, I'll do my best to make sure he feels at home.

'Thank you, Sally – is that what you want me to call you?'

'Sally is fine… Do you have a girlfriend, Kenny?'

'No.' He shakes his head.

'Do you know a girl named Charlie?'

He creases his face, trying hard to think. 'No. Not that I can think of.'

Tom arrives into the room, disturbing us, carrying a large box which he puts in the corner. Saoirse O'Neill places two smaller bags beside it. If Kenny didn't send that girl into the salon then who did?

'You have quite a lot of stuff, Kenny,' Tom says, standing back from the large box and stretching out his back.

'You should see what he left behind.' Saoirse chuckles before walking out to the hallway and beckoning me to follow. There seems to be a lightness to her step, a triumphant tone to her voice.

'This is everything you'll need.' She hands me a large brown envelope. 'I'll be back next week to check in on Kenny. In the meantime, if you have any questions, just give me a call. The number is in the envelope.'

Saoirse gets into her car and drives away from her instruction, leaving my family to live with it. Closing the door, I hear Amber's soft step coming down the stairs. Her hair is tied into a plait twisted up on top of her head. I wonder what is going on in her head. What does she really think about her new half-brother coming to live with us? She hasn't said much about it, in fact she's been very quiet lately, which is unusual for her. When asked directly, she said she had no objections but we'll wait and see if she thinks the same way when she can't get into the shower tomorrow morning.

'Is he in there?' Amber whispers, pointing at the play-room. I nod. 'Should I go in and say hello?'

'If you like but knock on the door, always knock on the door, Amber.'

'I wish you'd do the same for me, everyone seems to think my bedroom is a commune.' And she's back. My heart lifts. Maybe things will be okay.

–

The evening was strange. By the time the boys were asleep in bed and Amber in her room I'd almost forgotten there was a stranger living in the playroom at the side of the house. Tom poured me a glass of wine which I gladly accepted.

With my feet tucked behind me on the sofa, I search Netflix hoping for something to take my mind someplace else for a while. That's when I hear it.

The howls of pain coming from the playroom are unlike anything I've ever heard.

'Ring her, for fuck's sake, Tom. We can't leave him like that, the kid is in bits in there.'

I want Tom to ring the social worker and tell her the kid is not happy here, his heart is broken and they need to do something to help him.

'What do you mean ring her? He's our problem now, Sal. I can't ring her every time he gets upset.'

'That's not upset, Tom. I'm upset, that sounds like the kid is having a nervous breakdown or something. We can't just ignore it.'

'I'll go in to him.'

Holding my dressing gown tightly across my chest, I stand in the hallway, frightened by what I'm hearing. Amber is coming down the stairs again, her eyes wide with fear. 'Is he okay?'

The door won't open when Tom pushes on the handle, Kenny must have it locked. Tom attempts to talk through the keyhole.

'Kenny, are you all right, do you want me to come in?'

It's as if he doesn't hear us, that he has forgotten he's in someone else's house.

Amber stands at my side holding on to my arm, urging Tom to talk to him again but the results are the same. It's like we're not here.

A few more minutes pass, disguised as hours. The three of us remain standing like helpless fools outside the play-room door. There is a moment when things quieten down but then he starts again. Crying, crying, crying.

When the howling reduces to a whimper, Amber is the first to break up the assembly. She lets go of my arm and walks back up the stairs. Reluctantly Tom and I return to the living room.

'I hope to God he's not like that every night?' I say, lifting my glass from the coffee table and returning to my position on the sofa. 'I've never heard anyone cry like that. It's not normal, Tom, he's like a wolf howling.'

Tom doesn't speak but I can see the worry carving a whole new expression on his face.

Chapter Thirty-Four

Exhausted from lack of sleep and a head full of worry, I ring into work, asking for the day off. 'A family emergency' is how I put it, promising to be back tomorrow for the Friday rush. Megan tells me to take care of myself but she must be getting pissed off with my comings and goings of late.

Tom takes Kenny to school. First morning. Kenny can take the bus from now on. I'm not having our routine disrupted any more than it has to be.

After dropping the boys into the crèche I head to Donna's for a moment of me time. 'How is Mary Poppins doing?' Donna holds the door open, the usual big smile on a face ready to burst into laughter.

'Don't,' I say, lifting my open hand to her face while stepping into the hallway.

'Can't be that bad.'

'Well, it is.'

'A detective, Angela Burke, called here.'

'What?'

'Just for a minute, I asked her in but she hung out in the hallway.'

'What did she want?'

'She wanted to know If I could recall if you left the house at any time during the party? I told her you didn't.'

'When was this?'

'Two days ago?'

'Why didn't you ring me, tell me?'

'I was going to but then I said hell, the woman has enough to deal with I'll tell her when I see her.' I can understand Donna's reasoning but I wish she'd called me.

'Anyway, it doesn't matter now, they have their woman.'

On the front page of the newspaper, there's a passport photo which the cops must have got from airport security. Donna is holding the paper out for me to look at. 'Don't worry, Sal, they will find her, it's just a matter of time.'

'I hope so, my nerves are in pieces.'

Donna swings the conversation back to the day the woman was killed. The day Tom lied about his whereabouts. I tell her he'd gone to the house because I'd been shown a photo of him with Kenny. He went to confront the mother and she said she knew nothing about it. I sound like I understand and accept Tom's actions. Which isn't the case. Why he couldn't just admit Kenny's existence to me at the time is still bothering me. Did he think that he was going to be able to keep this from me forever?

'Who told Kenny that Tom was his father?' Donna says out of the blue. The question shocks me for a moment. I try to think.

'I guess the mother. I don't actually know.'

'But why now?'

'What do you mean, why now?'

'Why did she wait until now to tell him?'

'I don't know – guilt maybe, his age, I haven't a clue.'

'Does Tom know why?'

'I didn't ask him.'

Donna pulls the paper from my side of the island and flicks it around to look at the photo again. 'I don't like her hair,' she says, trying to defuse the atmosphere she's created with her question. 'Maybe when they find her you could give her a cut.'

I'm not in the humour of laughing but I chuckle anyway, then leave.

'What happened when you went to see the woman?' Tom is leaning against the counter top with a cup of coffee in his hand when I get home. White face, grey tossed hair and tracksuit bottoms tell me he's not having a good day, either.

'I told you, Sal, I went to ask her if she knew anything about the photograph that you were shown in the salon.'

'And what did she say?'

'She said no. That she never even wanted me to know Kenny was my kid. Never mind you.'

'If she didn't tell him – which we have to presume she didn't if she never wanted you to know about him – who did?'

Tom moves his eyes from me and stares into the space in front of him. Reality never settles that easily on the man. He has to give it time to register in his brain.

'I think you should ask Kenny, Tom.'

He's still staring into space when I suggest he takes Kenny for a coffee or burger or whatever sixteen-year-old boys like. Bring it into the conversation, see what he says. If Tom is right and Kenny's mother did not want the boy to know about Tom, then who told him?

—

That evening, Ellen arrives to the house like I've just given birth to a new baby boy. There's a card in her hand, 'Kenny' written on the envelope. I presume it's cradling some money.

'They're not here yet,' I tell her when she glides into the hallway smelling of Gucci and loosening a silk scarf from around her neck. Ellen seems disappointed, having come all the way to say hello to the boy and he's not here. 'But they should be here soon.'

I look at the clock and notice an hour has passed since I was expecting them. Tom must have taken my advice to take the boy for a chat, see what he can find out.

On realizing she's going to have to wait, Ellen goes out to Jack who's outside in the car, then comes back in. 'He'll call back,' she says. 'How are you coping?'

'I've no choice, Ellen. It is what it is and I have to get on with it… until I don't have to.'

'He's a lucky boy to have landed here and I'll make sure to tell him.'

'Don't, Ellen, please, I'm sure he doesn't feel a bit lucky at the moment.'

'Oh yes… Oh yes,' she says, remembering the circumstances that led to him being rehoused.

'And Amber, how is Amber taking it?'

The door swings open and Amber trots in tripping in king-size fluffy slippers.

'I'm under house arrest, Nan, so how do you think I'm taking it?'

I try to nod at Amber to say nothing about the woman looking in the window but I can't get her attention. 'She'll be all right. It's only for a few days… until things settle,' I say.

'Until they find the psycho, more like it.'

Ellen places the card on the table and I see Amber's eyes read the name on the envelope. She looks at Ellen. I can see disappointment written all over her expression.

Can Ellen? Clearly not, because the next thing she says is, 'What psycho?'

Amber walks out of the room without answering. My heart sinks. This is the sort of thing I did not want to happen. Kenny being made a fuss of, which is how Amber will see it. Ellen's favourite grandchild now has competition.

'Nothing, don't mind her. Do you want a cup of tea?'

'Is she talking about the woman in the paper that the police are looking for? What has that got to do with Amber?'

'Ellen, we're just being extra careful until they find her. Amber's not under house arrest, she's just exaggerating... The kettle is on, I'll be back in a minute.'

Amber is crying into her pillow when I open the door.

'Knock. You have to knock!' she shouts at me before dropping her face back into the pillow.

'Amber, sweetie, Ellen is just trying to be nice, she wants to welcome Kenny. You will always be your nan's favourite grandchild.' Surprised that she isn't shouting back at me, telling me I have it all wrong, I walk over and sit down on the bed. Dropping my head onto the pillow beside her, I let tears fall from my eyes without fighting back. Amber turns to look at me. Placing her warm hand on my cheek, she says, 'We'll be okay, Mam, we'll get through this.'

Chapter Thirty-Five

It's Amber who suggests we get our act together and go downstairs to where the welcoming party appear to be having a grand old time. Ellen's raucous laughter echoes up the stairway into Amber's room. Opening her stinging eyes wider, Amber's face breaks into a mischievous smile.

'The poor fella… I bet he wasn't expecting that.'

Releasing a much-needed chuckle, I slip off the bed and look into the mirror. My eyes sting. I take a make-up remover wipe from Amber's dressing table and attempt to erase the evidence of sadness. Lifting a bottle of tinted moisturizer, Amber squirts some onto her finger before handing it to me. 'This will do the job.'

When we've both done our best to look like we weren't crying, Amber walks to the door but before she opens it, I grab her close to me and hug her tightly. 'We're in this together, Amber, we're going to need one another. I promise you, I'll do anything for you. I love you more than you could possibly know.'

Not wanting to cry again, I push her away and follow her out the door to the sound of Tom rambling on about golf. He's probably got his one trophy in his hand telling Kenny about the 'hole in one' he got seven years ago while on a trip in Portugal. Poor Kenny, he has a lot of crap to catch up with.

Ellen is on her second cup of tea when I walk into the room. My earlier disappearing act isn't mentioned now that she's been distracted by her new grandchild. Kenny looks like he wants to be beamed up on to another planet. His polite nods and smiles are clearly forced, bearing no resemblance to the squirming taking place inside him.

'Is there any chance you could hang on for a while, Ellen? Tom and I want to pick up the boys from the crèche before it gets too late.' This is my opportunity to have a word with Tom out of Kenny's earshot.

Ellen looks at her watch before agreeing it's not a problem. Kenny's face immediately freezes, his eyes dart from side to side. The poor kid must feel like an animal at a circus so I suggest he goes into his room in case he has homework to do. The relief melts his expression and he immediately gets up from the table and leaves.

'We'll be back in half an hour, Ellen, if you want to ring Jack to pick you up then, or Tom can drop you home.'

Moving closer to her I whisper quietly, 'I wouldn't ask you to wait Ellen only I don't want him on his own in the house with Amber until I get to know him.'

Ellen nods a wink. 'That's fine, Sal, Jack will collect me when you get back. Take all the time you need.'

'They'll think someone's dead,' I say, getting into the car. 'I don't believe we've ever gone together to pick up the boys.'

Tom laughs, still under the influence of having had an opportunity to tell his 'hole in one' story.

When the car pulls away from outside the house, I question Tom about what Kenny said. Who was it that told him Tom was his father? Kenny is saying it was his mother, but Tom is becoming suspicious like me. He's convinced the mother didn't want Kenny to know and doesn't believe she would have told him. So who could it have been? Who told Kenny about Tom? Was it the mystery woman? The one the cops believe may be the killer. And if so, why?

–

The crèche vibrates with a completely positive atmosphere when we go through the door. Happy energy bursting out into the hallway from each of the busy rooms. Crayoned portraits hang on the wall to my right. 'Our families' is the heading above the display. Each picture is sketched in a rainbow of colour. Big people beside little people, one adult with one small person holding hands, two adults with three little people in the middle and other images with people in a row tallest to smallest. I wonder which ones are Cian and Aaron's. My eyes dart from one to the other but before I have time to locate my boys' masterpieces, Lorna the manager comes out of a room to see us. Her hair is tied back and she's wearing a pair of leggings and a T-shirt, skinny as a lollipop stick.

'Could I have a word before I call the boys?' she says, sending waves of alarm through my body. What is it now? Has Aaron pushed someone again or did Cian curse at his teacher? Something tells me, by the way she doesn't make full eye contact, that this is something else. And even though I don't want to go there I have a funny feeling I know what it is.

The cloakroom is the only quiet room where Lorna can talk to us in private. She makes small talk about the weather while we walk to the end of the hallway. Tom gives me a quizzical look before we go into the room and I brace myself for the one discussion a parent does not want to have with anyone who minds her kid.

'I'm glad I have the chance to speak to both of you together,' she says pushing a loose strand of hair from her eyes.

'What's wrong?'

My mind has become accustomed to hearing bad news of late so I'm not expecting her to tell me my boys are geniuses.

'I'd like to talk to you about Aaron's lack of progress.'

Her lips are moving but I'm finding it hard to get her words to register in my head. Tom seems more focused, nodding his head in agreement or acceptance, I'm not sure.

Like I need more shit on my plate, it turns out Aaron's teacher thinks he needs to be assessed. He's not doing the things a three-year-old should be doing at this stage and she listed a few markers. Tom tells her he's noticed, Cian tends to do a lot of things for him and questions, could this be the reason Aaron is behind?

I'm impressed Tom has noticed this and can back it up with some examples, the way Cian tells us when Aaron wants to go to the toilet, how he opens his snack bag for him. Once I even found him in the toilet with Aaron, pulling paper from the roller and handing it to him. I knew it wasn't normal but passed it off as something he'd seen the carer in the crèche do. Deep down I've been waiting for Aaron to catch up with Cian. Blaming Cian for helping Aaron too much is my mind trying to ignore the obvious.

There's also that part of me that believes children grow at their own pace, shine in their own time and I said this to Lorna. She agreed with me but still felt it would benefit Aaron immensely if we got him assessed. Early intervention is the most important thing, the magic ingredient, she said, before giving us a number to ring. Lorna expressed her commitment to working with the assessor and delivering any extra intervention that they suggested.

Lorna leaves to get the boys, Tom and I stand amidst a blanket of jackets and coats shoes and bags. Both of us are silent, Tom running his hand through his hair. The door opens a few moments later and in run the boys. 'Mammy, Daddy.' They seem extra excited that we're both here to pick them up and I'm reminded how easy it is to thrill a kid. Just be there.

Aaron is uncomfortable with the strength of the hug I'm giving him, trying to wiggle from my grasp so I put him back on the ground, tears stinging my eyes. Tom puts his arm around me while Cian pulls their two bags from the shelf below the coats.

'Sal, it's probably nothing.' But as I watch Aaron take his bag from Cian, I know it's not nothing. Aaron needs help and I'm damned if I'm going to let a dead woman or a homeless boy get in the way of it. I'm going to make sure he gets the help he needs before he goes to primary school.

His little hand grabs mine, eager to leave, as he pulls me to the door.

'Can we get ice cream?' Cian says as I strap him into his seat. Poor kid thinks it's a special occasion because both his mammy and daddy came to pick him up. I'm not about to disappoint him.

'Of course we can get ice cream, Cian, we'll go to McDonald's.'

Tom looks at me like I've said something mad while Cian and Aaron wiggle with joy.

'Ring your mother, Tom, she said she wasn't in a hurry. I want to take the boys for ice cream.'

At McDonald's, I watch each move Aaron makes as he successfully spoons every inch of ice cream into his mouth. Tom says he'll ring the number first thing tomorrow. Get the ball rolling but I'm still worried about putting my kid into the system. Will it go on forever? Will every little move Aaron makes be scrutinized and discussed like he's some sort of failure. I can't believe this is happening, that I didn't see it. But how could I, working full time to clear Tom's debts? I should have been here for Aaron, noticed what was noticed in the crèche. Maybe I'd have seen things sooner, got him earlier intervention. This is all Tom's fault.

Chapter Thirty-Six

Ellen is ready with her coat buttoned up, scarf wrapped around her neck when we get back to the house. Jack gives his usual wave as they drive away.

Sugar-fuelled, the boys run in circles, before following me into the house. Everything feels different but looks the same, the grey carpet on the stairs, in desperate need of a clean. The framed photographs hanging on the wall, dusty and tired. Reaching my hand to straighten one, Tom smiles from behind the glass. I smile too, my arms wrapped around the boys, while Amber's reaching over her dad's shoulder. Good times. I let go of the photo and it slips sideways again. Let it.

Every light is on in the house and there's a smell of something freshly baked. Now that's unusual. That must be Ellen's cupcakes. I'm just surprised she was able to find the ingredients in my kitchen. Lately with all the running and racing it's like old Mother Hubbard's cupboard. Bare.

Amber is in the kitchen with myself and Tom when Tom's phone rings.

'It's the cops,' he says, looking at the number before accepting it.

Amber and I move over to where Tom is standing but he waves us away, turning his back to us like our silent presence is distracting him from hearing the voice on the far end. A minute passes, Tom nodding and saying *ye, ye, okay, right, tomorrow at ten.* He ends the call then turns to update us.

'Well, what did they want?'

'They have her.'

'What?' Amber pulls out a chair and sits without moving her eyes off Tom.

'She handed herself in this afternoon and they are questioning her.'

'Does that mean I can go to the party?' Amber says but Tom ignores her.

'We've to bring Kenny to the station in the morning, they want to speak to him.'

'What about?' I say.

'They didn't say, Sally, they're hardly going to tell me over the phone.' His tone is dismissive, his face creased with stress.

'But I can go to the party... Yes?'

'Yes, Amber you can go to the party.'

With little else bothering her, Amber gets up from the chair and hurries out of the room. Clothes, make-up, false tan, the new priority. I'm happy to see her focus shift back to the normal worries a fifteen-year-old girl going to a party should have.

'I wonder what they want to talk to Kenny about?' Inhaling their warm smell, I lift the buns cooling on the rack from the table and put them on a plate by the sink.

'So do I.' Tom's voice is low and worried. 'She wouldn't say anything directly but she's adamant she speaks to him in the morning. I get the impression she thinks Kenny might be hiding something.'

'For fuck's sake, Tom, what is going on?'

'I haven't a clue, Sal, we'll know more in the morning.'

'I'm not going.'

Tom is walking towards the door and stops to look at me. 'Why not?'

'It's Friday, I promised Megan I'd be in work so I'm going into work.'

'But…'

'But nothing, Tom, I'm not letting the girls down again, I've had to leave the salon early, take days off, this is your mess you can bring him.'

With my colours nailed to the mast, I push past Tom and leave the room. My job is important to me, my clients are important to me and I'm not letting this mess get in the way anymore.

Chapter Thirty-Seven

My nerves rattle through three blow-dries, a colour, a cut and an upstyle. Tom still hasn't called. With a coffee break looming, I decide I'll call him, but first I have to convince this lady that blonde highlights are not the way to go when your face is as pale as a snowman's.

'But my daughter said they'd suit me.' Her daughter mustn't like her.

'With your lovely complexion I think a warmer shade of your own colour would suit much better but I'll do whatever you want.' I'll do whatever anyone wants today, my nerves are at breaking point waiting to talk to Tom.

'Do you think so?' she says, turning her head from left to right looking in front of the mirror. 'Show me.'

I go to get the colour charts, discreetly checking my phone. No texts, nothing. My mind wonders, what's going on at the station? Why did the cops need to talk to Kenny all of a sudden – and why is it taking so long? Rummaging through a shelf load of charts, I pick one, smiling at Sienna who is trying to hide her laughter at something her client is telling her.

I'm back standing beside the woman pointing at colours when the news airs over the speakers. The police are questioning a woman in connection with the death of Claire McCarthy. The woman the police had been searching for handed herself in at the station.

Thankfully my client is more interested in the colour chart than the breaking news. I'm barely able to communicate, pointing out possible colours while trying to curtail my emotions.

The decision is proving impossible for the woman to make. 'Highlights or colour? Highlights or colour?' *Hurry, I need to ring my husband.* Eventually she decides to take my advice and go with the colour.

'You're going to love it,' I say, walking to the press to prep the mixture. I check my phone again.

'That client's fucking mad?' Sienna rushes in behind me. She's holding her knees together, bent over trying not to piss herself laughing.

'What did she say to you, you've been laughing ever since she sat down?'

'She's telling me about a tinder date she went on... there was some mistake... the young fella was only half her age. Jesus, the things she said to him, I'll tell you later... she's a scream.'

Dabbing her eyes dry, Sienna goes back out on to the floor. Her long green dress floats like an angel. How she manages to look a million dollars every time she comes to work is beyond me. Always the same, never wearing her worries in baggy shirts, stretchy leggings or half applied make-up. The phone beeps. Tom.

Ring me.

When the lotion is fully applied, my client sits for twenty minutes worrying if she's made the right decision, before rinsing, while I go to the staffroom. Thankfully it's empty, so I take out my phone and ring Tom but he doesn't answer.

Back outside I check my client list for the remainder of the day. My phone beeps. It's Tom again.

You're not going to believe it?

I lean against the wall and take a deep breath. For a moment I consider not answering, pretending I never received it. Pretending there's no more bad news in store for me but I know I'm only delaying whatever it is he has to say. Deep breaths. I head for the staffroom which is empty and dial Tom's number. Opening the door slightly, I check to make sure no one is on their way in here. The coast is clear, everyone is busy.

'I can't tell you over the phone, Sal, can you not come home?'

'No, Tom, I can't, you know Friday is mad busy, I'm not leaving. Just tell me, is it bad?'

'I don't know about bad but it's definitely mad. The woman in custody is denying murdering Claire McCarthy, which is to be expected...'

He's talking in a low voice, so I presume Kenny is standing somewhere close by. 'What I wasn't expecting, and what the cops weren't expecting, was that she admitted to lurking around our house.'

'Did she say why?'

'Yes, and this is the weird bit. She says she was looking for Kenny.'

I'm confused now, what is Tom talking about?

'What does she mean? Why would she be looking for Kenny?'

The door of the staffroom opens. Megan sticks her head in. 'Your beeper's going off, Sal.'

I nod at her and say I'm on my way but my legs don't want to move, they're stuck to the spot.

'I have to go, Tom… I'll ring you back when I get a chance.'

What the hell is going on? Back out on the floor I try to concentrate but my mind is spinning. Why was the woman looking for Kenny?

It takes me forever to finish the blow-dry, my mind racing, my concentration lost to the turmoil in my head. Megan walks over to me when I hand my client her coat and thank her for the tip.

'If you want you can take your ten minutes now, Sal,' she says, even though my next client is already at the basin. Megan must have noticed my body screaming with anxiety. I hope she wasn't listening at the door when I was talking to Tom.

Leaving the salon, I walk down the busy street, phone to my ear, waiting for Tom to answer, ignoring the crowds pushing past.

'Sal, are you okay?'

'Yes, yes. What is going on?'

'I don't know but something has happened. The mad woman is apparently Claire McCarthy's sister. Angela Burke is coming to the house this evening to talk to us. Can you be here?'

'What time is she calling?' With my head heavy, my lack of attention causes me to bump into an oncoming shopper. 'Watch where you're going, love.' I want to shout back I wish it was that easy. I wish I had some control over where I was going but I don't. I'm being dragged along. Instead, I raise my hand to apologize.

'She said around six, will you be home?'

'Yes, I'll tell Megan I have to leave early. Jesus, Tom, this is mad.'

'I know… I know, I'll see you later, love.'

Love. The word echoes in my ear. Love. Why did you lie to me, Tom? Love. Why did you not share your secret, Tom? Love. Why do I feel like a fool, Tom? Love.

Turning to walk back to the salon, I watch the people passing by, everyone a wave, the ups and downs of life keeping them moving, until they reach the shore. I think of Tom, our relationship, how far are we from the shore?

Chapter Thirty-Eight

The rest of the day moves in slow motion. At 5 p.m., I put my jacket on and leave the bustle and excitement of Friday evening behind and head for home.

My heart skips a beat when I notice Burke's black car in my parking space outside the house. This time I'm more interested than nervous to meet her. I hope she tells us everything she knows and won't leave us with more questions than answers. If Joyce is a relative, this could be good for us. No more prodigal son in the playroom. We could get back to normal and Kenny could come and visit. Maybe call every second Sunday and have dinner with us. I know I can't wipe him out altogether, he's Tom's son after all. He's going to play a role in our lives from now on whether I like it or not. But I'd much rather it was planned from a carefully orchestrated distance.

When I find a spot to park the car, I put my bag over my head to dodge the shower of rain that decides to fall just as I get out. Tom already has the door open when I scurry up the garden.

'She's in the kitchen,' he whispers, closing the door gently. 'Amber is in the front room with the boys watching TV.'

Tom's face is pale, worried; his new look. He's wearing a loose T-shirt over track suit bottoms, which reinforces his state of mind, anxious. As a 'once upon a time' sports star for the local football club, Tom had learned to master the art of looking cool at all times by never wearing loose T-shirts and track suit bottoms unless you're about to paint a house or run a few laps around a field. Or as in this case, your life is falling to ruin. I can tell he hasn't shaved today either, another stress level indicator.

'Has she said anything yet?' I whisper, brushing the rain from my bag before unbuttoning my jacket.

'Nothing much, nothing important, will I get you a cup of coffee?'

'Ye, thanks.' I pass the front room door without going in. I don't want the boys to know I'm home yet. They'll be all over me if they see me, running around their shrunken house delaying me from hearing what Angela Burke has to say.

Inside the kitchen the atmosphere is strange, nerve-wracking and scary. Burke is sitting at the table and her quiet colleague – whose name I can never remember even though I've been told it a few times – is sitting to her right.

There are no folders or pictures or anything else on the table, just two cops eagerly waiting for me to join them.

'Tom tells me you left work early. Thanks,' Burke says.

I nod my head. 'It's no problem.'

'Shall we start?'

'I'll just make Sal a coffee, you go ahead, I can hear you.' Tom pours boiling water from the kettle into a mug. My favourite mug. The one with 'Best Mom Ever' printed on the side. Amber gave it to me four years ago for Mother's Day and I seldom use a different cup. It reminds me that she used to believe I was actually the best mom ever. Before she started giving suggestions as to how I could improve.

'Are you sure you don't want one?' Tom says, glancing quickly at the two cops before returning to the job in hand.

'No thanks.' Burke runs her hands over the table. She obviously does not like to be left waiting. Her eyes watch Tom's every move, I bet she's muttering, 'Hurry up, for fuck's sake,' in her head.

It's not often Tom makes me a cup of coffee. Not for any reason other than it never seems to work out that way. I don't often make him one, either, we both get our own.

He lifts the ceramic jar with the word 'Sugar' hand-painted on the front of it by some arty person who lives in a tree, then lifts the lid off. *Don't ask, Tom, please... don't ask.*

'Do you take sugar, Sal?' And there it is. The big reveal. Sally Cooper's husband doesn't know how many sugars she takes. I can almost see Burke's mind flashing back to the manual, *signs to look out for in a troubled marriage.* This woman puts me on edge, I feel like she's judging me. Looking for signs that all is not as it seems in the Cooper household.

'No thanks.'

With the coffee cup warming my hands, I sit facing Burke. Tom is on my right-hand side.

'As you know, we have interviewed Joyce McCarthy and yes, she was the woman who was at your house.' Burke is glancing from Tom to me. Keeping her voice low like she's telling us a secret. 'As I told you earlier, Tom, she said she was looking for Kenny.'

My hands are shaking, nervous of what the detective is going to tell us, so I put the cup down on the table.

'Did she say why?' Tom puts his hand on mine and squeezes it gently.

'Yes, she said Kenny was her son.'

Silence, both of us sitting open-mouthed, unable to respond. A thousand scenarios fly around in my head. This is unbelievable. If the woman is telling the truth there must be a reason Kenny was living with Claire, did Kenny know?

Tom speaks first. 'But how can that be – isn't Claire the mother?' He sounds as confused as me.

Burke leans back into the chair, her eyes fixed on Tom. 'Is she the killer?' I say.

'We don't know that… at the moment Joyce McCarthy is just a person of interest. Someone who we believe Kenny heard arguing with his mother at the house the day of the murder. Other than that, I can't and won't discuss the murder investigation. All I can do is tell you that Joyce McCarthy is claiming to be Kenny's mother.'

'But sure, how can that be? Has she any proof?'

'She alleges he was taken from her at birth.'

'And is it true?' My eyes are locked on her. Lifting the mug to my dry lips, I take a sip of coffee and listen with the intent of someone being told the winning lotto numbers before the draw.

'We don't yet know what's true and what isn't true but the reason she says she came to your house was she thought Kenny was here.'

'I'm confused. What made her think that? How would she even know where Tom lived?'

'I asked her that, she said she tracked him down using social media.' Burke turns her attention to Tom. 'Did she ever contact you?'

'Absolutely not.' Tom moves in the chair, pushing it back from the table. 'I never heard from that woman.'

'Did you know her name?'

'What do you mean?' Tom's growing agitation is showing in his quivering voice.

Burke puts her arms on the table and looks him in the eye. 'The night you had sex with the woman, did you ask her name?'

Tom looks at Burke, shaking his head slightly from side to side, his eyes are pleading with her to leave him alone.

'Well, did you, Tom?'

'I can't remember.' His voice is low, broken, embarrassed.

'So it could have been either of the sisters.' Burke places a photograph of the two women on the table. They both look alike, same dark hair, same green eyes.

'I don't know, it was so long ago…'

Turning to face him I smile, letting him know, it's okay, she might be judging him, I'm not. I know how things were back then. How a couple of pints would turn into a Tsunami of shots. How blackouts became the measure of a night's success. Placing my hand on Tom's leg, I squeeze it.

'Fine,' Burke says, pushing back from the table and moving the conversation on. 'Joyce McCarthy said she heard on the news that Claire had been killed and presumed Kenny was being taken care of by his father. Here. At this house.'

'But if she's nothing to hide why didn't she just go to you guys?'

'She said she wanted to speak to Kenny first, that was her priority.'

Tom pulls his chair in closer, resting his elbows on the table before joining in. 'I don't understand.'

'I know it's a lot to take in.'

'What did Kenny say about it? Does he know her? Did he meet her?'

Burke shuffles her feet, gliding her hands across the table again before lifting her gaze to me. Every time she looks at me I think she's going to accuse me of something. 'He says he doesn't know her, didn't even know she existed.'

'Do you believe him?' I ask.

Tom quickly turns his head and stares at me like I've just said something rude to the cop.

'It's a valid question, Tom.'

'At the moment we have no reason to disbelieve him but this investigation is only starting.'

'Did she say what happened? Why Kenny isn't living with her?'

'Joyce McCarthy maintains that Kenny was taken from her at birth by her mother who told her he had died at birth. Then she was sent to live with her uncle in the USA which is where she lived until coming home for the first time last week.'

'But…' Tom is speechless.

'Their mother is dead… look, it's a lot to get your heads around so I'll leave it at that for now. In the meantime, can I ask you to pay attention to what Kenny does or says. If he says anything that reveals he already knew the woman before she called to the house last week or anything you think might help the investigation, give us a call on this number.'

She hands Tom a card, another card. I think we have three of them already.

'Okay.' He takes the card and glances at it. I'm sitting here not wanting the detective to leave already. Why doesn't she question Kenny again instead of asking us to spy on him? Or listen and watch carefully as she puts it.

'Is she still in custody?' I ask, standing up along with everyone else.

'No, she left the station two hours ago.'

'But...' My heart stops. 'So she's back out on the street?'

Burke straightens her back and moves away from the chair. 'We have no reason to hold her.'

'I thought she killed the woman... her sister, isn't it?' I'm getting flustered now and losing my ability to remember the details.

'These are only allegations, we have no evidence yet, no reason to hold her.'

'What about stalking our house? What about that? What if she comes back?'

'She shouldn't come back we've made that very clear to her. If she does, you have the number.' The two cops are moving into the hallway now as a file load of questions build up in my head.

When the door closes behind them, I grab Tom's arm before he goes inside and tells the boys I'm home. 'Tom.'

'Ye.'

'Well... can you tell?'

'Tell what Sally?'

'Which sister you were with?'

'No, that was seventeen years ago on a drunken night in a dark alleyway, I can barely remember what I looked like.'

A dark alleyway, how fucking romantic. 'And you never saw her afterwards.'

'No, Sal, just that one night... I'm sure she told me her name earlier on in the club, the whole team were the centre of attention after winning the championship. The girls were all over us and…'

'Well, she certainly remembered your name.'

It wouldn't have been hard to track Tom down. The team photos were all over the *Evening Herald*, their names, the club. But why didn't she contact him when she found out she was pregnant? Unless she didn't want him to know. So why now?

'Do you think you should have a word with Kenny, see what you can find out?'

'I'm not sure, Sal, I think we should leave it to the police.' He pushes open the door and calls out to the boys. 'Mam's home.'

That's one way to end the conversation.

Cian jumps from the sofa, runs and hug me. 'Mammy, mammy, mammy.' Aaron pulls himself up off the floor and walks over, dragging a small bean bag with him. Releasing Cian from my hug, I put him on the ground then kneel to give Aaron a hug.

'They were fighting over that earlier,' Amber says, nodding at the bean bag that Aaron doesn't want to let go of. He puts one arm out to hug me. Holding him close I squeeze him a little tighter than I should, inhaling his innocence before releasing him back into his own little world. Pale blue eyes dominate his chubby face, blonde hair hangs like puppy tails across his forehead.

'Cocoa.'

'Of course, Aaron, Mammy's going to make you cocoa now… do you want some, Cian?'

Cian jumps. 'Yes. Yes. Yes.' They follow me into the kitchen, sit at the table and wait for their hot chocolate with marshmallows floating on top. Aaron always wants five exactly, no more, no less. Cian likes as many as I can fit in the mug.

'I think I should have my own TV in my room.' Amber walks into the kitchen claiming it's impossible to watch her programmes with the twins playing in front of the television. And if Kenny can have one, why can't she?

I never wanted a situation where everyone stayed in different rooms watching television instead of mixing with their family but things have changed. Once again I must lower my standards, I tell her I'll think about it.

'Maybe your dad can pick one up at the weekend.'

Amber thanks me then rushes out of the room before I can change my mind or attach conditions to it.

The smell of chocolate fills the air reminding me I haven't eaten yet. When the boys are in bed I'll ring for a take-out.

With the marshmallows on board I hand the boys two mugs asking them to be careful not to spill any when Kenny walks into the kitchen.

'Oh sorry… I didn't know you were in here.' He turns to walk back out.

'Kenny, come back.' He stops and turns to look at me. 'You can come in here whenever you like, you don't have to wait until the room is empty. If this is going to work you're going to have to feel at home. I want you to feel at home, so come on in, whatever it is you want, take it.'

Slowly, his eyes travel around the room like he's reassessing his needs.

'Would you like a hot chocolate?'

Kenny watches the boys pick marshmallows out of their mugs.

'Don't worry… I won't give you a Thomas the Tank mug.' He smiles at me. The kid has a lovely smile.

'Okay, thank you, Sally.'

I watch him trying not to slurp from the mug. I want to ask him if he knows Joyce? What he thinks about her story? But he's just a young boy, drinking hot chocolate at the table with his three-year-old half-brothers, making them laugh with his funny faces.

–

Later that night, after Amber made me sit and watch her try on every dress in her goddamn wardrobe before settling on what she'd wear to Sarah's party, I rest on the sofa with a glass of wine in my hand. Kenny is in his room, no howls of pain so far tonight.

Tom was itching to go for a pint with the lads, he didn't ask but I could tell, so I suggested he go out for a while. Truth is, I needed a break from him. I wanted him out from under me. I want to relax on my own, in my pyjamas, on my sofa with red wine. The remote in hand and a mind that needs to be ignored. It's impossible to do that with Tom in the room.

I thought about asking Donna to come around for a drink but I dropped that idea as soon as it arrived in my head. Knowing Donna, she'd sit at the end of Kenny's bed and drag his whole life story out of him. Probably have his bag packed and a one-way ticket to Joyce the mystery mother's manor in the USA. No. It's best I sit on my own tonight. Especially with that hair show on tomorrow night. I need to get to bed early.

I'll only have the two small glasses, which is what I'm doing when out of nowhere a thought crashes into my head. She must have told him. Joyce. She must have told Kenny who his dad was.

Tom is adamant Claire McCarthy did not want Kenny to know about him, so who else could have told him? She must have got in touch with him before now, contacted him from the States to tell him who his father was. It had to be her. Suddenly I feel a little scared of the hot-chocolate-slurping kid in the room a few feet away from me. If he's lying about that, what else could he be lying about?

Glass in hand, I quietly step out into the hallway and hold my ear against the door of the playroom. The only sound I can hear is the muffle of the TV on low. I consider knocking on his door, then decide against it. I'll talk to Tom tomorrow, see if he can get the truth out of Kenny, because I don't think he has so far.

Chapter Thirty-Nine

'It's important, Tom. I don't need you fucking this up.'

'I won't, I know what I've to do, first you, then Amber.'
Ellen is to be here at six thirty and wait until Tom is back
from picking Amber up from the party at ten. 'And I'm
not to leave the house once I get back from dropping you
to the RDS until I collect Amber.'

'Good, just make sure you stick to that.'

'I will, Mammy.'

'Don't mock me, Tom, I didn't ask for any of this.' A
quick reminder of whose mess this is and he's back in his
box.

Tom must perform like an army recruit in his final
exam. There's no room for error. Kenny is not to be left
here on his own until I'm certain he's telling the truth. It
might sound overly dramatic, do I care? No.

Amber has appointments the whole afternoon, nails,
hair, make-up. My own hair will get done sometime
during the day, whenever the chance arises. Sienna said
she'd do make-up for some of us before we go home to
change. The hair show starts at 7 p.m.

It's unfortunate that the two events landed on the same
night. I would have loved to drop Amber to Sarah's party,
even though it's only two blocks away. As it stands I'll have
a mere fifteen minutes to change before I'm back out the
door. Thank God for Ellen.

Maybe Tom and Ellen can have that all important what-the-hell-happened? chat tonight while they're on their own. Tom hasn't properly discussed the situation with his mother yet, so this will be their opportunity.

It just goes to show, ye think ye know people. I would have bet my house on Ellen being a lot nosier, that she'd ask a lot more questions about Kenny and how he came to be, but she hasn't. In fact, it's slightly worrying. Did she know already? *Don't be stupid, Sal, now you're definitely letting your mind wander.*

Tom is in the kitchen cooking sausages for his enlarged family, the sizzling smell filling the whole house. Amber comes rushing down the stairs.

'Ma.'

'What is it, Amber, I'm in a hurry.' Pulling my jacket on, I look in the mirror and make a plan to fix what I see looking back at me while I'm in the car on the way to work.

'Money.'

'What about money?'

'I need some.'

'Ask your father. I'm in a hurry.'

'Ye know him, Ma, he'll have a fit when he hears how much I need to get ready for the party.'

'Well, he's right.'

Actually, Amber's right. Tom will go on and on about how many rounds of golf he could play for the cost of getting highlights, or how many pints he can get for the price of a false tan. I don't want Amber to have to listen to that bullshit. Not at the moment. It's important she gets to enjoy this party, take her mind off what's going on at home.

I become aware of the closed door beside me housing Kenny and whisper the instructions.

'There's money in the bottom drawer of my jewellery box, Amber.'

'Thanks, Ma.' Running back up the stairs Amber shouts for her father to cook her two sausages and I head out the door.

–

The salon is already buzzing when I arrive. Hoping to finish earlier than usual to facilitate the staff getting to the hair show on time, Megan has timed the appointments so we can be all out the door by five at the latest. It's so busy I have no time to feed my worries. But they linger at the back of my head, a dark cloud waiting to drop its rain on me.

'Do you think Anna has a chance?' Marie says, both of us pushing the dregs of two chicken wraps down our throat that were bought in a hurry from the Spar shop on the corner.

'Yes, I think her presentation is fabulous, have you seen it?'

'No, but I heard it was good.'

Megan is referring to Anna's entry into the 'Fabulous Hairstyle' section of the show. She's one of three categories the salon qualified for. The 'Fabulous Hairstyle' category, the 'Long Hair' category and the 'Best Salon' category. It's the first time we've qualified for three so we're hoping to come away with at least one trophy tonight.

The black water flows between my fingers, colour disguising the passing of time on Mrs Rooney's head.

Rinsing until the water becomes clear, I wrap her hair in a towel and bring her back to her seat.

Megan catches my eye while I walk back, throwing her eyes to heaven at all the bodies gathered at the reception desk waiting to check in or check out.

In the mirror, I see Anna work away on the opposite side of the salon. It's impossible to keep my eyes from scanning her body. Looking for bruises, cuts, swelling. Very little of her skin is showing, her clothes cover her like a wannabe nun.

Anna sees me looking, fuck. 'Nice skirt,' I mouth before turning away. God, I'm paranoid. It's not like I could do anything to help her. Except let her know I'm here if she needs me. But that's not even true. I'm barely here for myself at the moment.

Pulling the plug on my hairdryer for the last time today, I finally receive a bit of pampering. The salon was so busy, no one got a minute to blow-dry my hair so I did it myself during my break. Sienna is now attempting to make my face look its best. Which it hasn't for a long time.

With my make-up done, I look at my face in the mirror. It resembles nothing like the turmoil boiling inside of me. Thanking Sienna for her work of magic, I leave the salon and head for home.

Chapter Forty

Amber looks eighteen. I hardly recognize her when she comes down the stairs. Her hair flows in waves around her heavily made-up face. False eyelashes dominate the look. I don't want to tell her she looks beautiful, which she does. I want to tell her, *take that off you, bring back my baby.* But I won't. I would have loved to have my mom to compliment me when I first started going to parties.

'Amber! Wow.'

'Do you like it?' she says, looking in the hall mirror while rambling on about who did this and who did that.

'You look so grown up.'

'Thanks, Ma.' It wasn't meant as a compliment but if it makes her happy.

'You look lovely too, Ma.' Amber moves closer to me, her eyes inspecting every inch of my face. 'I like the brown eye shadow.'

'Thanks, love.' She's still in her tracksuit, she hasn't put the dress on yet. Hopefully I'll be gone out the door by then. The thoughts of seeing my baby strutting her stuff in a twelve euro barely-covers-the-essentials dress, doesn't appeal to me. I'll let her father deal with that one.

With little more than half an hour before I have to leave, I check in on Tom who's feeding the boys in the kitchen. Aaron stares at me, trying to figure out if it's really me under all that make-up. Tom says, 'Woohoo,' while placing two plates in front of the boys.

'Where's Kenny?'

'He had a football match, someone is dropping him home.'

Home, the word hangs in the air. With no time to wallow in my torture I kiss the boys and tell them we'll do something nice tomorrow. It's important I keep things as normal as possible for the boys, spend more time with them. So much is going on I have to make sure all this turmoil does not affect them. I don't want them to ever feel neglected.

'Can we go to the playground?' Cian says, stuffing something that resembles a vegetable into his mouth before spitting it back onto the plate.

'We can go anywhere you want.'

–

Our World, that's the theme this year. The sign shines bright across the entrance to the venue, the coloured words floating on the backdrop of a deep blue sea. It's impossible to go anywhere without being alerted to the dangers facing the planet. What we should and should not do to save it. I think of *my world,* what I should be doing or not doing, how far am I willing to go to save it.

The magnificent space looms in front of me when I enter. Sound echoes in every direction. In the distance, I see Anna put the finishing touches to her entry. The model's hair wraps like coloured feathers through carefully manipulated hairbands that Anna made herself.

'The Peacock' is its name and I have to hand it to the girl, even though she has spent most of the past year throwing up from late nights in dingy venues, she's really pulled it off.

It does look like a peacock. Plumes of colour jut out in full circles around the model's face. How she manages to keep it all in place amazes me.

'I think we're over here,' I say to Marie, pointing towards Anna. We both walk in her direction.

Behind Anna's station we sit at a round table and wait for the rest of the staff to arrive. Sienna is first, walking in like she owns the place. Head held high, her pink dress flowing like candy floss. Sienna's hair is back combed so it's bouffant on top of her head, and wrapped with a yellow bow. Walking with the confidence of God, she arrives at the table.

'Looking good, ladies.'

'Sienna, you're like a fucking model. How did you do all that in such a short space of time?'

'Dedication, Marie, dedication.'

'You look fab,' I say, feeling like an old woman in the dated black dress that gets pulled out of the wardrobe for every occasion. It's beginning to look navy I've washed it that often. Pulling at the end of the dress, I promise myself when everything dies down, when my world is handed back to me, I'm going to go on a shopping spree. I'll buy myself some nice fashionable clothes like all the other staff wear. I used to be so fashion conscious and fussy about my image. I used to be a lot of things.

'Well, well, well,' Sienna says walking over to Anna, visibly impressed by what she sees.

'This is amazing, Anna.' She leans forward, careful not to disturb Sienna's creation and blows her an air kiss.

'She's here.'

'Who?' Marie turns to see who I'm looking at and without answering me, jumps out of her seat to greet her boss.

'Megan.' She waves her hands in the air like she's trying to alert a rescue team. Well, that's me put to one side. I can't compete with the boss.

My phone says 7 p.m. Amber will be shocking her dad at this point. I try to concentrate on the opening display of models, male and female, strutting their stuff on the catwalk. Their moves are accompanied by music unsuited to the echo in this great space. My head is bursting. I shouldn't be here. I should be at home, with Amber, with Tom, with the boys. Taking a few deep breaths, I tell myself to calm down, you'll be home soon. Hang on for a bit and then leave.

To my right, Megan sits, animated at the prospect of Meg's Hair Salon receiving the Best Salon award. It's very prestigious and would get the salon plenty of coverage. That means more business, which translates to more profit. Which is why Megan is animated.

Lights darken, music blasts out from the speaker behind me. Everyone is aghast at the wonderful peacock strolling down the catwalk. The shimmering blues and greens glisten under the lights as the model holds her head perfectly still in an attempt to keep the magnificent piece in place. The crowd reacts with delight, clapping and cheering with great appreciation.

Anna stands at the back of the catwalk, her eyes stuck on her creation. Her nerves are expressed in the way she holds her hands in prayer over her mouth. Her vulnerability is rarely on display, but in this moment, I see a stripped-down Anna. Gone is the hung-over, doesn't-give-a-shit party girl. Here she wants to be respected, wants her talent appreciated, *gives* a shit. I hope to God she wins.

The 'Fantastic Hair' category continues with some amazing displays and some not so impressive. The only one I can see that might challenge Anna for the trophy is the beehive. A traditional style, exaggerated in size and texture, dotted with paper bees bouncing on the end of wires from the centre of the hive. Someone's been following 'Save the Earth' on Facebook. The judges will have their work cut out. Style or content? I wouldn't want to be them... oh, but I would. I wouldn't mind being anyone else.

During the interval, Amy arrives at the table with a round of drinks that Megan bought to celebrate Anna's participation. Anna now has to wait until the end of the show when the winner will be announced during a finale of fanfare and glitter. With our fingers crossed we clink our glasses and congratulate Anna on her wonderful entry. Is that a bruise on Anna's chin? No. It's just some dark make-up, probably rubbed off the peacock.

With three gins swimming through my veins, I'm feeling a bit more relaxed. The room has become softer, the music more tolerable.

A woman about my own age passes by laughing, making her way to the bar like she hasn't a care in the world. I have. A wave of fear rushes over me. She looks like the dead woman, the woman who is now lying in a cold room, stitched up, the post mortem leaving its signature, all over her corpse. White faced, waxy skin, she lies there, staring at nothing. Her life taken from her at the hands of someone... someone I know maybe. What if Tom is involved? *Don't go there, Sal, you know he didn't do it.*

A fifteen-minute recess is announced before the judges pick their winner. Time to pee. I make my way to the ladies' toilets at the back of the hall. My head feels a little woozy but I'm not staggering. At least I think I'm not.

In front of me, a tall skinny girl stands in a multi-coloured, glitter-coated, swimsuit and silver tights. She's practically standing on the tip of her toes the heels are that high. Oh for the carefree days when I would have been that soldier. No pain, no beauty. The only pain I put up with nowadays is the awful pain on the inside. And that's because I have no choice.

My hand is about to tap the young woman on the arm to tell her I love her look when I sense someone arrive beside me. It's Megan.

'Enjoying the night?'

'Yes, Meg, it's great.'

She takes her phone out of her pocket reminding me to check mine. We were all told to put our phones on silent when the show started so I better... Shit.

Three missed calls from Tom. What does he want? Something's wrong. Holding my hand up to stop Megan speaking, I step out of the queue and dial the number.

'Tom.'

'Sal, you have to come home.'

'What's wrong, Tom? What happened?'

The space around me turns to darkness. My heart stops. Amber is missing.

Chapter Forty-One

Megan holds onto me when I stumble.

'Sal... Sal.' Her voice sounds miles away.

'Sal.' She pulls me to my feet and takes the phone from my hand. Megan speaks to Tom but I don't understand what she's saying, everything is spinning around in front of me.

'Come on, Sal, I'm taking you home.'

Amber is not answering her phone. 'Answer the phone, Amber.' The cops are already at the house when we get there. The front door is open wide. The brightly lit hallway stands like a beacon in the dark night. *Where are you, Amber?* Megan walks me to the door asking if there is anything she can do. But I tell her to go back to the show, to the girls. It's probably nothing. Amber will arrive home, I know she will. 'Just go, Megan, leave.' I don't want her here.

Tom comes out to the hallway when he realizes I've arrived. 'Sal, Jesus, Sal.' He rushes to me, pulling me into his grip. 'We'll find her.'

He doesn't have to tell me that. I won't entertain any other outcome. We will find Amber and she will be safe.

Angela Burke is holding court by the fireplace. They came as soon as Tom rang the number on the card because of Joyce McCarthy, the woman who had been stalking our home. The woman they let out of custody.

Her partner stands sheepishly by her side. The house feels empty, something is missing. Amber.

'How are the boys?'

'I just checked on them, they're asleep, they don't know anything is going on.'

My fingers struggle to press the contact on my phone. 'Answer, please answer.' Nothing. 'Why isn't she answering, Tom, she never has that phone out of her hand.' He shakes his head, tears gather in his eyes as he drags in air, breath after laboured breath.

Behind me Kenny sits on the sofa. His pale face, nervous, his hands gripped together between his knees like he's secretly having a word with God. His eyes avoid contact with mine when I turn around to face him.

'Do you know where she is?' I say, taking a step closer to him.

He shrugs his shoulders, shakes his head, looks at the floor.

'Sally, no one knows where she is at the moment but we will find her.' Burke moves over to my side and puts her hand on my shoulder.

'Well, she isn't here,' I say shrugging her off. 'What are you doing here? Shouldn't you be out looking for her?'

'There's a car combing the area, Sally, we're here trying to find out her last movements… figure out where she could be.'

'She was at Sarah's party.' I don't recognize my high-pitched voice, the words barely making it out of my mouth.

'She didn't arrive at the party,' Tom says, putting his arm around my shoulder again. Why does everyone think I need them to touch me. I push him away too. Then fear digs deeper. 'What are you talking about, Tom? You dropped her to the party. How did she not get there?'

'That's the thing…'

Oh sweet Jesus, I do not believe what he just said. Amber changed the plan, said she was meeting her friends at the corner so she didn't need Tom to drop her there. So Big Bad Fucking Tom just let her go, even though I'd been adamant that he was to bring her.

Expecting that man to perform is like running a fucking puppet show. If I'm not here with my hand up his rear end, conducting his every move, he flops.

There's no point in confronting him now, time is too precious, no room for anger, we have to find my girl.

At seven thirty she left the house, didn't arrive at the party, which means she's been gone nearly five hours. *Breathe, Sally, breathe.* I'm doing my best to control the horror that's building up inside me.

'I'm going out to look for her, Tom.'

Burke walks over to me. This time, I take a step back putting my hands in the air.

'What?'

'Sally, I don't think you should leave the house. If Amber arrives back it's better that you're here.'

'I'm very sorry, detective, but I'm not in the humour of taking advice from someone who told me my family was safe. If I want to go and look for my daughter, I will go and look for my daughter.'

She doesn't say anything. It's about time that woman knows who she's dealing with. She should not have presumed my family was safe while that mad woman was still out there.

'What about the boys?' Tom says, his sentences an encyclopaedia of problems, never a solution. I look

237

towards Kenny on the sofa and think, well, that's not going to happen. I'm not trusting him to take care of Cian and Aaron. Taking my phone from my pocket, I dial Donna's number.

I try Kenny once more. 'Do you know anything at all about this?' I say, standing in front of Kenny while I wait for Donna to answer my call.

Kenny shakes his head.

'Are you sure, Kenny? … Think.' My voice is loud and I know Tom probably thinks I'm out of order. Which is where I'll stay until Amber is at my side.

Within five minutes, Donna arrives. Then I'm about to walk out the door, ignoring the advice of Angela Burke, who'd prefer I sit and wait like a helpless fool, when I see two people coming up the driveway. It's Sarah and that must be her mom. Tom had gone to collect Amber from the party as planned so they know she's missing.

'Sally,' she says, putting her arms out when she reaches the doorway. 'I can't imagine what you're going through.' The woman hugs me, her body shaking as much as my own. 'I think you should talk to Sarah.'

Sarah is whiter than an anorexic ghost. Dressed in pyjamas and wrapped in a dressing gown, the party make-up still clinging to her face, she walks through the door, hovering in her mother's shadow.

'Do you know where she is?' I say, leading them both into the living room.

Sarah shakes her head.

Her mother speaks. 'No, but she does have something to tell you. Go on.'

Sarah looks at me, eyes filled with tears.

'Tell her,' her mother repeats.

238

Tears everywhere. Her mother continues, 'I asked her why she wasn't surprised when Amber didn't show up to her party and—'

Sarah interrupts. 'I don't see Amber much anymore, so I just thought she didn't want to come.'

'What do you mean you don't see Amber, she's always over at your house.' As the words leave my mouth, the truth hits me, I'm wrong, Amber has been lying.

Sarah mumbles something else but I can't hear. Her mother tells her to look at me and speak more clearly.

'She often sends me texts, asking me to pretend she was with me but she isn't. She goes to meet him.'

'Who's him?' I say, thinking Amber must have a secret boyfriend. Maybe she's with him now, maybe she'll arrive home any minute pretending she was at the party.

Sarah turns her head slowly, like it's the last thing she wants to do. Removing her hand from the pocket of her dressing gown, she points towards the sofa. At Kenny.

Chapter Forty-Two

The room falls silent. Everyone is looking at Kenny. My head drills with pain, my mind begging my body to stand strong, do not fall to the ground. Kenny lifts his eyes and looks at me.

'What? … What is she talking about, Kenny? … Meeting you? When did Amber meet you?' I've moved without realizing it and I'm now standing in front of the boy, staring down at this little shit who has made my daughter lie to me.

'Tell me, Kenny, this is too important for lies. Amber is fucking missing, we don't know where she is. She could be in danger.'

'I met her a few times.' The mumble barely disturbs the air but it disturbs my anger.

Leaning forward I pull on the shoulders of his T-shirt. 'Where is she, Kenny?' I shout. Tom is beside me now, pulling me away from the boy.

'Sal, relax, Kenny doesn't know where she is.' My hand moves without my consent, slapping Tom across the face. 'This is all your fault.'

Burke has moved over to the sofa next to Kenny. 'Kenny, when did you start meeting up with Amber?' His face stays in position but his eyes travel up to meet mine. He's afraid I'm going to jump on him again. He should be. My eyes are fixed on his lips, eager to get the truth. What has been going on behind my back?

'Probably about two months ago,' he says, coughing slightly to clear his voice.

'And how did you meet with Amber? I presume it was you who contacted her.'

'Of course it was him,' I say, not giving him the chance to invent some story.

'Sorry, Sal,' she says, 'I need you to stay quiet.'

His eyes glance to check on me. 'Yes, it was me, Face-book.'

I'm holding myself back with all the strength I can muster. I knew he'd met her the once at some football game. That's what Amber said, she saw him once. She never told me she kept meeting him.

It all makes sense now, Amber's secrecy, her distancing herself from me. The endless smartass comments, treating me like the fool she thought I was for not knowing what was going on around me. I had put it down to her being a teenager, those re-aligning years, the usual errors parents make when they're trying to understand a sudden change in their kid's personality.

'Do you have any idea where she could be now?' Burke says in a tone a hell of a lot gentler than I'd use on him. This time Kenny looks up at Tom, he's preparing to disappoint him.

'Maybe she's with Joyce.'

'Joyce?'

'Yes, the woman who said she was my mother?'

I'm ready to pounce but she puts her hand up to stop me.

'Why do you think she might be with Joyce, Kenny?'

'I'm not saying she is.' Kenny creeps to the edge of the sofa, his face ashen, his legs shaking.

'What are you saying, Kenny?'

'Just… well…'

Jesus, I want to get a hurley stick from the back garden and beat the answers out of him. Tom is equally as impatient; moving forward to within an inch of Kenny, he says, 'Amber is missing, answer the police.'

Tears are now flowing down the boy's face. 'I don't know, it's just something she said.'

'Who? What did they say?'

'Joyce… After my Mam was killed. I told her I didn't want to live with her.' He's rushing now, words falling like rain from an overburdened cloud.

'Go on.'

'I told her I wanted to live with my dad, that's when she said it.' He looks up and speaks to myself and Tom. 'She said she wondered how you'd like it if someone took your child away.'

The room darkens. Below my feet the ground feels like sponge. The mad woman has her. I know it. She's taken her to get even. Oh my God, she's with a murderer. Amber is in real danger. Rushing from Tom's side, I pull a Lego bucket from the pile of kids' toys in the corner and puke.

'Sal, we'll find her,' Tom says, his voice crackling with fear.

In the distance I hear Burke telling Kenny he did well, just to hang in there and we'll find her. *He did well,* is that woman for real? Kenny is the whole reason we are in this mess, he's not an innocent victim here, he lied about how long ago he contacted Amber. He made her lie about meeting up all the time. It's now two hours since Amber was supposed to be home from the party and he's only telling us what Joyce said now.

Angela Burke goes to the hallway talking on the gadget in her hand. When I take my head out of the bucket, I notice Sarah still here with her mother, standing in the corner of the room. She is answering questions the quiet cop is asking about Amber's friends. Who she knows. Who else does she hang with?

When he's finished, Sarah and her mother fall into silence.

'If there's anything else you think of, Sarah?' I say, wiping my mouth as I walk over to them.

The kid is scared and there's nothing more they can help us with so I tell them to go home now, to contact me if Sarah thinks of anything, no matter how small, that Amber might have said or done in the last couple of weeks that was strange.

Sarah's mother gives me another hug. This time I hug her back, the heat from her body soothing my nerves, putting my panic on pause for a brief moment. I don't want to let go. If I let go, I have to deal with this nightmare.

Eventually I pull away and thank Sarah for coming and talking to us. She'll never forget her fifteenth birthday, poor kid. Huddled into her mother's side Sarah walks out the driveway, both a little more appreciative of what they have.

Burke continues to question Kenny. They've sent a car over to the hotel that Joyce is supposed to be staying in. The car isn't there yet.

'I'm going to look for her. Tom?'

His eyes are red with fear. He grabs my arm. 'Sally, we don't know where to look for her.'

'She's not here.' My voice soars across the room filling the space with desperation. I'm frantic. I can't help it. Amber is missing. I move towards the door. Tom follows. Glancing down at the boy on the sofa, I see a stranger, a liar. His head bent down, afraid to look at me.

Out in the hallway, I remember Donna is in the kitchen. She must be telepathic. She opens the door before I get to it. 'Don't let him out of your sight,' I whisper.

Donna winks at me before pushing me out the kitchen door. 'Go find your baby, I'll hold the fort here.'

Chapter Forty-Three

Driving down the road my eyes jump to every shadow, every movement searching for her. Could she be lying dead somewhere. *No. Don't go there, Sal, you know Amber is still alive. You would feel it if she wasn't. Something would leave you, drag itself from your body and fly out into the night. As of yet, that hasn't happened. I know my baby is still alive.*

Tom sits beside me silent, fear stiffening his body. I manage to utter the address of the hotel, which I overheard Burke mentioning on the phone. Tom nods.

I shouldn't have gone to the hair show, not with every-thing that's going on. Megan would have understood if I didn't go. I should have stayed at home, taken Amber to the party, collected her when it was over. But it's too late now. Too late for 'I should have'.

My phone beeps, it's Megan, texting to see if Amber is home yet? I don't answer her.

The streets are quiet until we reach the centre of the city. The hustle and bustle of Saturday nightlife evident everywhere I look. O'Connell street is full of people, most of them drunk. A young man stumbles in front of the car when we're stopped at the lights. He's out of his head, slipping to the ground before his friend steps out to help him back to his feet. Jesus, he doesn't look much older than Amber. Where the hell are his parents? Irony slaps me in the face.

The more vulnerable people I see out of control, the more nervous I become. The madness scares me. Amber should be in her bed by now, dreaming sweet dreams. Breathing softly on her pillow, wrapped comfortably in her pink duvet. So should half of these kids.

One after the other, I conduct each breath in and out of my mouth. In… out… in… out. Unable to sit easy, my body shifting in the seat. 'Can you go any faster?'

'I'm going as fast as I can.'

'Faster.'

'Sal, we don't know for sure Amber is with the crazy woman. She may have gone someplace else, fallen asleep in someone's house, on the sofa. It happens all the time with teenagers.' Tom is clutching at straws, slippery straws, trying to keep the worst possibilities from drilling a deep dark hole in his head.

'I know… I know.' I don't know.

The police are searching Amber's laptop hoping to find some insight as to where she could be. A contact that we haven't given them, someone we don't know about.

According to Sarah she was able to meet Kenny regularly for two months and we never noticed that. Christ, we must be brutal parents. Our own daughter, meeting a stranger on a regular basis and we didn't have a clue. I feel so guilty. When I get her back, things are going to change. I'm not spending my life chasing my tail and blow-drying everyone else's hair, while my kids run around doing whatever they want behind my back.

After what feels like a lifetime, we pull up outside the Hotel on Burgh Quay. There's a cop car parked outside, yellow stripes, lights flashing. Tom pulls in behind the vehicle just as two policemen walk out of the hotel entrance. One of them is holding a phone to his ear.

Before Tom has a chance to switch off the engine I jump out of the car.

'Is she here?' I say, running towards the man in uniform. He hasn't a clue who this mad woman is shouting at him. 'I'm Amber's mother. Is she here?'

The cop shakes his head, extinguishing the small flame of hope that gently shimmered inside me. For a moment I think I might collapse. My legs wobble beneath my shaking body. Vision blurs. Stop. I can't. I don't have Amber yet. *Pull it together, Sal.* More deep breaths, in out, in out, dragging strength on board. I can't lose it now. I have to find Amber.

Tom leans forward, his hands pressing on his knees, his eyes staring at the ground. Is he going to be sick? Putting my arm across his back, I find myself consoling him for the first time since Amber disappeared.

The cops explained to us, no woman called Joyce McCarthy had checked in to the hotel. They double-checked with the station, this is definitely the hotel they have on file. Joyce McCarthy told them she was staying here, she lied.

My mind fills with darkness. Visions of Amber lying scared on the floor of some barren room enter my head. Her eyes wet with tears, her hands and feet tied. Her little body shivering with cold and fear, wondering when we'll get there, when we'll come to save her. 'We're on our way, Amber,' I say out loud to the night, hoping my words will somehow reach her.

I want to ask how could that happen? How could someone, a suspect in a murder case, get away with giving a false address? But feeding my anger will only use up my energy, distract me from what I must do, so I let it go for now. I'll come back to it.

'So, Tom, what do we do now? Where do we go?' Tom's eyes are emptier than a field in a famine. I've never seen the man this broken.

'C'mon, Tom, don't give up, stay strong. Amber needs us.' Dropping his head back, his eyes stare to the stars twinkling above us. His mouth opens, groaning with fear. The pain travels into the night sky drowning out all other sounds on its way.

'Stop it, I need you. Stop it.' My pleas float past him. He's like a werewolf howling at the moon. I don't know what to do.

Eventually he stops, looks at me. His eyes full of energy, fuelled by fear.

'C'mon, Sal, let's find our baby.'

Just as we're about to get into the car, the second cop, the one who was on the phone, walks over. He must have reported back to Burke that we arrived at the hotel. She's saying she wants us back to the house, they need to co-ordinate a search and they need our input. After seeing how hysterical Tom has become, the cop tells us to leave our car where it is and travel with them.

Search… Search. The word shakes my very existence. It echoes of dead bodies, buried bodies, bodies hidden in fields, sprawled amongst the brambles, bodies floating head-down in water, still waters, fresh waters. Tom is holding me up now. I'm trying to stay alive.

Chapter Forty-Four

Not all roads should be travelled and this is one of them. Sitting in the back of the police car, sirens blaring, moving us swiftly through the city to where we don't want to go, I think of Amber. Sweet Amber.

The day she was born was the best day of my life. Her tiny lips, pink skin, eyes like jewels gleaming up in wonder. Amber was a good baby, ate and slept when she was supposed to, not like the boys. It was hit and miss with Cian and Aaron. One sleeping while the other cried for food. One being bathed while the other covered himself in muck. But maybe that was my fault. There was no real routine until they got to the crèche. With Amber, there was more time and I was more besotted by my new job as mammy.

In the weeks coming up to Amber starting school, she would stand at the front door every day with the school bag Ellen had made such a fuss of buying her and practise walking out the door with the bag on her back.

No practice prepared me. I cried the whole way to the school. It was the first time I saw that look, the one she gives me when she wants me to stop embarrassing her.

My eyes are closed. I allow my head to sink briefly against the car seat headrest and pray to God that my little girl is okay. 'Did you ring Ellen?' Prayer reminded me of her.

'No. I didn't think of her. There's no point waking her up in the middle of the night now. There's nothing she can do. Wait till the morning. We may need her to mind the kids tomorrow.'

–

Outside the house, two more police cars, lights spinning, are parked up on the path. A few neighbours hover by the garden gate, talking, staring at us as the car comes to a halt. Rena from next door is the first to approach me.

'I'll take the boys in with me, don't worry about them.' She follows me up the garden path. *The boys, the boys.*

'But they're in bed, Rena, they're okay.'

'Not anymore,' Donna says when we reach the hall door. Aaron is flopped over one of Donna's shoulders and Cian is standing by her side holding her hand.

'Mammy, Mammy, why are the police here?' Bending down, I hug Cian, telling him everything is going to be okay, it's just a little problem that Mammy and Daddy are going to fix. His eyes are wide with confusion. 'Rena is going to bring you into her house so you can have a sleepover with Owen.'

'But Mammy—'

My body feels like it could collapse onto the floor in front of me and sleep for a month, but I won't let it.

'Sorry, Sal, they woke up.' I smile at Donna, letting her know it's not her fault, sirens outside the window and heavy footsteps on the stairs will wake kids up.

Turning around I manage to utter a 'thank you' to Rena before walking into the living room where Angela Burke is sitting with some technician guy searching through Amber's computer. Kenny is still on the sofa.

The police have already searched Amber's room but found nothing to guide them. I want to scream, tell them to get the fuck out and look for her but my energy is drained and I'm not sure they'd listen anyway. I hope they know what they're doing.

With a mouth as dry as chalk I walk to the kitchen to fill a glass of water. Outside the window, the moon's shadows remind me of my brief encounter with that woman.

Does she really believe Kenny is her son? She must, if she's doing all this. But surely that's easy to prove, DNA, birth records. Why the madness? And why did she kill Claire McCarthy? There must be something we're missing.

What if she's telling the truth?

As the cold water flows down my throat, I picture the moment Amber is back in my arms. The heavy embrace, the tears, the smiles. Her soft hair brushing my face, her scent floating up my nose like cocaine to a junky. I let the vision hang in my thoughts long enough to recharge my battery. I will see her again.

Donna walks into the kitchen. 'How are you holding out, Sal?' My tears have dried up but the pain in my heart is piercing every inch of my soul. I turn to answer her but there are no words, so I shake my head. Donna reaches out and grabs my shoulders. Staring straight into my eyes, she speaks in a slow definite tone.

'You will find her, Sal, nothing bad is going to happen to her.' Her words stick to me, I won't let them go.

Back in the front room the main hub of the investigation continues. It's two in the morning now, still no Amber. Burke is going from phone to laptop to maps to things I know nothing about. Kenny is in his room being questioned by someone else. I have to go, I have to find her.

I throw a rope around everything I know so far, pull It together and try to make sense of what could have happened. How did Amber end up in that woman's company? She's no fool. Amber is not going to get into a car with a stranger. Then it hits me like a stray arrow. Maybe Joyce is not a stranger. Maybe Amber has already met her. After all she seems to have met everyone else. If Amber didn't know this woman, why would she go with her? Get into a car or whatever happened. It's just not Amber!

'Kenny.' I push open the door of the playroom and see a woman in uniform writing in a notebook. Kenny must think he has been dragged into the dark ages. Notebooks that don't plug in.

'Kenny, how often did you meet Joyce?'

The woman turns to look at me. 'Sorry, we're in the middle…'

'How often did you meet Joyce, Kenny?'

'I… I…'

'Kenny?'

'Just the once…'

'Was Amber with you when you met her?' Tom has come into the room and is standing behind me. Both of us waiting as Kenny lowers his head.

'Yes.'

Chapter Forty-Five

It's four in the morning now and there's still no sign of Amber. Every beep and call offering empty hope. Amber's phone cannot be tracked by the police. So they are now searching Kenny's phone to see if they can get contacts from the messages Joyce sent him on Facebook. It's all down to technology at the minute, combing fields with dogs has yet to come.

Donna is making me drink coffee. Keeping me alert. I'd rather drift off to sleep and never wake up. Live in a dream world where nothing goes wrong, where Amber lives with me. Then I remember Cian and Aaron, the poor guys don't know what's going on. With Donna in tow, I go to their room and fill a bag of clothes to send in to Rena's.

'I better not forget the trains,' I say, returning to the toy box in the front room to select Thomas and four of his pals to help them through the day.

Angela Burke calls for attention. 'We'll start the search with the first sign of daylight.' Placing a map on a makeshift board that she's created from a chair and a clothes line, Burke points at the area surrounding our house on the map. 'We will need more bodies, neighbours, family, friends?'

Tom takes his phone from his pocket. 'I'll make some calls.'

Burke kneels down to talk to me. 'This must be very frightening for you, Sally, but you should know, I do not expect to find Amber this way. I believe she's alive and we will keep looking for her until we find her.'

I hope she's telling the truth, that she doesn't believe she will find Amber in a field, or a shed, or a river. I really do hope so because if she does... if she does... *Don't go there, Sal.*

Eventually the sun peeks over the top of the houses on the far side of the street and the search gets underway. Police mainly but some local people as well. I'm about to join them, putting on a yellow vest that somehow landed in my hands, when I look down the street and see them arrive. Oh my God.

Megan is leading them, all of them, even Anna. They're all waving at me as they march up the street. At the back of the group I see Elsie, her two bags dragging along the pavement. How the hell is Elsie with them? I smile for the first time since this nightmare began. Something hugs me. Hope. The girls are here to help.

They walk up the driveway, last night's make-up still evident on some faces. Sienna is the first to suggest we bombard the social media sites, confidently walking into the room like she's a real detective who has come to save the day.

'You can go ahead and pound the pavements,' she says to Burke. 'We'll sit here and conduct our own search via the phones.'

Anna takes my cell, lifts my finger to unlock the code and sends a picture of Amber to each of the girl's phones. They send it to their friends asking them to send it to their friends and so on. Facebook, Twitter, LinkedIn. etc., etc.,

etc. Within fifteen minutes half of Dublin knows Amber is missing.

'Now… sightings,' she says, pulling her chair in closer to the kitchen table where the cyber search is well and truly underway. 'We'll probably get a lot of shite and we don't want to waste time, so triage them, like they do at the hospital. Put them in order of the likelihood of the tip being possible. Sienna you can do that. Louise you help her.'

Suddenly Anna is running the show. Telling everyone what to do and keeping tabs on all comments, shares, etc. Poor Elsie is sitting at the table, no phone, no friends to share messages with on social media. I feel so sorry for her, but she seems content to be here, to be part of something, anything, even something this horrible. Megan is making everyone tea, which might be the first cup of homemade tea Elsie has had in years.

Suddenly, Elsie stands up. I think she's going over to help Megan give out the tea but her hand doesn't reach for a cup. It reaches for the drawing of Joyce, the mad woman, the one the cops gave us to show the kids. It's on a shelf below the counter. Elsie holds it in her hand and stares at it. My heart skips a beat. 'Do you know her, Elsie? Do you know this woman?'

'She was outside the salon.'

'When, Elsie? When was she outside the salon?' I can't stop shaking. Could this be true? Did Elsie see that woman? For some reason this gives me hope, energy. This could be something.

'A couple of times, last week or was it the week before?'

'Did you talk to her, Elsie? Did you see where she went?' I hold my breath to hear her answer. My eyes glued to her lips. My hopes glued to her words.

'I followed her.'

My legs are struggling to hold me up but somehow make their way over to Elsie. I hug her. Cling to her before lifting my face to look at her. 'Can you show me?'

She takes my hand, squeezes it tightly and nods.

Anna is suggesting we don't involve the cops, that we take Elsie ourselves to where she says she saw the woman enter a building.

'We'll have a better chance of sneaking up on her, catching her off guard. A convoy of police vehicles and uniforms could send her over the top and if she has got Amber with her, she could...' She stops then, knowing the rest of the words should not be spoken out loud.

I understand what Anna is saying but I don't agree it's right. What if she has a weapon? How would we disarm her?

I look at Sienna, a weapon of mass destruction when she wants to be. She had no problem kicking the gun out of the hand of the scumbag who tried to hold up the salon last year.

And Anna, the night she closed up shop on her own. She was pulling down the shutter when a guy approached her from behind and grabbed her. I doubt he's been able to walk in a straight line since.

'I'm not afraid of anyone, Sal.' Amy speaks for the first time since entering my house. 'Thanks, Amy.'

I'm still not convinced it's the best plan. What if something goes wrong? But they have a point. The mad woman will not be expecting us. We can take her by surprise.

'I can pick locks.'

'What?' Everyone turns to look at Louise who is standing behind Elsie.

'Yeah, my brother taught me when he was a dickhead. He's okay now.'

Everyone laughs, momentarily, forgetting what they're planning.

'Thanks, Louise. That could be very helpful,' Anna says turning her eyes up to heaven.

'But what about Tom, I'll have to tell Tom our plan.' Tom is out with the search party at the minute but I can ring him.

Everyone stares at me, the silence deafening. It seems no one is agreeing to that. I glance from one stern face to the next before conceding defeat. The girls are right. Telling Tom is a stupid idea. He's bound to tell the cops or want to come with us. He's bound to find his own unique way to balls it up.

I'm still not convinced it's the best idea though. This is not some stupid crusade, this is Amber, my baby, my daughter.

'I'll go along with it for now but if at any stage I want to bring the cops on board, you're not to stop me.'

Everyone nods.

Burke walks in. 'How's progress?'

Sienna answers her. 'Great. We've shared her picture all over the place, thousands of shares. If she's out there to be seen. Someone will see her.'

In the corner of my eye, I notice Elsie slipping the drawing of Joyce the mad woman from the table and holding it underneath so Angela Burke doesn't see it. I don't know why she's doing that. She must have her reasons.

I lead Burke out to the hallway, Elsie's revelation hovering on the tip of my tongue. Do I tell her or do

I put my faith in my colleagues? 'Have you any news?' I plead.

'The search is underway, Sally. We're waiting to hear back from the station to see if they've had any success locating Joyce. There's a big team on this, we will have some results soon.'

I decide to tell her what Elsie said, get the cops out to the location as quickly as possible but Donna walks through the open front door. She had gone home for a few hours and now she's back.

'How are you?' She pulls me by the arm away from the detective and into the kitchen. Burke is stunned by Donna's actions. An inquisitive expression creeps onto her face as I disappear behind the wooden door. She knows we're up to something.

'I can take six with me and Sal, of course,' Donna says in a low voice. I wasn't aware she'd been updated with the plan but Marie rang her while we were discussing it. She wanted to get Donna's opinion and Donna said she'd be around in two minutes with her husband's big fancy SUV. And that's not all.

Chapter Forty-Six

The gun is heavy, black and scary. 'What the…' I'm lost for words. Donna leans her back against the kitchen door holding it out in front of us. No one's mouth is closed.

'I know what you're thinking,' she says, 'and you're right… fabulous, isn't it?'

'Donna?'

'Oh, don't worry, I don't have actual bullets for it, he's not that stupid but *she* won't know that.' By she, I presume she means the mad woman, by he, I presume she means her husband.

'When did you get that?'

'We'll talk on the way.'

I call Tom, tell him I have to leave and ask him to come back to the house in case Amber arrives while I'm gone. I convince myself that telling the cops could take them on a wild goose chase, take their attention off the search. I'm better off going and seeing if Elsie is right before involving them. If there's a chance this takes us to Amber, I'm ringing Burke straight away.

Burke isn't happy when I tell her I'm going to join the search party. She doesn't want me to leave the house, telling me how important it is for me to be here when Amber returns. I explain Tom will be back shortly and so will I.

My thoughts are twisted: what will I do? I really should tell Burke what Elsie said. She should know what we know. My mouth opens, but Sienna pulls me by the arm, stares into my eyes. 'Are you ready?' Deep breaths, in out, in out, *what will I do?*

'I have my phone, I'll come straight back if you hear anything.'

Burke says nothing, nods her head at me without losing eye contact. She still has her eyes on me when I look back at the house.

Louise and Amy squash into the small seat at the rear. Anna, Sienna, Marie and myself push into the middle. Elsie's up front with Donna. My mouth fills with water, bile, something; I'm going to be sick. I can't believe I'm doing this. I've been dragged along with this plan without fully comprehending what could happen. Am I making the right decision? Following a lead without the police. Anna sees doubt in my eyes.

'Ten minutes in the kitchen and we have the lead, Sal. Ten hours in the house, the station, the best technicians working for them and the cops have nothing.'

True, very true. And she's right, if the mad woman sees the cops arriving, she might harm Amber. *Oh Amber, hang in there, baby.*

The city's hangover is reflected in its silence. Traffic is almost non-existent. Elsie told us she followed the woman who'd been staring into the salon two days in a row to the back of Christchurch cathedral. Here, she saw her enter a blue door. A door Elsie believes leads to apartments. We'll soon find out. I'm beyond myself, existing out of my mind. Words of comfort and support fly past me. I stare out the window. *Oh God. Help me help to find Amber.*

The city looks like a picture postcard. Blue sky, white bridge, green river. We cross the bridge. Donna is being very liberal with the rules of the road, ignoring lights, signposts, directions. She tells us the gun in her pocket was a present from her husband four years earlier, for security reasons, to scare any potential intruder off the premises. He never gave her any bullets though. 'He knew better,' she said. 'If he had, he'd have got one back by now, via the chamber.'

'Up here.' Elsie points towards a little side street. We see red bricks, coloured doors, sash windows and many entrances to the apartments lining both sides of the street.

'That one,' she says, pointing at a blue door. My heart sinks. Is Amber somewhere behind that door? Craning my neck, I look out the window to the top of the building. There must be at least four floors of apartments. How the hell will I find out where she is?

Elsie gets out of the car first, the look of a homeless person gone without her two bags weighing her down.

We're all out of the car now, standing, heads tilted, staring at the building in front of us. Is it possible Amber is behind one of those windows?

Could it be that one? The one with the white shutters just like her doll's house. My body shivers.

In the corner of my eye I see Marie whispering to Donna.

'No, I'm coming,' I say, guessing what they're saying.

'But Sally, what if...?'

'What if what, Marie? What if Amber is dead? Don't you think I've thought about that?' I *have* thought about it, Amber lying dead on a floor, Amber in a coffin. A part of my brain has not been able to ignore this outcome since my baby went missing.

I try to shut it down, push it away but it keeps coming back. *What if Amber is dead?*

Everyone looks at me, silently, the reality bringing a lot more gravity to the situation. 'Okay, what's the plan?'

The door of the apartment block opens while we're standing, wondering what to do. A man in cycling gear struggles to push his bike out through the narrow entrance. Anna rushes over and volunteers to hold the door open for him, keeping it ajar when he exits.

'What's she doing?' Sienna says watching Elsie walk over to engage with the man.

Her head is shaking from side to side. The cyclist doesn't recognize the woman in the photo Elsie is holding out for him to look at.

'Did you say this woman has only been in the country a few weeks?'

I nod. *What is Sienna planning?*

'Well, that means she has to have booked somewhere to stay.'

'Ye, the police thought she was staying in Jury's. They were wrong. She wasn't.'

Sienna takes her phone from her jacket pocket and starts to type. 'Someone get me the exact address of this place.' We all respond. Each of us huddled in a narrow hallway in a strange building on a Sunday morning, heads down, searching Google Maps. Except Elsie. Elsie has no phone. I must remember to buy her one.

'Aston Quay Apartments!' Louise shouts, like she's answering a question on a quiz game. Sienna continues to concentrate on whatever she's doing. I'm trying to concentrate on breathing. The thought of Amber being somewhere in this building and not being able to find her haunts me. We have one shot at this before I ring the cops.

'There's two.'

'Two what?'

'Two apartments listed on Airbnb for this building.' A sigh of admiration. How did she think to check that?

'15 and 10… So, which do we try first?' Sienna looks at me for an answer like I have an extra sense at play here. I don't. '10… but what do we do, knock?'

'We'll see when we get there.' Donna moves towards the elevator. We're all about to step inside when Amy says, 'Maybe some of us should wait here. In case she makes a run for it or something.'

Good thinking, Amy. But I think she's just scared to come in. I don't blame her.

'You and you.' Donna points at Marie and Amy.

'And me,' Elsie says, handing me the picture. She doesn't want to come either.

'Good luck.'

The door of the elevator closes and there's silence. Each of us watching the buttons light up until we get to the third floor where apartment 10 is located. The corridor is empty when we step out. Not a peep. The air smells stale like a room after a party. My legs begin to wobble beneath me but I think of Amber, take a deep breath and move on. When we locate number 10, we look at each other. The door is grey like all the others. I put my hands together in prayer and hold them to my mouth. Every part of me is shaking.

'What do we do now?' Anna says with her ear to the door. 'There's no sound.'

'Hold on…' Sienna is back on her phone, checking the Airbnb site again. According to the bookings, apartment 10 is still available to rent at the moment. So she's not in there.

'Let's go to 15.'

My heart is not able for this. Amber could be anywhere. She might not even be in this building. We're wasting precious time. Amber could be injured or worse. If that woman has done anything to my baby, I will find a bullet for Donna's gun.

Outside apartment 15, Louise asks has anyone got a hair clip. Seriously, five fucking hairdressers and no clips? But Donna pulls one out of her hair. Louise fiddles with it. Holding it up to the lock before saying. 'Will I?'

'I'm not sure that's gonna work,' Anna says. 'There's bolts and all sorts of security things on doors nowadays.'

'Just someone do something or I'm calling the police.' I'm hopping from one foot to the other, sorry that I didn't tell Burke. We haven't a clue what we're doing.

'Do you want me to knock?' Louise whispers at Anna, through gritted teeth.

'Try it. Try it.' Donna moves forward watching Louise manoeuvre the clip. Sienna puts her arm around my shoulder and squeezes me. At this stage I don't know if I'm crying or not. Is my face wet from old tears or new ones? 'Hurry, Louise. Hurry.'

'Click.'

'What the fuck?'

Louise looks at Anna and whispers, 'You're welcome.'

Pushing gently on the door, Sienna is the first to creep inside, quickly followed by the rest of us. Donna squeezes my shoulder. My body rattles. My heart thumps. No one is saying anything. Tiptoe. Tiptoe.

The hallway is tiny, wooden floorboards, grey walls, a door. Sienna places her hand on the handle and nods at me. I nod back. The room is dark, scrambling on the wall she finds a light switch and presses it. The first thing I see is the body on the sofa.

Donna moves over, *it's not her*, she says, *too big*. The body turns when they hear Donna's voice. It's Joyce McCarthy. I run over to her, grab her, shaking her arms, her head, her shoulders anything I can get a grip on. 'Where is she? Where is she?'

I can hear my voice, a witch, howling in the night. The woman manages to pull out from my frenzy into a standing position holding her hands in the air as Donna points her gun. I run at her. Then stop, look around the room.

There's nothing in the room except the TV and the sofa the woman was lying on. Her hair is splayed all over her face. Her eyes stare out from behind the veil. She says nothing.

'Where is she?'

There's a second door in the room. A key dangles from the lock. Sienna is pointing at it. She wants me to open it. With my hand on the handle, my heart in my mouth, I close my eyes and pray. *Please let my little girl be safe.*

'Mammy. Mammy.' I hear her voice in the darkness. Sienna switches on the light. Amber is pulling herself off the bed. She rushes to me when I collapse to the floor.

'Mammy!' she cries, falling to the ground by my side. 'I'm okay, I'm okay.' I can hardly hear her over my own relieved sobbing.

Chapter Forty-Seven

Burke is standing in the apartment with another cop hand-cuffing Joyce McCarthy when I come out of the bedroom with Amber huddled under my wing. Nobody called her. She followed us.

Amber is trembling in my embrace but has no physical injuries. She's saying nothing, clinging to me, wiping a mountain of pain away with her embrace. Burke nods at me, smiles a little before mouthing, 'Is she okay?' I nod back, there's plenty of time to talk later. Now I must get Amber out of this building.

An ambulance is parked behind one of the police cars when we get outside.

'I'm not getting into that.'

'You don't have to, Amber. You don't have to do anything you don't want to.'

Her face is swollen, red from the tears she must have been crying all night.

I'm wiping Amber's face with a cold towel kneeling against the wall when she tells me that Joyce assured her she wasn't going to hurt her. Amber believed her. She begged and begged, asking to go home, knowing myself and Tom would be worried sick. But Joyce said she had to wait until the morning. She wanted us to be worried sick.

I want to ask Amber how she ended up with Joyce in the first place. Why she lied about meeting Kenny. I want to apologize to her for taking my eye off the ball, for not being there when she needed me. But not now. Now I need to hug her. Make her feel safe.

A few minutes later, Tom jumps out of a car, eyes searching for his daughter. Tears slide from down my face when I see him, the man is lost. I wave at him, let him know where we are. On seeing her Dad, Amber pulls from my side and runs into his arms. I'm so happy.

For the first time since Amber went missing my body feels like my own. I slump into the stone step I'm resting on.

Donna is standing a few feet away telling a detective her version of what happened. There is no sign of the gun.

Neighbours gather in my garden, cheering, welcoming Amber home like she'd been gone for over a year. Amongst them, my father. What is he doing here? How did he know Amber was missing? I didn't ring him; who did?

He walks over to us when we get out of the car. 'Is she okay?' Dad rubs Amber's head.

'Yes but...' I don't ask, I'll wait until things calm down. 'Are you coming inside?'

Looking around at the crowd, he declines. 'I'll ring you later when all the fuss dies down, I just wanted to be here in case you needed me.' Dad leans in and hugs us both before walking out of the garden. Turning my head, I watch him leave, his step slower, his shoulders slumped.

The cops have taken Joyce to the station and this time they won't be letting her go. They still have no knife, no proof she murdered her sister. She's being held on abduction charges.

Amber is saying very little about it all. Which is unusual, I do hope she's not broken. That she hasn't left her sarcastic smart answers behind in that apartment. I don't want her to change. Amber is Amber. She's what I love.

Tom hasn't left her side. He's like a puppy following her around. She had to ask him to get out when she went to the bathroom.

-

Later that day when the police have left the house, things relax a bit. I relax a bit. Two hours of sleep should be enough to help me paddle through the day.

I'm well aware there are still questions to be answered. The biggest one being, who killed Claire McCarthy? But for now I need to be alone with my family and just enjoy the fact that we're all together again.

That evening, Amber is in her room scrolling down the screen on her laptop when I walk in.

'I hate that picture.'

'What picture?'

'The one of me that's been shared across the whole of the country. Could you not have got a better one?'

'Amber, you were missing, it wasn't a beauty contest.'

'Still.' Closing down the screen she pushes the laptop to the side and turns to me. Her head resting on the pillow, her eyes half closed. 'Were you scared?'

'Yes, Amber, I've never been more scared in my life and I never want to be.' I move closer and sit on the side of the bed.

'Did you think I was dead?'

'No, I never thought that.'

Amber turns to lie on her back, her gaze fixed on the ceiling. 'I think she's telling the truth.'

'Who.'

'Joyce, my abductor.'

'What truth?' I'm on high alert again, blood rushing through my veins.

'About Kenny, I think she is his mother.'

'What makes you think that?'

Amber yawns, pulls at her hair then turns herself back to face me. 'I'm tired.'

I pull the duvet up around her neck. 'Sure they'll find out soon, Amber, they'll do DNA tests.' She moves position and pulls her arms out over the duvet. Suddenly I realize Amber spoke to this woman so what else does she know? I don't want to push her to talk. The social worker who phoned – didn't call to the house, Sunday, overtime restrictions – told me not to hound her for answers, that she'll talk herself when she's ready.

But Saoirse O'Neill doesn't know Amber Cooper like I do. There's a risk she'll have moved on in a couple of days. Have lost interest, tell me to mind my own business. She's already begun to refill her tank with attitude. I can hear it creeping back into her comments.

'What else did she tell you?'

'She told me she got pregnant and her mother went mental. She'd been in trouble with drugs already and her ma had wanted her to go to America to live with the mother's brother. Joyce's uncle. Joyce didn't want to go but when she gave birth to a dead baby... that's what they told her, that the baby was dead. Imagine that, Ma, telling someone their baby is dead.'

Amber believes this woman and she's not usually one for getting people wrong.

'So she went to America.'

'Yes and stayed there. Then, two years ago she found a picture of her sister on some social media page. She had a boy with her. He was being presented with a trophy for some under fourteen's football game… Joyce did the sums.'

Holy fuck; I'm trying to act calm here but my heart has stopped.

The dim glow of Amber's bedside lamp is casting a warm shadow across her face. The room feels cosy. The story is anything but.

'And?'

'She got the address and sent him stuff, all the time, she said, but when she heard nothing back from her sister, she located Kenny's Facebook page and that's how she contacted him… and she told him about Da being his father. Can I go asleep now, Ma?'

'Yes, love, of course.' I lean over and kiss her on the forehead. 'Sweet dreams, baby. I love you.'

She smiles, wrapping the duvet tighter. 'I love you too.'

Good God, what happened? I try to act like Amber's story didn't shock me. I hope she doesn't see my hand shaking. I'm about to walk out the door when I remember Charlie, the girl who showed me the photo.

'Just one thing.'

She turns around to face me. 'What, Ma? I'm knackered.'

'Do you know if Kenny has a girlfriend, someone called Charlie?'

'What?' Amber jerks up into a sitting position. 'Charlie?'

'Yes.'

'Ma, don't kill me—'

Oh Christ, what is she going to say?

'That was me who sent her into the salon.'

Speechless, I step closer to the bed.

'I didn't know what to do, Ma,' Amber cries. 'And… and… I wanted you to know what was going on.' Her eyes are glued to mine, waiting for my reaction. 'So I…'

'It's okay, Amber.' I grab the duvet and wrap her in it. 'Go asleep now.'

Out on the landing I consider what I've just heard. Amber sent Charlie in to alert me. God, she could have just told me instead of putting me through that nightmare. The poor thing, faced with that dilemma, she did not know to tell me. That's my fault. But at least she wanted me to know. She cared enough.

And Joyce McCarthy, the madness of it all. Trust Tom to find the nut in the nightclub. He couldn't have shagged someone less problematic.

Walking from Amber's room, I check in on the boys, happy to be snoring in their own beds tonight. My body aches with tiredness. My mind aches with energy.

'How is she?' Tom calls up to me in a soft voice.

'She's asleep.'

A part of me wants to go down to question Kenny but I know I'll make a mess of it. I'm too tired and confused. I didn't get to ask Amber how she ended up in that apartment and not at Sarah's party. Tomorrow, the cops will be arriving early to speak to her. I'll find out then.

Chapter Forty-Eight

Amber wants to go to school. She's not about to miss out on all the attention she'll get from her new celebrity status.

'I'll drop you there as soon as they've finished,' Tom says, taking his keys from the hook by the door.

Megan told me to take the week off work. But I don't want to. I need to get back to some sort of routine or my mind will crumble and it will cheer me up to see Anna's trophy on display in the front window of the salon.

Donna said she's not getting out of bed for the day, so unless Amber is abducted again, I'm not to ring her.

--

The following morning, after the best sleep I've had in a long time, Burke arrives at the house. I'm not nervous. She's here to talk to Amber, to find out what happened.

'Coffee?' God, Tom, can you not think of something else to say, it's always coffee? The man is still a bundle of nerves. Grey face. No hair gel. He probably feels responsible for what happened to Amber. And yes, he did set the ball in motion, but he could never have anticipated how far it would roll.

Angela Burke is sweet-talking Amber, attempting to relax her before hitting her with the big questions. I know all the tricks now.

When we move into the kitchen, she takes Tom up on his offer of coffee, one sugar, while we all wait anxiously at the kitchen table.

Amber tells her all the information she gave me last night, except for Charlie and the photo bit, but I still don't know how Joyce got Amber to go with her. Burke must be reading my mind.

'How did Joyce McCarthy get you to the apartment?' she says, holding her cup in the air for Tom to refill it. I wish that worked for me.

I'm holding my breath. Amber's gaze moves from Burke to the table. I can tell she feels stupid.

'No one is judging you, just tell the detective what happened.'

'She told me she had proof, she wanted me to give it to Kenny.'

'Proof of what?'

'That she was his mother.'

'So you had met her before.'

'Yes, once with Kenny.' She glances over at me briefly. I nod, assuring her I'm fine with whatever she has to say.

'So you weren't afraid of her?' Burke says.

'No. I said I'd meet her but I had to be quick, I had to go to a party.'

Amber continues. Joyce met her in a taxi, said she was coming from someplace else and asked if she would come to the apartment to collect the proof. She promised to have her back in Sarah's within half an hour. Amber believed her.

There is a moment in life when you realize how little control you have over things. Most of it's luck, stars aligned, angels, karma, whatever your thing is. But very little of what happens is in your own hands. Ten per cent

273

maybe. This is one of those moments. Knowing my child was in such danger — and how easy it happened — scares me. It's too much to process. Pain shoots up my back. I want to get sick.

'I knew she wasn't going to hurt me, Ma.' Amber looks at me. 'I knew after the first few minutes in the apartment.,. she just wanted someone to believe her.'

'Okay.' Burke sighs. 'That's probably enough for now. Is Kenny here?'

'No we sent him to school.'

'Well, I need to talk to him.'

Amber is about to step on to the stairs when Angela Burke says, 'Just one last thing, Amber.' Amber turns, looks at me, then Tom. Why is she so nervous all of a sudden?

'Yes?'

'Amber, did Kenny ever say anything about the things Joyce McCarthy claims she sent him over the past few years?'

'No, he said he didn't know what she was talking about.'

'Do you believe him?'

'What?' Amber doesn't know what to say, her face turns white.

'I think that's enough,' Tom says, telling Amber to go and get ready for school before opening the hall door for the detective to leave. She walks out, saying she'll need to speak to Kenny when he gets home. Tom tells her we've had enough commotion in the house so he'll bring him to the station.

There's no real proof that Joyce McCarthy killed her sister. Either she admits it, or they find the knife? Which could be at the bottom of the Liffey by now, floating among the rocks and fish, the empty cans and plastic rubbish. But what if Joyce McCarthy didn't kill her sister... who did?

Tom is in Amber's room screwing her new TV to the wall. I'm sitting with a pen and paper trying to make a list of stuff we need in the supermarket. Milk, bread, pizza, spaghetti, cheese, tomatoes, tuna, everything, everything, everything. My memory has gone to pot. Two weeks of heightened anxiety will do that to a girl.

Being on my own in the house with Tom is very unusual. Normally one of us is at work or the kids are here. In the earlier days we'd be straight in the sack, going at it like we were on a spousal visit. Hurry here comes the guard... Not anymore.

More and more I find myself asking, do I love him? Like really love him. I love Amber. I know that. But Tom? Would I have married him if I wasn't pregnant? Probably. I thought he was great. Do I still think that?

I'm measuring my love for Tom with his value on the world around me, not my heart. To love him keeps the family together. To love him means I have someone to share things with, to go home to at night. To love him means I can grow old with him. It's easier to love him than not. I love him because it's easier.

Dropping the pen on the table, I massage my hands into my face, through my hair, down my neck. Why did the cops ask Amber if she believed Kenny? Do they not believe him? I need to find out more about Kenny, see if he's telling the truth about never having known about his real mother. After all, he's living under my roof, sharing this space with my family. If his head is messed up and he's constantly lying, I don't want him here. I'd never be able to relax knowing I couldn't trust him.

His room, I suddenly think. Kenny isn't here. I'll check his room. I feel sure I'll find my answers there.

Chapter Forty-Nine

The curtain is closed so I flick the light on. Bags, cases, boxes, all lined up against the far wall where the kids' toys used to be. It seems Kenny isn't in a rush to unpack. I don't know what I'm looking for. Evidence of what?

In the corner a small cardboard box filled with comic books and schoolbooks sits on the floor. Bending down, I rummage through the contents. All pretty normal stuff. Leaning my hands on the ground, about to push myself into a standing position, I notice something hidden under the bed. It's pushed right into the corner. Scurrying across the floor I reach in and pull it out. My hand brushes across the carving on top of the wooden box. It's old, a strange thing for a young boy to have, unless of course it's his mother's, something to remember her by. Pulling on the lip, I attempt to open it but the box is locked. Now I'm really interested.

'What are you doing?' Tom is standing in the room by the door.

'I want to know what's in this box.'

'For fuck's sake, you can't do that.'

'I can and I will.'

'But...'

'But *nothing*, this box was hidden under the bed, our bed, in our house, I want to know what's in it.'

Tom pauses, shaking his head before walking over to where I'm sitting with the box at my side on the bed.

'Here, give it to me.' He wants to know too.

'I can't open it, it's locked.' I hand Tom the box which he inspects from every angle.

'If we break it open he's going to know, he'll never trust us.' For a moment I let Tom's concern linger in my thoughts.

'Don't you think we should know what's in our house, especially when it's in a locked box, hidden under a bed? Remember, Tom, we know fuck all about this kid. What if it's drugs? We have to protect our own kids.'

He relents, takes the screwdriver from his back pocket that he's been using in Amber's room and holds it to the lock.

'I don't know if this will work, I might have to—'

Ouch, he broke the lid, it's cracked right down the middle. There's no going back now. After a bit more tugging and twisting the box is open.

'Got it.' Tom pulls on the lid. Both of us stand back from the bed like a bomb is about to explode. Well, it's not drugs. It's letters. *Cards and letters from people I don't even know.* The song swirls around in my brain. 'What the...'

Tom is the first to put his hand in, lifting out a pile of envelopes and cards. They're addressed to Kenny McCarthy. Birthday cards. Christmas cards. Letters. Tom opens a letter to Kenny, it's from her. Joyce... Mammy.

Sitting on the bed, I read her words.

> *Dear Kenny,*
> *You don't know me, but I know you. I held you in my womb for nine months before they robbed me of you. I've been trying to get Claire to tell you*

the truth but she won't answer my letters or calls. I am your mother, Kenny. I did not abandon you or choose to leave you in the hands of my vicious mother and weak sister. They sent me away, told me you had died. I hope you get to read this, that Claire doesn't keep it from you like I presume she did all the other ones. I'll keep trying to contact you. Soon we will be together.

    Your loving Mom, Joyce.

And there's more, lots of letters, lots of cards. According to the dates they were all sent over a two-year period which ties in with how long Amber said the woman knew about her son. If he is her son. She could be just mad. Or devious.

Lifting a second pile out of the box, I notice the writing is different and the date stamps go way back, back to… I pull out the card. *Happy 1st birthday, Grandson.* Then another. *Happy 2nd birthday, Grandson.* Are these from Joyce's mother, the woman who sent her away to America, the woman who told her the baby was dead?

Opening the card, I hold it over the bed in case money falls out. It's a hard habit to break. Years of expecting nothing else on my birthday has me this way. When I was young, Mam used to buy me toys but when the job of getting my birthday present fell into my father's lap, money fell into mine.

I read the inscription.

LOVE, ELLEN.

The card falls from my hand and lands on the floor at my feet. I try to say Tom's name but nothing will come out of my mouth. Tom… Tom… no, nothing. He notices my distress, walks over and picks up the card, reads it.

He reads it again, this time turning it upside down and around and up and it's like he can't believe it's real. I can't believe it's real.

'Tom?' Eventually I hear my own voice.

'Sal... I...' He lifts a second card and opens it. 'I can't believe this, what is this? Does this mean what I think it means?'

A cold imaginary blanket wraps itself around me. Ghosts circling me.

Tom is still staring at the name ELLEN. 'She knew... but how?'

'Did you know, Tom?' He's shaking his head slowly from side to side still holding a card in his hand. His face has turned green, his eyes locked open in shock. Tom didn't know.

He makes the call immediately.

Chapter Fifty

'What's wrong?' Ellen arrives in the door all flustered. We take her to the kitchen to where the cards are laid out on the table. On seeing them, she staggers.

'Oh God… Oh God.'

'What's going on, Ellen?'

'I… Oh God…'

'Here, sit down, Ma.' Tom pulls out a chair and Ellen drops into it. Her face pales, her eyes fill with tears.

'I'm sorry… I'm sorry.'

'Just tell us what happened?' Tom sits on the chair beside her while I hover at the opposite side of the table. Ellen doesn't know where to start, her eyes are darting from Tom to me.

'She came to me.'

'Who?'

'A young woman, the week before your wedding… She told me about Kenny being born, that he was your baby, she told me.' Ellen looks at Tom. 'I didn't know what to do, Tom. I didn't want the wedding cancelled. I wanted you to marry Sally.' Ellen lifts her eyes to look at me. 'You were so good for him, I didn't want it ruined.'

'But why did you believe her? Why didn't you tell me?' Tom's voice is growing in anger.

'I know. I should have… but I just panicked.'

'What did you do then? Why did she go away?'

'I offered her money.'

'You *what*? Did Dad know?'

'No I never told him. I gave her money and she promised to leave you alone.'

'You paid her off... Ma... is that what you're saying?'

'I didn't know what else to do, I couldn't let her ruin your life.'

'Why did you think it would ruin my life?'

This sounds a bit concocted, a woman knocking on the door saying Tom was the baby's father.

'Why didn't you ask for proof, Ellen?'

She lifts her head to answer me. 'I did... I did... I told her that I didn't believe her but...'

'But what?'

Ellen bursts into tears. 'Oh it just got so complicated.'

'Okay, Ma, take a breather. Do you want some water?'

Tom nods at me to get her a glass of water. Turning the tap on, I look out the window to the empty garden to the spot where Joyce McCarthy climbed the wall.

I curse the night the senior footballers won the championship. One mistake, one stupid mistake. For the past sixteen years Ellen has lived with this, dealt with it on her own and for what? Now we're in the middle of a murder investigation.

Tom walks over and takes the glass from my hand. He's shaking.

'I still can't understand why you never said anything, Ma, we could have dealt with it.' Handing her the glass he sits back down beside her.

'I know, I know, I should have but...'

'But what, Ellen?' I'm finding her story hard to believe, there has be more to it. 'Ellen, why didn't you ask for proof that Tom was the father before you paid the money.'

'I should have. I know but…'

I'm getting annoyed now, the woman is not stupid, there something she's not telling us.

Ellen shakes her head slowly from side to side. Tom stares at the cards on the table. This is going nowhere. I move closer to the table, anger directing me, lifting one of the cards I read out loud. '*Lots of love, Ellen*. How could you do this to us, Ellen? How could you lie – year in year out, sit at our table with our kids and all the time you were keeping this from us. Did you not know it would eventually come out?'

'I did, I worried about it every day. I wanted to tell you but the longer it went on the harder it became. I was afraid.'

'Afraid of what, Ellen? We're family, we could have dealt with it.'

'Afraid of her!' she shouts.

Tom looks at his mother, takes her hand in his. 'Why were you afraid of her?' Rubbing her eyes with a tissue, she takes a deep breath. 'She threatened to say you raped her.'

Silence. After a few minutes Ellen sniffles into her tissue. 'I knew it wasn't true, Tom, but I also knew that all she had to do was say it.'

My heart sinks, Ellen has been paying for peace.

'So where did you get the money? How much did you give her?' Tom wants answers.

'Two thousand pounds.' Ellen's voice is getting quieter like she doesn't want us to hear.

'Two thousand pounds. Where did you get that sort of money?'

Ellen is clenching her teeth. She doesn't want to say but Tom won't let up.

'Ma, where did you get the money?'

Sniffling into a tissue, she moves her head slowly from side to side before lifting her gaze to look at me. Why me? What's going on? Oh no.

'I had no choice, Sally, I had to tell him. I knew he wouldn't want his daughter's wedding destroyed...'

I feel weak. Leaning against the counter, the room spins, I'm going to be sick.

'He wanted to help, he offered, he said he was glad I told him.' She's rambling on but all I can hear is muffle.

I can't believe my father knew about this child. No wonder he's been showing up lately. Ellen must have alerted him to what was going on. Claire McCarthy must have warned her that Tom knew.

Tom walks over and wraps me in his arms. I pull away.

'Amber's due home from school any minute now,' I say, gathering the cards from the table and telling him to take Ellen home before she arrives. I can't believe she hid it from us for sixteen years. That my father knew.

It hits me then, like a train. Did Claire McCarthy ask for more money? Did Ellen pay Claire McCarthy a visit? *No. Stop, Sal.* You know Ellen didn't stab Claire McCarthy. Ellen was here the day of the party until Jack picked her up... except when she left to get the candles.

But my father wasn't here all day. He just called in for a few minutes. He had plenty of time to visit her.

Chapter Fifty-One

Later that evening, the boys are in bed and Amber is around at Sarah's house. I checked.

The cops arrive when Tom calls them about the box of letters. He also told them about the money our parents gave Claire McCarthy to shut her up. They'd find out anyway. At this stage we don't need to be holding on to any secrets. Plus, it shows the type of woman Claire McCarthy was, how manipulative and dangerous she could be. Maybe she has more enemies out there.

Angela Burke takes the box in her hand like a baby just pooped on it. Arms straight, she holds it out while her colleague manoeuvres it into a big plastic evidence bag. She now has proof that Kenny knew Joyce McCarthy. That she did contact him. It means nothing, except Kenny is a liar and as a young boy who suddenly discovers his mother is not his real mother, and then she's killed; maybe he could be excused.

He says he found the box of secrets in his mother's room one day, hidden at the bottom of a wardrobe. His mother said the letters were from a crazy relation who was in an asylum somewhere in America. He wasn't to pay any heed to them. Kenny didn't think much more about it until he was contacted last year by Joyce on Facebook.

'This will be them?' Burke takes the phone from her belt and holds it in the air before answering it. She nods…

nods and nods again, eventually thanking Dr Grimes at the far end of the phone before cutting him off.

Pushing her thumbs into the black leather belt, she shuffles on her feet, straightening her back before announcing that Joyce McCarthy is most probably Kenny's mother. The autopsy guy told Burke that Claire McCarthy had never given birth to a baby.

A sense of dread envelops me. My head, bang, bang, bang. Moving to the kitchen I swallow two painkillers. Part of me is relieved they now have a motive for Joyce murdering her sister.

Kenny says there were two people who came to the house on the day of the murder. Both fighting with Claire. Tom and Joyce. Both suspects are denying killing her. If only they had the weapon. Tom's fingerprints will not be on that weapon. I know it, my husband might be a lot of things but he's not a killer.

I lean my head back against the sofa, my eyes close softly, shutting off the world around me. This day is endless. The kids still have to be picked up yet. Tom and Kenny are down at the station being interviewed again. Maybe Kenny will remember something that will put this whole thing to rest.

An hour later, Cian and Aaron run through the hall door. Donna is behind them.

'I know I wasn't supposed to ring you, Donna, but I just couldn't drive to pick them up, my nerves are shot and now Tom is down the station with Kenny and…'

'My dear, sweet friend, never apologize for asking for help. Anyway, I got as much sleep as my body could handle. I'm better awake.'

The boys are playing on the floor in front of me when Aaron comes over to my side. He puts his hand on my face, trying to soothe me, comfort me. Aaron knows that something is wrong with me. Placing my hand on top of his I feel the heat of his kindness pass right through me. 'Be okay, Mammy.' He makes me want to cry. I wish Lorna and her early intervention could see this.

'Mammy is going to be fine. Thank you, Aaron.' I kiss him on the cheek, inhaling every last inch of his sweetness. 'Mammy loves you.'

'And me.'

'And you, Cian.'

The night eventually arrives. When Amber is in her room and the boys in bed I sit on the sofa and open a bottle of wine. The more I let the situation fester in my mind, the less I understand it. Kenny has not been playing ball. Hopefully Angela Burke will go a bit harder on him tonight. Remove her gloves and question him in detail.

I think it strange that he did nothing when Joyce contacted him. It doesn't add up. Especially when he went behind Claire's back to contact Tom. Surely when Joyce told him Tom was his father and the DNA proved her right, surely *then* he would have believed her. Unless of course he didn't want to. Didn't want her in his life. Maybe Claire told him all sorts of stories about Joyce that scared him off wanting to know her. I hope he's down there now telling Burke the truth, the whole truth and nothing but the truth. Our family has been put through enough. Kenny should know that, do what he can do to help.

With the second glass of wine heating my veins, I relax. *Forget about it, Sal. Leave it to the cops.* The television entertains from the corner of the room but I'm not paying any attention to it when the phone rings.

'Sal.' Tom is whispering.

'She admitted it.' He must be still at the station. I can barely hear him so I ask him to speak up a little.

'Joyce McCarthy has admitted guilt. She killed her sister.'

Relief. If God was here, I'd thank him personally. The end; no more shit. I feel like a sack of stones has been lifted off my back. I want to cry. To hold Amber, to hold Tom, it's over.

'They were going pretty heavy on Kenny, starting to question whether he was involved. When they told Joyce they were questioning her son, she just admitted it.'

'What?'

'That's it… it's all over.' He sounds happy for the first time in weeks. I want to go to him. Hold him. Tell him everything will be fine. I know it will… I love him.

'O… okay. Will you be home soon?'

'Hopefully.'

Tom hangs up the phone and I go back into the living room. Why does that not sound right to me? What did Tom just say? The cops told Joyce that they were questioning her son about his involvement and then she admitted to the murder. That'll do it. With the next glass of wine en route to my stomach, I rest my head on the back of the sofa.

My eyes close. Visions of the murdered woman lying dead on the ground fill my head. Poor Claire McCarthy. Bitch Claire McCarthy. How could she do that to her sister? Even if it was her mother's doing, she had an opportunity to undo it when the mother died. And now, lying in a pool of blood. I'm not sure she deserved that.

–

Hours later and I'm awake. My head is in pain. My mouth feels like a rat slept in it. Pulling myself into a sitting position, I squint my eyes to look at the clock. Four am. Where's Tom? Out in the hallway, I notice slits of light coming through Kenny's bedroom door. Tom must be in bed already. He must have arrived home, found me sleeping on the sofa and decided not to disturb me. The house is locked up, the alarm on.

Switching the small lamp on the hall table on, I walk into the kitchen to get something to drink. Water. Turning on the tap I look out the window. Joyce McCarthy was here. In my garden. The killer. She was looking for her son. I can't blame her for that. If someone took Amber from me, I'd hang around gardens in the middle of the night looking for her. I've done worse.

A part of me feels really sorry for Joyce and now she's going to spend her life in prison. Well, some of it anyway, she'll probably be charged with manslaughter. I wonder will Kenny want to visit her?

Something tells me he won't. That he'll stay playing happy families here until the social worker lets him off on his own. To live in Sycamore when he's seventeen. One year away, all according to Saoirse O'Neill's plan. Let's hope it works out that way.

Instead of going upstairs, I tiptoe back to the sofa. I'll wait here for the morning, wrap the throw around me and dose off. After a few minutes my eyes are heavy. I'm falling… falling… falling. What's that noise?

Chapter Fifty-Two

Peeping through the little gap in the door, I see Kenny standing in the hallway. He doesn't know I'm here. Quietening my urgent breathing, I watch. What is he doing? His jacket is zipped up like he's going somewhere. Where is he going at this hour of the night?

His tall skinny frame takes a few steps up the stairs, then he stops. Listens. He's checking to see if the coast is clear. Kenny comes back to the hallway and walks to the front door. My heart beats like a bass drum in my ear. Thud. Thud. Thud. Holding my chest, I step back into the darkness, the gap in the door still allowing me to watch Kenny. He doesn't seem to know what he is doing. He was about to go out the door and now it looks like he's changing his mind. He goes back into his room but doesn't close the door behind him.

Maybe the kid is just confused, worried, unable to sleep. He's had such a hard time. Or maybe he's planning on running away. The bitch inside me considers letting him. *Stop it, Sal.* He's been through so much... what's that in his hand?

He's coming back out of the room, this time holding a bag. Not a rucksack or schoolbag. It's a small black plastic bag. The kind that will be illegal in a few years. What has he got inside it? I hope to hell we didn't bring a drug dealer into the house.

My heart skips another beat. *What is in that bag?* I want to ask him. Catch him in the act. Pounce. But something is telling me to wait, watch, see what he does. If it is drugs, he'll be meeting someone, I guess. Giving them a supply... or money.

My nose itches. Shit, I'm going to sneeze, he'll know I'm here. Holding my nostrils tightly, I almost choke trying not to make a noise. Water fills my eyes blurring my vision so I wipe them on the sleeves of my pyjamas and wait. *What are you at, Kenny McCarthy?*

He takes one last glance up the stairs before pushing the alarm code, which I'm surprised he knows. Then he opens the door.

Shuffling across the wooden floorboards I move to the window to continue my observation of the boy. I don't hear the front door closing. Is he leaving it open? The little shit. He's going to head off and leave us at the mercy of the criminals. Jesus, I'll have to do something now.

The gap in the curtains allows me to watch his shape move like a black shadow under the street light. His movements are slow, gentle, like a dancer. When he gets to the end of the garden he stops beside the black and green bins at the wall. Kenny lifts the lid on the black bin, then the green bin. But he doesn't leave the black bag there. He looks around making sure no one is watching him. He glances back at our house before stepping into Rena's garden where her bin stands behind the pillar.

Kenny drops the black plastic bag inside. He rummages around as if trying to cover the package up. What is Kenny McCarthy trying to hide?

With his hands stuck in his pockets and his shoulders hunched, he comes back into the house. Does he wait now for someone to come and pick up the package or is that his part done?

Beep, beep, beep, beep. The alarm is set. He's back in his room. What will I do? Wake Tom. No, I'll wait and see if someone comes to pick it up first. Sitting on the armchair by the window, I widen the gap between the curtains… and fall asleep.

'Mammy, Mammy.' Aaron is climbing all over me. My head is woozy, what happened? I know something happened. Kenny, the bin, the drugs, it all comes flooding back to me.

With Aaron in my arms I pull the curtain open. I probably missed the pick-up. I'll tell Tom, he can confront him, there is no way Kenny can stay in the house now. Drugs and kids, not a chance. Saoirse O'Neill will have to refer to her manual and come up with another solution. Jail maybe.

Aaron runs barefoot ahead of me into the kitchen. I can hear Cian's patters across the floor above my head. The world is stirring. Today has arrived.

I don't know how I feel about what I saw last night. I'd come to accept that Kenny would be with us for at least a year and I was willing to do my part to make it work but… Jesus. Suddenly a thought crashes into my head.

Fumbling before eventually knocking off the alarm, I whisper, 'Wait, Aaron, wait.' I open the door and run down the driveway into Rena's garden. Aaron is following me barefoot.

'Mammy, Mammy.'

'Go back inside, Aaron.'

Cian is running out the hall door after us.

'Go back inside, Cian.'

'What's going on?' Tom is standing in the doorway in a pair of track suit bottoms. 'Take them inside, Tom.'

'What are you doing out here?'

'Just take them inside.' He's still half asleep when he grabs Cian and Aaron under his arms.

'Sal, are you all right?' I don't answer him. I lift the lid on Rena's bin, rummage in the rubbish until I find it. My heart is threatening to blow up. I open the bag.

The knife glimmers.

Two Weeks Earlier

JOYCE

They told me he was dead. They lied.

'Do you think this is what I wanted?' Her voice is loud, eyes bulging from the far end of this tiny room. 'Do you think I wanted to raise a child that wasn't mine?'

I want to say, *I never asked you to*, but her anger is palpable, changing the air, changing her face.

'Why did you?' I say. 'Why did you take my boy and raise him like I didn't even exist?'

'Well, you didn't exist. You were gone.'

Her hands are gripping the edge of the table. Her piercing eyes boring holes in my head. 'I didn't choose to leave, she sent me away.'

'But you left and I was stuck here with her, while you were off living the life I had dreamed of. Stuck here in your shoes, raising your child. And now you decide you don't want that anymore.' Her voice soars.

'I never wanted this, you lied to me, Mother lied to me. I wanted to raise my baby but she had other plans, didn't she, and you went along with them.'

Claire steps back from the table, leans against the wall. A bitter smile creeps onto her face.

'I went along with her,' she says, bending forward, her eyes burning. 'Do you think I had a choice? Do you think

I said, "*Hey Ma, let's tell Joyce the baby is dead, let's pretend it's mine?*" Do you think that's what happened? Have you no idea the pressure I was put under, the fear I lived with. No, you don't, because you were either drunk or drugged up to your eyeballs, always the drama queen, always trouble.'

'I still should have been able to raise my own kid.'

'Should you? *Should you?* Maybe you should but that's not what Mother thought. No, she thought she'd send you to have a better life keeping me here to look after your big mistake.'

She turns her stare away from me, picks up a knife from the counter beside her and runs her finger along the blade. I'm getting nervous now, I've never seen someone so angry. I move closer to the door.

'But what about now?' I plead. 'You have to tell him the truth, he's seen the letters. He knows who his father is.'

'You just couldn't stay away, could you? Trouble, trouble, trouble.' She's moving towards me now, holding the knife in her hand. Sweat seeps from my forehead into my eyes blurring my vision, my heart is in my mouth. I have to get out of here.

When I leave the house, she's alive.

TOM

They never told me he was born.

I should have told Sally straight away when he came to my office that day. But I was afraid, afraid of what it would do to our marriage. Things were good following the dark spell when I lost all her money. She forgave me and I didn't want to land another bombshell on her, not yet. I had to wait until the time was right. Sal is everything to me I don't want to lose her or break up my lovely family.

'What do you want?' She turns her back to me before I have a chance to see her face and walks down the hallway into the kitchen. I follow. When I enter the room she's standing at the far end against the table. She stares at me, her eyes red, tired, like she's having a rough day.

'I thought we had an agreement,' I say, walking closer to the table, trying to make eye contact. She grunts a laugh. 'You agreed to wait, I was supposed to tell my wife but now she's seen a photo of him. Why did you do that?'

Claire looks like she's in a trance, swaying slightly, looking through me. 'It wasn't me.'

'But who else could it be? No one else knows?'

'You're sure about that?' she says, in a tone that suggests I could be wrong. 'I never wanted him to know about you.' Her voice is sharp, cutting the air with its edge. 'He was happier before you came along filling his head with ideas. So why would I show your precious wife a picture? None of this is my doing.'

'If you didn't, who did?'

She huffs, smiling to herself. Then leans over the table gripping the edge with both hands. 'You think you can just come along now, into my life after all this time.' Her voice fills the room with anger. 'I never even got a "thank you". I raised your son for sixteen years on my own. All those nights pacing the floors with your child in my arms when I should have been out, having my own life.'

Her words unsettle me, what is she saying?

'He was your child too.'

Another smart chuckle before her eyes bore into mine. 'You know nothing, Tom Cooper.'

'I know what you did was wrong.'

'I did my best for that boy, gave up my whole life for him and now the two of you show up and think you can replace me.'

Claire turns her back to me and walks over to the window. What does she mean the two of us? Sally has nothing to do with this.

'I didn't just show up. I was dragged into this.'

Silence. Claire looks out the window. I came here to make sure she stays away from Sally and my family. But now I realize she wants nothing to do with us.

'Kenny came to me, remember,' I say. 'He wanted me in his life. You weren't enough.' The words hang between us. I should not have said that. Claire turns slowly, looks at a knife sitting on the table. This woman is mad, I better get out of here.

When I leave the house, she's alive.

KENNY

They never told me who I was. They lied.

So it's true. Joyce McCarthy is my birth mother. Sitting on the ground in the back garden below the window I hear everything. Words. Lots of words.

Mam didn't even want me, it's clear from what she said to her that I ruined Mam's life. She had to stay in all the time to mind me. Maybe I should leave.

I'd like to live with my dad. Like a real family, brothers, a sister. I wonder what Amber's mam is like. I could go to school from their house. Dad could bring me to my football matches and I could teach my two little brothers how to play. Everything would be great. And there'd be holidays. I've never been on a holiday. I wonder what their house is like? Amber said she'd sneak me in someday.

Lifting my head, I close my eyes and dream of what might be when I hear his voice. Dad is here. What's going on? He's fighting with Mam. This is not good.

Everyone is angry over me. Nobody wants me.

The door slams. Dad's gone. Will I run down the side passage and stop him? Ask him not to leave, ask him will he still want to see me? He probably doesn't now. I want to cry but I'm too angry. This is all her fault.

When I get to the front of the house, Dad's car screams down the road. I'm too late. With my hand on the door-bell, I wait for her to answer.

'Did you forget your key?' she asks like nothing has happened. I wonder how often she does that, pretend. All the time I guess, all her life.

I follow her into the kitchen and that's when I see the knife.

When I leave the house, she's dead.

A Letter From Jackie

Thank you for taking the time to read my second novel, *The Secrets He Kept*. If you enjoyed it, and I really hope you have, I would love to hear your thoughts via a review. Knowing what you think of the story is important to me.

Social media affects how and where we receive information these days and was the inspiration behind the story. How do we know if what we're looking at is true?

Sally is just an ordinary woman, married to an ordinary guy, when a photo on someone's camera changes all that. What should she believe? Her eyes or her heart?

I hope you enjoyed this journey with Sally as she discovers the truth behind the photograph.

This story is not true and all the characters are fictional.

Thank you for your support. I would love to have your continued support as I progress on my writing journey.

You are welcome to contact me with any questions or comments anytime. I'm available on Facebook and Twitter.

Best Wishes

Jackie Walsh

www.twitter.com/JackieWalsh_ie

www.facebook.com/jackiewalsh.ie

Acknowledgments

I would like to thank everyone who has supported my journey so far. In particular, all the people who read my first novel, *Familiar Strangers*. Thank you for your kind words of support and great reviews. Every positive reaction you send my way pushes me forward.

To my publishers at Hera Books, Keshini and Lindsey. Thank you for all your hard work. Knowing you have my back makes the experience a lot more pleasurable.

For Patricia Gibney, who is always at my side with her encouragement and help. We have such fun together, long may it last.

To the writers who previewed my first book; in particular, Patricia Gibney, Louise Phillips, Andrea Carter, Niamh Brennan. Thank you for taking time out of your very busy schedule to help me.

To my family and friends, whose reaction and support for *Familiar Strangers* could not have been better. Keep it up. And the girls in Lollipops who continue to make my life easier, you are the best staff anyone could ask for.

For the people on the street, my neighbours, who stop to wish me luck. Every word of encouragement cheers me on.

The writing community in Ireland is one of the friendliest places to be. Special thanks to Vanessa Fox O'Loughlin, who gives tirelessly to this community helping shape it into a place of support and encouragement for all writers at any stage of their journey.

Paul, Layla, continued love.